Praise for IN TWO WEEKS' TIME

"Lassen's writing is vivid, blending humor and tension as the story progresses. The interplay between Sam's personal trauma and professional life adds a lot of depth to the character. The flashbacks to her military life were also intense and capturing. The description of the backdrops and the brilliant use of symbolism for the protagonist's chaotic life throughout the story showcase the authors' potential. ... With mild spice and lots of flirting, it scratches the itch for a cute thriller-rom-com work for readers. ... *In Two Weeks' Time* is a robust offering by the author. It will successfully capture the interest of readers who like a blend of thriller and thematic character-driven stories."

– Rashmi Agrawal on *Reedsy Discovery*

"This must-read adventure is strengthened by the author's real-life military experience, bringing a powerful authenticity to Samantha's character, making her journey both thrilling and heartfelt."

– M.Z. Medenciy, author of *Island Eight*

IN TWO WEEKS' TIME

A NOVEL

REBECKA LASSEN

atmosphere press

© 2024 Rebecka Lassen

Published by Atmosphere Press

Cover design by Matthew Fielder

No part of this book may be reproduced without permission from the author except in brief quotations and in reviews. This is a work of fiction, and any resemblance to real places, persons, or events is entirely coincidental.

Atmospherepress.com

To my best friend and the best ex sister-in-law, Rachel.
I'm sorry I made you read all the sex scenes I wrote,
over and over and over and over again until they came together.
I love you.

Chapter 1

Samantha Reeves didn't need an alarm to tell her it was five o'clock in the morning. Even after a restless night of sleep, her body woke her up like clockwork. She rolled out of bed and onto the worn carpet, knocking out her morning workout of core and strength exercises since a gym wasn't an option at the Lakeside Motel.

She cursed as she pushed her face away from the musty stench of the carpet. *I have to remember my yoga mat next time.*

She would have liked to go for a run instead, but Jeffrey Lindahl, her current subject of surveillance, was attending a morning golf gala, and she needed to be there. She was able to procure a ticket to the fundraiser through some friends of friends who knew a guy. It was one of those types of back-alley transactions that she was quite accustomed to at this point in her private investigative career.

After a quick shower, she pulled her long, dark, thick hair into a high ponytail, dabbed on a bit more makeup than usual to fit in with the crowd, and put on the designer golf dress she bought last week. Having never golfed, she wasn't sure what to wear, but the perky saleswoman at the store insisted on the dress because "the soft coral color would be splendid with your jet-black hair."

Sam checked her appearance one more time in the oversized frameless mirror hanging over the bathroom sink. She had to admit the saleswoman was right. It was a great color on her. Her summer tan still held, giving her usual pale skin a bronzed glow against the soft pastel color of the dress. Sam fussed over the pleats and hem of the dress. Her tall frame had the hem of the figure-hugging dress landing mid-thigh, which was much shorter than she appreciated, but she'd be blending in with the golf crowd, so it would have to do. *I'll be just like them, so who's going to notice?*

A knock on the door made her nearly jump out of her dress. She took her pistol from its holster that sat on the bathroom sink. She forced herself to even out her breathing as she made her way across the dingy motel room. As she reached the door, it rattled once again with rapid knocking, followed by a familiar voice, "Ms. Reeves, it's Juan from the front desk."

Relaxing slightly, but never fully, she exhaled and steadied her breath as she inched the door open slightly, keeping her leg pressed against the back to prevent it from being shoved open and someone forcing their way in.

"Hi, Juan," Sam said through the two-inch crack that the flimsy door chain lock allowed.

Juan held up a small manila envelope so Sam could see. The printed label read, *Samantha Reeves – 7B – Lakeside Motel.*

"Hi, Ms. Reeves. There is a package here for you."

"Oh, that's odd." She unchained the door and opened it another inch, motioning Juan to slide the envelope through. "Thank you. Did you happen to see who dropped it off?"

"No, ma'am. It was sitting on the front desk this morning when I got here."

Sam nodded. "Thanks again," she said as she shut the door and slid the lock into place.

Sam walked over to the bed and carefully laid the envelope on the faded maroon bedspread along with her pistol. Sam squatted down and leaned back on her haunches as she considered this perplexing package.

Maybe it was Maggie Lindahl who sent it, she pondered. Sam would label Maggie as a trophy wife: well, ex-trophy wife, who had hired Sam to surveil her now ex-husband, Jeffrey Lindahl. Maggie felt her ex was increasing in violent behavior, and she was worried he would do something to hurt her or their two young daughters. Sam had been on this case for a few weeks, researching and looking through divorce papers, court transcripts, social media, text threads, and any other documents she could find. Most of what she found was some delicious upper-class tea, but nothing led her to believe Jeffrey was becoming violent. Just a straight-up d-bag lawyer. Which is what led her to the Lakeside Motel. Nothing in the digital world was adding up, so surveillance was the next step.

Jeffrey Lindahl. Sam's lips curled up to one side, and her eyebrows squeezed together in annoyance at just the thought of him. "Gross," Sam huffed out as she let her bottom fall to the floor and sat with her legs crossed in front of her.

She met this d-bag lawyer once briefly, about two years ago, just after he, his wife Maggie, and their two young daughters moved to the Twin Cities from Manhattan. It was at a fundraising dinner for the families of fallen police officers that Jeffrey's law firm hosted every year. She had never attended before but ended up being a last-minute date for her mentor, Chief Mark Crane, when his wife was sick and couldn't make it.

The tea at the time was that Jeffrey's law firm had transferred him for nefarious reasons, but the happy cover story was a promotion.

"You fuck up, you move up," Sam said to herself as she laid back stretching her legs out in front of her, never letting her eyes drift away from the mystery envelope on the faded bedspread.

Apparently, corporate folks used that tactic, too. She considered. You can't really fire soldiers, so leaders would often promote the worst soldiers to get them out of their unit. Then they were someone else's problem. To Sam, especially after researching and surveilling him the past few weeks, Jeffrey was indeed, a problem that was promoted.

Jeffrey was last year's up-and-coming hot new corporate lawyer, according to the *Minneapolis St. Paul Business Journal*. He was a regular at the Mendakota Country Club which was just down the road from the motel Sam was staying at. If he wasn't in a courtroom or golfing, he occupied himself in various ways, often with the club president's daughter or the wives of some of the other club members.

Sam leaned forward, resting her elbows on her thighs and her cheeks against her hands. Besides being a morally-questionable lawyer and a narcissistic, controlling, cheating asshole, that's all she could find so far. Nothing to support Maggie's allegations of Jeffrey's increased violent behavior.

She had spent the last few days tracking and following Jeffrey's movements, which were very predictable at this point. Yesterday was a long day of loitering around the courthouse, following Jeffrey to the gym, then to a downtown bar for late-night drinks and listening to him compare case sizes with other lawyers, "Case sizes. Ha." Sam giggled to herself. "Yeah, that's what they were getting in pissing matches about."

Thankfully, Jeffrey didn't stay long. Sam's patience had run dangerously low. Not enough food or evidence had been gathered yesterday. She was ready to be done with this case.

Sam followed Jeffrey to his house, and after he was in for the night, Sam returned to the Lakeside Motel, to her usual room 7B, with a late-night dinner, the empty take-out containers from the past few nights now filled the undersized garbage can by the front door.

But there was no way Jeffrey knew she was here at the motel. Sam guessed if Jeffrey had known she was following him, he would have approached her. Even if he had caught on to her following him, he still wouldn't have known where she was staying.

And there was no way Maggie knew she was staying at this motel. Sam was careful never to share too much information about her processes or plans with her clients. Once Sam resolved a case, she would share some details but held onto most of her processes and never shared locations. So, it couldn't have been Maggie, either.

She picked up the envelope, turned it over, and pinched the small metal tabs together so they slipped through the punched hole. The glued edge didn't allow the envelope to open, so Sam tore the edge with care, letting the sound of the tearing paper echo over her breath. Her eyes caught sight of a bundle of folded, crisp black tissue paper. She tipped the envelope over and let it fall onto the bedspread. She sat at the foot of the bed and picked up the packaged bundle. A short, torn piece of clear tape held the tissue paper together. She pulled the tape and peeled back the layers of the black paper.

Inside, a stitched, subdued military police patch lay on her lap—the kind sewn onto the arms of army uniforms. She'd seen patches like this on hundreds of soldiers. She used to wear one every day when she was enlisted. This one, though, was well worn, with dark stains spattered on the tanned stitching.

Sam's breath hitched as her vision blurred.

Sam could still see the patch as her vision started to clear, but now the patch was on Specialist Justin Sommers's arm as she tried to pull him out of the overturned armored Humvee. His all-black sunglasses hung crosswise across his forehead. Shards of metal and glass riddled his camouflaged body armor like confetti. A steady stream of blood dripped from his ear, forming a bright red river flowing down his dangling arm. Sam leaned closer to Justin to cut him out of the seat belt that was holding him in place in the now upside-down truck. As she leaned across his blood-coated face, her sight caught on a large piece of sharp, fragmented metal sticking out of the small vulnerable gap between the chin strap of his

helmet and protective collared vest. Sam closed her eyes and took a deep breath.

When she opened them back up, she saw the scuffed walls of room 7B. She rushed over to the window, dropping the patch in her haste. She peeked out the dusty vertical blinds to the small square parking lot. The Lakeside Motel was a U-shaped building. 7B was on one top end of the U. Sam could see the motel lobby directly across the way on the other side of the parking lot. She saw her rented black sedan right out front of her room. She never used her car during surveillance cases. Sam parked her car a few blocks away in a park and fly lot for the airport. She didn't need any angry ex, con artist, or cheater coming after her in the unlikely case someone spotted her. Always vigilant and prepared was her motto.

A few other cars were parked in front of the various rooms—the usual mix of high-end SUVs and then the ones with rusty duct-taped bumpers. The fancier ones usually only stayed for an hour or so before heading back home to their supposed loved ones. She had her fair share of cases that brought her to this hotel before. She met Juan from the front desk on the first case here, and he was helpful and discreet and continued to be Sam's ally. He was known to avert his eyes, and considering why Sam was often there, she appreciated his discretion.

She exhaled meditatively to calm her accelerated heart rate. She stepped away from the window as she wiped her damp forehead with the back of her hand. Nothing was different outside, and Sam knew that. Sam bent over, picked up the patch, and sat back down. She peered inside the envelope, searching for more clues, but nothing was inside. Still, she knew. She knew what it was: a military police patch from her team's failed mission in Afghanistan. It was nearly ten years ago when four young men lost their lives, and it was all because of her.

"I can't process this right now. I have to get going." She wrapped the patch back into the tissue paper and placed it in the envelope and shoved it deep into the bottom of her overnight bag. She grabbed the keys to her rental car and walked out of the motel room. As she pulled out of the lot, she hoped she had buried the patch deep enough in her bag so that she could forget about it for a long, long time.

Chapter 2

Sam parked her rental car in the overflow lot at the Mendakota Country Club. She purposely arrived an hour after the first round of golf started. Most golfers would be out, letting her entrance go mostly unnoticed.

"Today's the day I close this case," she told herself as she walked up the clubhouse. She'd gather all of the information she needed to finalize her report for Maggie, and be done. This was far from Sam's favorite case. Maggie Lindahl was a difficult woman to read, with little presence on the digital side, aside from a social media account filled with filtered selfies and posed family photos on luxury vacations. Jeffrey was a narcissistic asshole with no loyalty to anything but himself, but again, nothing to suggest he'd become violent that she could find.

She had half a dozen other cases sitting in her queue that she had accepted and needed to focus on. Maggie had paid Sam quite a handsome amount to get her case pushed to the top.

The beer carts were already making rounds for the early morning golfers like usual at these events. By the time people were back in the clubhouse, the liquor would have loosened their lips and helped out Sam more than they ever realized. She got more information at these fundraisers than any interview or online research could provide.

The elegant clubhouse was a far cry from the Lakeside Motel. It wasn't much of a motel. Nor was it by a lake. The thin bed sheets had been washed one too many times. The dingy brown carpet had seen better days with its goat trails worn between the two beds, to the small front table, and back to the bathroom. Juan must have attempted to give the bathroom a facelift with a new white plastic shower curtain and liner, but it just emphasized the coffee-stained-teeth color of the dated floor tiles.

Here, at the clubhouse, she was greeted with beautiful cathedral ceilings with rich oak millwork and panoramic views that overlooked the expansive outdoor space and brilliant greens of the golf course. The patio was bustling with breakfast diners in collared shirts with their light beers and mimosas. The late-summer morning sun was still bright and full of heat, with a bit of dampness holding on. The clubhouse was empty for the most part when Sam walked in, with the majority of golfers and guests enjoying the weather while they could.

A few shoppers were in the golf shop as she walked past. She strolled easily to the open bar nestled at the back of the gallery room. As she waited for her light beer, she watched a group of older women as they sipped on mimosas around a white linen table, gossiping with wild gestures and gleeful laughs as their spouses golfed the day away.

Sam smiled at them with fondness as she walked past with her drink in hand. She hadn't many friends, really. Her life and schedule didn't allow it. Most of the time, she accepted this reality the way it was. But every once in a while, seeing a group of women enjoying life with each other made Sam wonder if she would ever find a friendship like that.

She once had a best friend, but he didn't come home with her from Afghanistan.

Sam shook her head and took a sip of her beer. That damn patch was sneaking in thoughts that she hadn't cared to think about.

"Focus," she scolded herself as she stood in front of the

full-size window overlooking the course and outside patio. She watched the golfers go by on the course and looked through the diners outside, trying to find Jeffrey among the crowd. She recognized local celebrities and business leaders, but no sighting of Jeffrey so far. She recognized a gentleman she surveilled for an insurance company, but she was confident he wouldn't know her. Nobody would know her here.

Unless, she thought as she stilled, *what if someone does know I'm here? What if whoever sent that military police patch was here?*

Her eyes scanned the crowd more feverishly than before. *Who would have sent it and why?* she asked herself. Was it a warning or a thank you? Why would someone...

"Who are you looking for?" a deep, commanding voice asked that seemed to come out of nowhere, interrupting her meandering thoughts.

"Shit," she cursed to herself. She was so lost in her thoughts that Sam didn't see anyone approaching her. She counted to three before turning her head toward the voice. Remaining calm on the outside while her mind whirled inside came with years of discipline and training.

Sam turned and connected the deep voice to the dark green eyes that were focused on hers. Her insides whirled again. His stern cheeks were covered in a clean-cut beard with almost invisible flecks of gray. He had unruly wavy hair that he tried to wisp back with no success as strands lay loose across his forehead and around his ears. His eyes never wavered as they pierced through Sam in a way she never experienced. She had to count to three once again to regain her composure before responding.

"I'm sorry, what?"

The stranger smiled with brilliant white teeth gleaming through his trim, dark beard. "I asked... Who are you looking for?"

Sam gave him a questioning look. He gestured out the window. "You've been standing still at this window for quite some time now." He paused as he studied her face. "Yet your eyes never stopped moving."

Sam raised her eyebrows as she tilted her head, revealing her shock despite her best efforts to maintain control.

He shrugged. "One would assume," he paused a beat and kept his eyes trained on hers, "you must be searching for someone."

Rarely was she speechless, but this stranger rendered her so. She observed other people, not the other way around. All the energy of his piercing stare settled on top of her chest at this realization. She inhaled through her nose, trying to replenish the oxygen that had seemed to escape her body. She smiled to cover her angst as she hummed a quiet grunt and allowed her eyes to dare him before asking, "Aren't you quite the observer?"

He shrugged one shoulder and grinned. "Depends."

What is with this guy? she thought. His intense gaze was far beyond the appropriate amount of time and now into the uncomfortable zone.

This man has to be into men with that amount of intense eye contact, she mused. Straight men didn't look at her with that intensity. They looked at her eyes for a brief moment before trailing down and landing their eyes on her chest. *Men. Ugh.*

Shame, though, she thought. He was gorgeous.

"Fine," she said as she averted her eyes from his. She allowed her eyes to drift over his broad shoulders, down the muscular arms that stretched the sleeves of his golf polo, before she dared to go any lower.

Oh my gosh. Sam realized she was being "that guy." She cursed herself and turned back to the window to regain her focus and control. Taking a breath, she pushed off her wandering thoughts, ignored the bad behavior, and dove into her rehearsed lines.

"I didn't get a chance to register, but I still wanted to

show my support. This event does so well in raising money." She turned from the window and looked at the man through her lashes. "Sadly, I missed the past few years." Her voice remained even and smooth despite the dryness that began to cling around her teeth. She took a small sip from her almost-forgotten beer to ease the cotton-filled taste in her mouth. Sam couldn't tell if it was the lie or his proximity, but heat flushed up into her cheeks, and her ability to control her body responses remained thin.

She hoped her lie would hold; she hadn't expected to be approached by anyone. She had researched Jeffrey's friends and acquaintances, and this guy didn't look familiar. She studied him while she waited for him to accept or dispute her cover story. She would have remembered this guy for sure, she thought. You don't forget eyes like that, or hair, or face, or firm chest, or massive arms and probably a huge... *shit*, she thought to herself. She was ogling this guy like he was a delicious block of cheese or something. *Get it together, Sam*, she scolded. She said a quick prayer, asking that her body not give away her thoughts as they traveled down a dirty road.

He eyed her for a moment more before he stuck out his hand. "Casey Parks."

Phew. He bought it, she thought as she mentally high-fived herself.

She rotated her beer bottle to her other hand and took his. "Samantha Reeves," she said as his hand engulfed hers. "A pleasure to meet you, Casey Parks."

After the firm shake and zap of heat that went pulsing through her arms, she quickly pulled her hand out of his grip. Sam nodded toward the pristine manicured greens through the floor-to-ceiling glass. "Shouldn't you be out golfing?"

Casey heard her question, but his whole body reverberated with the pleasing sound of Samantha Reeves saying his name.

Why did that sound so good? he thought.

Sam turned from the window and met his gaze when he didn't respond.

He had to force his brain to function again. "I'd love to, but they frown upon golfing when working." His brain may have stopped responding, but dammit, his other body parts were responding with intensity. He wanted to know what she would sound like if she were saying his name from under him.

She was still staring and studying him, which wasn't helping. *Get it together, man.*

"I am the club's marketing and brand manager," he said. "I guess that means event coordinator as well." Casey shrugged. "So here I am, making sure the event is coordinated."

Jesus, the event is coordinated? If he could have smacked his forehead for sounding like an idiot, he would have.

"Interesting," was all Sam replied.

Gaining back his composure, he continued with a smirk, "So, are you going to tell me who you are looking for?"

He watched her face pass through a few series of expressions that he wasn't sure meant if she was annoyed or impressed by his question. He hoped impressed.

"Jeffrey Lindahl," she finally said with an even tone.

"Oh really?!" Casey questioned with a raised eyebrow. "Friend, foe, or jaded lover?"

He really hoped it wasn't a jaded lover. He hated Jeffrey Lindahl and couldn't imagine a woman like the one in front of him with a guy like that.

He watched her face once again pass through a quick flicker, and this time, he was certain it was annoyance. And that made him smile.

"Friend." She then quickly added, "Of a friend, really."

Casey breathed a sigh of relief; for what? He wasn't sure why he was even holding it.

"Ahh... well, if that is the case, you'll be looking for him all day but won't find him. He didn't check in this morning for his tee time for the tournament."

"What?!" Sam opened her mouth to say more but quickly closed her lips into a pressed thin line.

How did she miss that? *Dammit.* She hadn't even checked the sign-in roster when she arrived at the golf course. "Shit." She shook her head as the image of the police patch flashed to the front of her mind. Apparently, she hadn't buried it deep enough in her bag, as it seemed to be messing with her more than she wanted to admit. "He's never missed a tee time," Sam said out loud but mostly to herself. "He's too type A for that."

Sam looked up and found Casey staring at her—and she could only presume studying and analyzing, too—as she'd done to people her entire life. She knew that look. Game recognizes game. She needed to get away from his gaze and focus back on finding out where Jeffrey was.

"I guess you do know Jeffrey well," Casey said.

Sam tried her best not to roll her eyes. "Well, crap," Sam said.

She turned and looked around the immaculate clubhouse. This day was not going as she planned. A stranger, albeit an alluring and handsome one, was too curious about her, and now she had lost her main subject of surveillance. And without Jeffrey around, she'd have a hard time bringing him up in conversations to get more intimate details.

"Something isn't right," she told Casey. "I better go make some calls."

"He didn't answer when the club called," Casey offered. "But here's my card with my number. Call me when you get a hold of him, please?" Sam looked at Casey with an eyebrow raised. Sensing her hesitation, he added, "He's a club member, and we care about everyone here."

"Oh really?" Sam asked. "Was he a friend, foe, or jaded lover for you?" Sam smirked with a wink.

Casey's eyes widened at Sam's tease. The side of his mouth

lifted in a grin. "None of the above."

"Interesting," Sam said with a teasing smile.

Maybe he's not into men after all, she thought, feeling oddly relieved. *Dammit, Samantha Jo*, she cursed at herself. *Are you seriously trying to flirt with him right now?* She shook her head to clear her thoughts. She didn't have time for this. What was she doing still talking to him?

"It's not my place to update you." Sam threw her full beer in the nearby recycle bin before stepping around Casey, ignoring the card in his hand.

"Okay. Fine. You caught me." He gently grasped Sam's arm above the elbow before she got by him. "I just want you to call me, regardless." Casey pressed his card into her hand.

Sam looked down at his hand on her exposed skin to make sure his touch was real. The heat seemed to be amplified tenfold from their handshake earlier. The sensation traveled across her skin as if his hands were moving under her golf dress and grazing her whole body. She hoped she was hiding her reaction to his touch, but she knew whatever control she had left was running low.

She was worried her inside thoughts would be exposed. Her eyes trailed up along his muscular arm and traced his sharp jawline under his scruff. His smile faded into an intense line as his eyes deepened to an impossible green.

She froze and seemed to lose all of her senses. It felt like she and Casey Parks were the only people in the room.

Sam blinked a few times rapidly to snap back to reality. She couldn't lose sight of her surroundings. It was too dangerous to do that. She had to get away. She stepped out of his touch and steadied her voice as she stuffed the card into the hidden pocket of her golf dress. "Good luck with the rest of the tournament today, Mr. Parks."

Sam turned on her heel and out the main oak doors without daring to look back.

As soon as she was outside, Sam pulled out her phone and

scrolled through, looking for the right contact. She shook her head as her finger swiped through her contacts.

"What the hell was that all about?" she asked herself as she tapped a name on the screen and waited for the call to connect. It wasn't even lunchtime yet, and she was exhausted and confused by the day—and by Casey. She didn't need another distraction right now, and something about the last few minutes told her this guy would be.

Chapter 3

Casey watched Samantha sprint away from him and out the door. His hand still hummed from touching her arm and the soft skin that he never wanted to stop touching. Her large brown eyes imprinted in his memory the moment they connected with his. He tried to look away but was pulled into the depths of Samantha Reeves and couldn't escape. Casey's face relaxed into a smile as he thought of Samantha Reeves and those investigator's eyes. They darkened as he noted her processing everything, including him, but her face expressed little to nothing. Well, almost nothing, he thought. A slight narrowing of her eyes as she let them roam over him. And the way her lips pursed together as she was organizing her thoughts. He admired that control.

His ex-wife was never in control. She expressed everything—loud and overly exaggerated. He loved her passionate nature at first, but the overt passion masked her actual personality. It didn't take long to discover that. The marriage was a short-lived, fresh-out-of-college marriage. He thought it was what his family wanted. Looking back, he realized he'd married for his family's sake, not for himself. His momma wanted grandbabies, and his little sister Nikki wanted to focus on school and becoming a doctor, so as the older brother, he felt obliged to try. But after a few months of marriage, he knew Lucinda wasn't the motherly type. She wasn't the wife type either; he learned too late she wanted more of an open relationship. He was fine with one partner. She was not. The last he heard about Lucinda was that she was remarried to a nightclub owner and living a life that offered endless nights of opportunities for her and her now husband.

Seven years later, he was still looking for someone that made him happy, not his family. Not that he didn't love his family. Whenever he called his parents back in Cuba, every conversation with his momma started with, "Mi hijo, when will you give me nietas?" Then, she would go off on a tangent. "God blessed me with two beautiful babies to keep this family's heritage alive and growing." He could hear the whole conversation before picking up the phone. He would roll his eyes and pull the phone away as she continued her routine plea, which ended with, "No voy a vivir para siempre amor." That was his cue to tune back into the conversation, "Yes, Momma, nobody lives forever; you'll get grandbabies when the time is right." Casey would hear the puff of exasperation and some words muttered under her breath before any further conversation could happen.

He loved his family and missed his parents dearly. His dad, Joseph Parks, originally from Florida, visited Cuba when he was eighteen. His parents had a love-at-first-sight marriage. Joseph met and fell in love with Aletha in Cuba and stayed. Joe worked at a local golf course, one of only three remaining golf courses, after Fidel and Che flattened and destroyed most of them. Casey was born a few months after they were married, and Nikki followed less than two years later.

As a young boy, Casey often joined his father after school and helped around the course, where he developed a deep love of the game, eventually leading him to leave Cuba to study the game and profession. His sister came with him to the States to study medicine, leaving his parents back in Cuba. Momma said they would only consider moving if nietas came about. Otherwise, Cuba was home, and Dad did whatever Momma said.

He reminded himself to call his parents as he followed after Samantha to the front entrance of the Mendakota Country Club. He peered out the front window facing the pull-through driveway. There were no palm trees or the calm claps of the crashing waves of the golf course of his younger years. But this club was beautiful. He looked over the neatly trimmed hedges surrounded by summer blooms of red, blue, yellow, and white, planted purposely for the upcoming Tee It Up For The Troops Tournament. Coming from a war-torn country, he understood the sacrifice of soldiers and their families. Even with all the happy, beautiful events, weddings, galas, and fundraisers, the Tee It Up For The Troops Tournament was the one he looked forward to the most.

He caught sight of the soft pastel dress as it swished around Samantha Reeves's body. She had her phone pressed against the side of her face as she paced along the front circular drive. Frustration was evident as her free hand waved around as she spoke, with more animation in her facial features now that she thought nobody was watching her.

"What are you gawking at?" Will Pinsonneault asked as he walked up on Casey, straining out the window.

"Nothing," Casey said as he leaned back from the window, feeling a flush of heat rise on his cheeks.

"Right," Will said as he eyed Casey before he leaned to look out the window in the direction that Casey had just been looking. "Okay, so what am I looking at... Oh... I see now," Will said with a laugh.

Will was the reason Casey was working at the country club. They had known each other since college at UW Stout in the golf management program. They became inseparable friends during their first year of school. Casey had been chatting with a gorgeous fraternity sister at a frat party when Will introduced himself to the girl and started hitting on her in front of him. Instead of what Casey thought was going to be a fistfight, they ended up drinking a few rounds, chatting golf, and that was it. The girl was forgotten, and their friendship cemented—until Will tried to talk Casey out of marrying Lucinda. They didn't speak for a long time. Casey always chalked it up to Will, not wanting to lose his wingman because Will had no intention of marrying—and still didn't. His life was golf, drinks, and women.

"A wife would just nag me for spending too much time at the golf course." This was the classic Will response whenever someone asked why a handsome, successful man like him was still single. Will worked hard to earn his way as the Head Golf Professional. Shortly after being hired, he brought on Casey as the director of Media and Marketing.

"Have you seen her before?" Casey asked as he leaned back into the window next to Will.

"No." Then Will added, "And I would have definitely remembered her."

"It's strange. I feel like I know her," Casey said mostly to himself, "but I don't think I've ever met her before."

Will popped his head back at Casey's comment. He just stared at the back of his friend's head as Casey stared out the window.

He looked over and realized Will was eyeing him carefully. "What?" Casey asked incredulously as he sat up straighter, pulling away from the window.

Will went wide-eyed and pointed his finger at Casey's chest. "You like her."

Casey huffed a laugh as he swatted Will's hand off of his chest. "I talked to her for two minutes." Casey shrugged. "I mean, yeah, she is drop-dead gorgeous. And smart." Casey smiled as her image came to mind. "She's funny, too."

"When was the last time you talked to a woman for two minutes and then stalked her through a window looking like a sad, lost little puppy?"

Casey turned from the window and pushed Will's shoulder as he walked past. "I'm not stalking her. I just wanted to make sure..." he trailed off. "Hell, I have no idea what I wanted to make sure of." He looked at Will before turning back into the clubhouse. "Shit, man, I think I do like her."

Chapter 4

Jeffrey Lindahl was dead. Minneapolis PD confirmed it as Samantha arrived at his Minnetonka house just after lunch. Sam worked a lot with the MSPD and had a good rapport with them. She found the chief investigator, Mark Crane, standing by the front door of the house as what she assumed was Jeffrey's body rolled out covered with black plastic on a yellow-legged stretcher.

"And what do I owe the pleasure of being graced by my favorite PI?" Chief Crane said as Sam approached. He hugged her with his big arms and his growing belly, which grew bigger every year. The closer he was to retirement, the bigger his belly got. Thankfully, Sam thought, retirement was just a few years away.

"Well, good news and bad news for you, Chief." Sam smiled as she stepped back. "The good news is that Jeffrey Lindahl was the subject of my current case."

His face went from a soft greeting to a tightened grimace. "Go on with the bad news."

Sam mirrored the change of expression. "Well, that depends. Does this look like foul play, natural death, or suicide?"

"Well, considering there is a bullet hole in the center of his head and through his pillow, I'd say we're looking at a murder."

"That is bad news," she said as she shook her head. "I haven't noticed anything out of the ordinary the past few weeks. I followed him home last night, and everything was routine.

I expected to catch up with him at the golf course this morning." She gestured to her clothes as she stood in front of the chief on the front lawn, watching the stretcher disappear into the awaiting ambulance. "Obviously, he didn't show up."

Chief just grunted a throaty acknowledgment as he crossed his arms over his chest.

"Damn," Sam cursed. This was not good. She lost Jeffrey between last night and this morning. If she had been thinking clearly, she would have noticed he wasn't at the golf course right away and could have been at Jeffrey's house sooner.

Sam put her hands on her hips as she turned to the chief. "In fact, I was investigating him for a supposed increase in potential violent behavior toward his ex-wife and kids."

"Interesting," he said. "Find any?" he asked.

"No."

Chief Crane uncrossed his arms and put a hand on Sam's shoulder. "Well, it seems we'll be working on this one together, huh?"

"Yup," Sam agreed with a smile. Chief Mark Crane was the only friend she had and could count on. If she couldn't figure out something, he could. He asked her many times to join the police force, but after years of serving in the army, she was happy to be her own boss and work on her own terms. She was done taking orders.

"Chief." One of the sergeants appeared at the front door. He looked at the chief, and his eyes landed on Sam and widened. "Excuse me, Chief, you better come see this." His head bounced back to Sam before turning back to the chief. "Maybe she should wait out here."

Chief looked at the officer and then at Sam in confusion. Sam shrugged, just as confused.

"She's on the case, Officer Williams. She's fine."

With an accepting nod, the young officer led them through the luxury, gray-on-gray decorated home and up to the main bedroom. Sam noted all the crime scene techs that buzzed around with their equipment. Each focused on their mission of finding that vital piece of evidence that would solve the mystery and close the case.

They continued to follow the officer into the oversized bathroom off the main bedroom. A giant tub hugged the corner under oversized windows with views of the mid-day sunlight casting slices of light through the thick suburban trees. The clear glass shower with luscious, black rectangular stone tiles gleamed clean and fresh with no signs of a morning shower or shave. She noted the single electric toothbrush charging on the double-sink marble counter. She analyzed he must not have had any long-term or even an overnight "girlfriend."

The chief stood in front of the bathroom counter as Sam watched the sergeant hand him a piece of paper, keeping his eye trained on Sam. She glared back at him, not sure what to do with his odd behavior toward her. As the chief held the paper, she looked down and realized, no, it wasn't a piece of paper. It was a photograph.

"We found this on the mirror here, Chief," the officer said as he straightened his back slightly taller.

The chief peered down at the photograph, then at Sam. He held the photo up to his face, trying to get better light on it, Sam presumed, and then he turned to her. "Sam, is this you?!"

"What?" Sam leaned closer to the photo. The blood drained from her face as her heart fell to the bottom of her stomach. The chief held the last known photo of her team: her army brothers and teammates just before they left on the fatal mission in Afghanistan. They stood shoulder to shoulder, their rifles slung across their body-armored chests. Only this photo wasn't just a photo. It had an angry, drawn circle with a red slash over Sam in the image as she stood with the team. At Sam's feet, the word "Murderer" was scribed in the same angry red ink.

Sam was faced with the four people she failed and let die.

She should have prevented their deaths, but her carelessness cost them their lives, and she lived on. A thickness built in her throat that she couldn't swallow away. She couldn't speak. She couldn't breathe.

"Sam?" Chief prodded.

She mindlessly nodded as she stared at the photo.

"Sam," Chief said her name, but it was more of a question.

Sam looked at the chief. She waited for her vision to clear. Finally, she was able to swallow the bile that had risen. She cleared her throat before mustering up a whisper response. "Yes, Chief. That is me in Afghanistan. With my team." Sam choked on the last word as she tried to control her emotions.

Chapter 5

The unmarked police cruiser dropped her off at the Lakeside Motel in front of the crooked 7B door. It took the Minneapolis police department all day to interview and dissect her files and notes on Jeffrey Lindahl. Her only break was to drop off the rental car since it was her final day of surveillance. After Juan confirmed her alibi, she went from suspect to co-investigator. Sort of.

Not all of the detectives appreciated her relationship with Chief Crane and her working so close with the police department on cases that were deemed police business. It took all of her willpower not to roll her eyes as certain detectives attempted to wield their badges over her. Overcompensating for sure, she thought throughout her day.

She was used to working with male-dominated industries; she let it stop fazing her a long time ago.

She collapsed forward onto the dingy motel bed face first and exhaled a long and exhausted breath. She had planned to check out after the golf tournament, but now it was too late, she thought as she checked her watch. It was after nine.

Sam rolled onto her back with a moan and closed her eyes. She wanted nothing more than to let the exhaustion take over and fall into a deep, dreamless sleep. Sam sighed, "But first..." She popped open her eyes. She reached out her hand, clutching her bag closer to her on the bed. She rooted around until her fingers wrapped around her phone. She held it above her face as she lay on her back. She hadn't figured out what to tell Maggie Lindahl yet. Technically, her case was over with Jeffrey no longer needing to be surveilled. Still, she would wait until it was better timing to close out the contract with the final payment. Normally, her closing out a case didn't involve a dead subject, so she didn't quite know how to close this one and didn't think that today would be the day.

She sent off a text sending her condolences and let Maggie know that all of her investigation material had been turned over to the police to help find out who had done this and that she would be in touch soon.

Sam forced herself to sit up. She needed a shower and food. Other than stale vending machine food, she hadn't eaten anything all day. She caught sight of herself in the frameless mirror. She was still wearing her golf dress from this morning. She chuckled at her reflection. She had never even swung a golf club before, but she certainly looked the part today.

She found Casey's card from this morning in her dress pocket. It was thick cardstock with a gold-embossed golf emblem and lettering—simple and clean, with his number inked in deep black balancing the gold. She thought about calling him to let him know they'd be one member short this year.

"Better not." She tossed the card on the bathroom counter. "And why would I?"

Casey Parks hadn't crossed her mind all day. "Okay, fine." Sam picked up the card again. "Okay, maybe once or twice, those evergreen eyes popped into my head," Sam said to her reflection. She pointed the card at the mirrored image of her. "But it was when I was talking about golf so that it totally made sense." She threw the card back on the counter. "Obviously."

She should just go home. It would be late enough that traffic would not be an issue, and she could be home in thirty minutes or so. She walked over to the window and peered out the blinds. Across the lot, the front office sat dark.

"Well, crap."

Any plans to check out were officially squashed. She'd have to spend one more night here before heading back to her home. She loved her little townhome and had designed it to be comfortable with warm, neutral tones that she could relax into. It had been nearly a week since she was home. As excited as she was to crawl into her own bed, she knew nothing else awaited her there.

Her cabinets looked as if the Grinch had slunk through her house, leaving nothing but a crumb that was too small for a mouse.

She tried to keep a pet fish at one point. After she found her rainbow betta, aptly named Sushi III, floating upside down, she called it quits. It is much better to come home to an empty house than a dead fish.

She had put the rest of her cases on hold. They waited in her inbox, and they could continue to wait until tomorrow. She thought about the mysterious military police patch at the bottom of her bag waiting for her, too. As far as she was concerned, that could continue to wait forever.

"Ugh." Sam dragged her hands over her face. "What a fucking day." She made her way across 7B back to the bathroom. "Before anything else, a shower."

The hot water sprayed a sad light mist from the fixed showerhead and did nothing to help Sam's achy shoulders relax.

She closed her eyes as she succumbed to the images of her team from the photo earlier. She explained each of them to the police investigators earlier in the day. Specialist David Voss was just out of college and lived with his mom before deploying. He had a brother and sister, if she remembered correctly. He was new to the unit, so Sam had only just started to get to know him.

Private First Class Brian Lewis she knew well. They shared a lot about their families (or lack thereof). He had an on-and-off-again girlfriend back home that always stressed Brian out, but Sam stayed out of it. The girlfriend was young and didn't understand military life. His family was Southern Christian, the "praise Jesus, faith is life" type. Months after she returned home from Afghanistan, Brian's parents sent her a letter saying, "God felt it was time for our son to be close to him, so He sent him home." Sam appreciated the gesture, but it had yet to bring her much peace. Brian was still dead.

Sergeant Erik Danu was married and had two kids at home. Sam heard his wife had since remarried and had two more kids. For Erik, family was everything. Rarely a day went by he didn't email or call them.

Sam's closest friend and confidant was Specialist Justin Sommers. They spent endless days playing card games, reading, discussing life, and how it would be when they got home. Justin had a relationship with someone else in another company, but Sam didn't know much about it. He was very hush-hush about it. As much as she tried to get him to talk about it, he just shelled up. Sam assumed it was fraternization with an officer or married woman. Neither was good, but stuff like that happened on deployments, so she let it go. She assumed he would talk about it when he was ready.

Justin grew up on a Minnesota dairy farm just two hours north of the Twin Cities, with a two brothers and two sisters in what Sam teased was the "stereotypical" farmer family whenever he showed pictures of the family. They had this tradition where his mom would decorate their big wraparound porch for every holiday season. Justin's mom, Patty, was proud of her hand-painted tin milk containers. She'd email Justin a picture every time she finished a new one. Sam loved seeing Justin show them around to the team. A pumpkin surrounded by white wispy ghosts for Halloween. For Thanksgiving, Patty had turned the milk container on its side and painted a cornucopia and a turkey holding a sign that said "Beef. It's what's for dinner."

Those men were the closest thing she ever had as a family. She just had her mother growing up. Calling her a "mother" was being generous.

Sam finished washing the shampoo out of her hair and then let the conditioner soak in.

"There has to be something I missed."

Besides the roadside bomb. An intrusive thought penetrated her head.

Sam groaned as she grabbed the sides of her head, squeezing tight, trying to stop the revisiting voice and visions that crept in.

She should have seen the signs of the ambush.

That was her job.

She was the lead vehicle, the spotter.

She was the team leader.

How did she miss it?!

They were heading west outside of Kandahar. They were providing security for troop movement and supplies to Kabul. She was in the lead truck, as usual, with her squad in the truck behind, followed by three more vehicles and rear security. Sam spotted an overpass ahead and was doing her surveillance scans when an explosion from somewhere behind rocked her forward, smashing her Kevlar helmet against the thick windshield of the Humvee. The truck slammed to a stop. It was quiet for a split second until she heard the fast rhythmic clink, clink, clink, clink of small arms fire as they started to pelt the armored vehicles with gunfire. Everything began to play in slow motion. Sam heard shouting, then the familiar steel grinding as the gun turret spun above her head. The gunner, now in position, lit up the hillside where the small rounds of fire were coming from. No more thinking was necessary. Training took over. She closed her eyes as she waited for the noise to quiet and the all-clear to go back and save her team... her family.

When she opened them back up, she was standing under freezing water in the dank yellow-stained motel bathroom shower.

"Get it together, Sam," she scolded herself as the memories faded back into the darkness.

She toweled off and stood in front of the bed. She needed to go to bed but knew the memories of her team would follow her there. She needed food "and a strong drink," she said as she finished her thought out loud. Sam confirmed her decision by slipping on denim jeans and a simple, black V-neck shirt. She no longer had the rental car and had her car parked a few blocks away, so she called for an Uber. She dabbed on some mascara and concealer to hide her exhaustion the best she could. Her ride pulled up, and she was ready to find some food and a drink.

Chapter 6

Casey Parks was closing things out in his office at the country club. He couldn't believe how late it was already. The day had gone really well, so it flew by. His team kept the golf pros and local celebrities to their schedules, and the event went off as planned. He smiled as he thought of how intriguing the beautiful stranger Samantha Reeves was. He didn't want to admit to himself how often he checked his phone to see if he missed a call from an unknown number. When his phone finally did ring a couple of hours ago, it wasn't Sam who called, much to his disappointment; it was the Minneapolis Police Department.

"Jeffrey's dead? Really?" Casey spoke to the chief investigator—Mark Crane. "Haven't heard from him since..." Casey trailed off, pausing to think of how to phrase what he wanted to say.

"Go on," Chief urged.

"Well," Casey continued, "I had to ask him to leave the club a week or two ago. He had one too many drinks and was being," Casey paused. "How do I say this politely? He was being an ass-wad dickhead toward our other members." Casey remembered the putrid wet smell of piss and whiskey as he and Will practically carried Jeffrey out of the country club. The whiskey scent came when Jeffrey sucker-punched his girlfriend's husband while holding his drink. The piss scent came after the husband bounced back and knocked Jeffrey out cold. The board had planned on banning Jeffrey after that incident, but a sizeable donation came in a few days after the incident, and he was allowed to stay.

Just thinking about all that drama made Casey happy he'd kept single after his impulsive college marriage. But then he thought of the beautiful woman by the window in the soft pink dress.

"There was a woman here earlier this morning at today's golf tournament," he told the chief, "looking for Jeffrey." Casey explained about his encounter with Samantha Reeves.

"Thanks for letting me know about Ms. Reeves, Mr. Parks." Chief Crane chuckled. "I actually know Ms. Reeves quite well. She is an interesting person." He cleared his throat. "But not a person of interest in this case," Chief Crane said. "No need to worry about her."

"Interesting is one way to describe her," Casey said. "I'd add compelling and beautiful, and..." Casey stopped himself. Why was he saying all this stuff to a complete stranger? He shook his head as he heard a gruff laugh come from Chief Crane.

"She is all those things, son, but add hardheaded, stubborn, and..." This time, it was the chief who trailed off.

"She is single, then?" Casey pressed.

Chief cleared his throat uncomfortably. Casey wasn't sure if it was his reluctance to share information about Sam or if it was guilt for sharing what he already had.

"Go on," Casey mimicked the chief's tone from earlier.

Chief cleared his throat once again. "Well, don't worry about Ms. Reeves. She's a private investigator." His tempo changed as he attempted to change topics. "Well, I appreciate your time, Mr. Parks. Let me know—"

"Private investigator, huh?" Casey cut off Chief with his spoken thought.

Casey's mind drifted into a dreamy state as he thought about how much he wanted to investigate every interesting, soft and sexy inch of PI Samantha Reeves. His mind and body responded in unison, and he knew for sure he needed to see her again. His next sentence came out faster and higher pitched than he wanted. "How do I get in touch with her?"

He cleared his throat, trying to regain his composure. "What I mean is, I'm sure you are busy. I could ah... er... just reach out to her directly. You know..." He cringed as he heard the desperation in his own voice, so he added, to save any face, "For the case."

Casey swore he could hear the chief smile through the phone. His suspicions were confirmed after he heard the short, grunted cackle. "Ha. I've been a detective for nearly thirty years," the chief continued now in more of a fatherly tone. "I wasn't born yesterday, son, but no."

"Please, Chief, I have to see her again." Ugh, Casey hated pleading, but he couldn't shake her out of his head.

The moment of silence seemed to stretch as Casey waited for the chief to respond. Twice in one day, he felt compelled to express himself emotionally to complete strangers. Casey shook his head at his own stupidity. He had to be losing his mind.

Casey heard the chief inhale deeply before he spoke, "Why, Mr. Parks? What is so important that you'd need to speak with her instead of a police officer?"

Casey tried to think of anything reasonable. Anything that would be considered a rational response to a seemingly simple question. Casey hung his head and rubbed his forehead with agitation.

"I have no idea, Chief." He ran his hands through his thick hair and down the back of his neck. "I just need to."

"Son, if I had a dime for every time someone asked for Ms. Reeves's number..." He chuckled. "Mind you, most of them were handcuffed when they asked."

"Well, I assure you, I have never been handcuffed, Chief Crane." He smirked and almost added, "I've used handcuffs," but thought better of it.

"Hmm, well, you seem like a savvy guy, Casey."

Casey's heart jumped a bit at the chief's change of tone. "Yes, sir, I am."

"I'm sure you'll find a way to find..." the chief paused, "... Raven Investigations' sole owner, Samantha Reeves's, contact information," Chief said with a wink in his voice. "But as I said before, I'm not looking to get in trouble with her and won't share her number."

Casey couldn't help but grin and thought he might have fallen in love with a police chief today. "Thank you," he practically shouted into the phone. He regained his composure, evening out his tone before adding, "Please let me know if there is anything I can do to help with your case."

"We'll be calling with any follow-up information we may need, Mr. Parks." The chief paused before adding, "Good luck, son."

"Thank you, sir. I appreciate it." Casey pulled the phone down and was about to end the call when he heard the chief's grunted laugh say, "You're going to need it."

Chapter 7

Her phone buzzed on the bar as the bartender put a shot of tequila and Coke in front of Sam. An unknown number after ten o'clock was never a good sign. Sam sighed and answered anyway, knowing how the day had gone so far; it couldn't get much worse.

"You never called me." A familiar, deep tone instantly brought intense green eyes to her mind.

"How'd you get my number?" Sam asked, annoyed by Casey's lack of proper greeting and her increased heart rate at just hearing his voice. Damn her betraying body.

"You're not the only one with investigative skills, Ms. Reeves." Sam could hear a gloating tone in his voice. He clearly figured out who she was. Still, she smiled at the impressiveness of him taking the time to do it. Ugh! She didn't have the time or the patience to deal with this guy right now. She had a mile long list of cases she needed to get to and still support Chief Crane on this investigation. She was letting the police take the lead, but she knew she'd still do her own work. They had their way, and Sam had hers. She could do things and go places they couldn't. And she didn't need Casey taking time away from her work.

She threw the tequila shot back and signaled the bartender for another.

She smacked her lips, tasting the tequila as the smooth agave coated her tongue.

"Welp, I'm busy right now," she explained louder than she meant. "I have to go."

"Did I just hear you pound back a drink?" Casey asked. "Busy, huh?"

Sam smacked her head. Damn, this guy was good. Good looking and... No. She shook her head. She needed to stop her mind from going down that path again.

"You heard correctly. I am busy. And I did throw a shot back." She can't have distractions right now. The police patch and a murderer blaming her were plenty enough. "Congratulations, you're practically an amateur sleuth," Sam deadpanned. "And now I hope you hear correctly once again when I say 'Goodbye, Casey.'"

"Ah, please don't hang up, Sam."

There was something in his voice that made her pause from ending the call. "Why not? Give me a reason why I should keep talking to you?"

"Damn," Casey cursed. "That's twice in one day; I don't have a good reason."

Sam kinked her eyebrow up. "Huh? What do you mean?"

Casey smashed his palm on his forehead. "Never mind. Anyway, I found out about Jeffrey today. Since I know now you were looking for him, I wanted to talk to you about him."

"I just spent all day talking about Jeffrey, among other things," Sam said. "Your offer is not enticing."

"Okay, I'll only talk about Jeffrey briefly; the rest, we'll talk about you."

"Hmm," she hummed her disbelief.

"Besides, I have some good info on him that might help your investigation. I wasn't sure if it mattered, but maybe you want to know, being a private investigator and all."

"I don't have the energy for games, Casey Parks. Just tell the police."

"Please, Samantha."

"Flipping A, Casey," she said as her hand came to the temple and rubbed with vigor. She wanted to get to the bottom of what happened to Jeffrey, mainly because it involved her somehow, but she wasn't sure about Casey. The pleading in his voice sounded genuine, but she couldn't understand why he was intent on seeing her.

"Sam," he pleaded her name once again.

Maybe it was the long day, the tequila, or just her morbid curiosity, but the following words out of her mouth surprised her.

"I'm at McPaddy's in St. Paul. I'll be here until my dinner and drink are gone."

"I'll be there in twenty."

"I eat fast."

"I'll be there in ten."

Sam put down her phone and threw back the second shot the bartender had dropped off a second ago. Curiosity was going to get the best of her. Sam decided she would have to put aside whatever feelings were meddling with her mind about Casey and the military police patch and focus. She had to find out who killed Jeffrey, why she was involved, and most importantly, if they planned anything else.

Chapter 8

Sam nibbled on the last bit of her fish and chips when a platter of chicken wings, mozzarella sticks, and other appetizers landed in front of her with another shot accompanied by a Coke. "I didn't order this," she said, confused, looking around the bar. It was quiet when she arrived, but the crowd was picking up. A few tables were full, and people were filing in every few minutes or so. None of the growing crowd offered her an answer, so she looked back to the ponytailed, lanky bartender with full tattooed sleeves.

"No," he answered. "But a guy called and said to keep food and drink in front of you until he arrived." He shrugged. "So there you go."

"And you listened to him?" Sam said open-mouthed.

"Yeah." The bartender's gray eyes looked over Sam for a brief moment before he added, "For a 100-dollar tip"—he grinned—"I sure did."

"Which was well earned, my friend," Casey smiled as he breezed up to the bar with perfect timing. He slapped the cash on the counter and winked at Sam. He wore an off-white scout jacket over a black t-shirt with well-worn jeans that hugged his muscular thighs.

"Any time, man," the bartender said as he put a beer in front of Casey. Casey nodded at the bartender as he plopped himself down on the bar stool and spun so he was facing Sam.

Sam tried to ignore the sensation when his knees grazed by her thigh.

Keeping his eyes locked on Sam's, Casey leaned within inches of Sam's gaping mouth, snagged a mozzarella stick off the platter, leaned back, and shoved the whole stick in his mouth. Sam watched him as he chewed slowly, and his mouth formed into a slow-burn smirk.

She felt her body flush with heat. Probably from the tequila, she told herself.

"I couldn't risk you finishing before I could get here." He looked at his watch. "Twelve minutes." He smiled at himself. "Not bad."

Sam shook her head, trying to comprehend what the hell just happened. "I need to go to bed."

Casey grinned, letting his perfectly aligned teeth beam as he slid the platter closer to him, grabbed another bite of food, and winked. "Happy to take you there."

"Ha." Sam rolled her eyes. Now she knew why he wanted to see her. "I'm sure you would."

Sam popped the last fries in her mouth, trying to get control of the conversation. "However," she said and licked the salt off her fingertips. "Once there, you would be wildly disappointed." Sam smirked as she licked the last bit of salt off her thumb with a popping smack. "I snore," she added a long snort to affirm her snoring statement.

Quite pleased with herself, she turned to Casey, expecting to see the light, humorous look in his teasing eyes. Instead, she found his eyes were darkened and focused on her mouth. Sam was overcome with an immediate sense of self consciousness and bit her bottom lip to stop her tongue from darting across her lips.

"So do I." His voice was sultry and low. It hummed through her body and echoed through her thighs. She took a sip of her Coke, hoping to distract herself from the trembling heat that coursed through her.

After a few more sips, the sugary soda freed her mind, "Oh, you snore too?" She hoped she sounded cool and calmer than she actually felt.

Casey raised his eyebrows at Sam with a smirky grin.

She smirked back. "Okay then."

She shoved her empty plate to the bar edge, wiping her hands on the napkin before throwing it on the plate. "Was there something you wanted to tell me, or can I go home now?"

Casey nodded toward the back wall. "Let's grab a booth."

Sam narrowed her eyes at Casey. He wasn't leaving as easily as she first hoped. Casey's eyes were challenging her to say no again. She grabbed the tequila and tossed it back, smacking the empty glass on the bar. Never backing down from a challenge, she grabbed the Coke and marched over to one of the few remaining booths as Casey grabbed his beer and shoved another cheesy breadstick in his mouth before grabbing the food platter and following Sam to a wooden oak booth in the corner.

Apparently, Sam thought as she slid into the booth, Casey hadn't had dinner tonight either, as she watched him stuff another mozzarella stick into his mouth. Damn, it wasn't fair that a man should look that sexy with melted cheese and grease dangling from his scruffy beard.

"What?!" Casey said with a mouthful as he caught her staring.

She wanted to scold herself for thinking it but surprised herself by laughing when he asked. "Nothing. You're just acting like you haven't eaten all day." She pressed her lips into a thin line to stop her laughter as she gestured to his chin.

"I haven't," he said after he swallowed his mouthful. Sam watched as his tanned hand cupped his beard and wiped the dangling cheese away. Casey unrolled the napkin from the silverware roll and wiped his hands before reaching for a sticky chicken wing. "I get caught up in work, and before I know it, it's late, and I'm hungry."

"I get that," Sam said. The past week, all her meals had been after thoughts and late nights.

Casey readied the tangy barbeque wing for a bite. "Jeffrey Lindahl was cheating on Maggie." He took the bite and looked at Sam expectantly. "You know, when they were still married."

Sam sipped her drink with zero reaction. Apparently, Casey thought this was big news. *Amateur.*

"They showed up together often to the country club." Casey pointed the stripped wing at Sam. "Which I thought was a grade-A asshole move. I think he thought having an affair was part of his status. Part of his charm. Gross." Casey tossed the finished wing down and grabbed a fresh one.

"Interesting," Sam said, sounding like Chief Crane, unaware she was mimicking her mentor.

Before taking a bite, he said, "It's not our place as a club to meddle too much into personal affairs, but when Jeffrey's escapades, we'll call them, started becoming the center of attention instead of our social events and fundraisers, we thought as a club staff, we'd better step in before the board would need to."

Sam realized Casey was waiting for her response to this "shocking news," which it was not. She knew of this affair on the first day of her investigation. As well as Jeffrey on the verge of losing his country club membership. The contact that got her on the list for the golf gala that morning happened to be excellent at hacking into certain software undetected.

"Go on," she waved her hand as she sipped the last bit of her Coke.

Casey let out an exasperated sigh. To Sam, it sounded like giving up on the shock factor of his news. Instead, he seemed to be enjoying Sam's challenging silence. He took a long pull from his tall tap beer. Trying to prove to her he wasn't in a rush, she mused. He set down the empty glass, never once taking his eyes off Sam's.

"Another round?" The sturdy, short waitress appeared, breaking their silence.

"Yes, No," they said simultaneously,

"Welp," the waitress said, "the woman is always right. I'll bring the check." She left with a short nod.

"Fine," Sam caved, turning back to Casey. "What did you do about Jeffrey and his personal affairs being flaunted all over the club?"

"I pulled him aside one day and asked him about it directly." Casey wiped his hands on his napkin. "He told me to *fuck off* as I expected, but I warned him to keep his personal life—personal. That he should be careful."

"Did he take that as a threat?"

"No, I don't think so." Casey thought momentarily. "He just seemed pissed that I dared to challenge him. Jeffrey was 'the shit,' or so he thought of himself. Most of our club members aren't like that."

"But you saw through him, didn't you?" Sam asked in a soft tone.

"Yeah, I guess." He shrugged. "Most of the other staff wanted just to let it go. They said Jeffrey just needed to get it out of his system." Casey's eyes closed just a moment as he seemed to consider his next thought. "But I couldn't." Casey continued explaining to her about dragging Jeffrey out of the club, the same as he told the chief. And how he nearly lost his membership rights.

The waitress dropped the check, which Casey quickly snatched up. "My sister dated her fair share of *Jeffreys*." Casey shook his head. "Nobody deserves that."

He has a sister that he cares about. An electric ping zipped through her body. Oh, hell no, she thought as she tried to shake off the flutter that landed smack in the center of her chest. Good looking and sounds like a good brother. Sam forced her eyes to look away from Casey. She focused on the growing crowd around them. Saturday night in St Paul; it was bound to get packed in here soon. She was guessing there was a concert at the Xcel Energy Center, and the concertgoers would rush out to get a drink as they let their ringing ears subside before making their way home.

I need to get out of here, Sam thought as she turned her attention back to Casey.

"Look, Casey, I'd love to tell you that you brought to light some great, case-breaking intel." She slid cash across the table to pay for her food and drink. "But sorry, you haven't." She looked at Casey with sympathy in her eyes. "And I'm not officially investigating this case anymore." She shrugged as she grabbed her phone and pulled up the Uber app. "I better go."

"You may not be officially investigating, but something tells me it won't stop you from digging further into it," Casey said as he pushed the cash back to her and put his hand over the phone in her hands. "Let me drive you home."

Sam paused as she scanned Casey over again. She tried to pretend his touch didn't phase her. "That's not necessary."

She went to pull her hands away from his, but as she did, he squeezed gently. "I know it's not. But I want to do it regardless if you find it necessary."

Sam now sat with the zap from earlier pulsing once again through her chest. In her head, she stood firm and thought *no*. But her mouth betrayed her resolve. "Fine," she said as she put down her phone.

They sat in comfortable silence as Casey drove her back to the Lakeside Motel. She watched out the passenger window as the various buildings and lights blurred until her thoughts were in oblivion. "None of today makes sense."

Casey reached over and squeezed Sam's hand as it sat on her lap. It startled her out of stupor as she turned toward him. Like she was seeing him for the first time here. Casey smiled and pulled his hand away. "I'm sure it will eventually."

Confused, Sam asked, "What will?"

"Today," Casey explained, "You said none of today makes

sense. I'm saying it will eventually."

Holy hell. Sam thought she was losing her mind. Now she was thinking out loud, and somehow, in his presence, she'd lost all sense of her surroundings each time. They had pulled into the parking lot and she had no clue. This was not good.

Casey's shadowed gaze locked with hers under the dim lights of the motel parking lot, each trying to get a read on the other.

Casey Parks was an attractive human being for sure, she thought. Everything about him caused her body to pulse in places she assumed were permanently dormant. Sam was a master at controlling her emotions and mind, but today, around Casey, her body had a mind of its own.

"I... I need to go to bed," she stammered. Before Casey could respond to her, she pointed a finger at him and added, "Alone."

Casey threw his hands up, feigning innocence, and chuckled. "I wasn't going to say anything."

Sam gave a halfhearted grin and fumbled for the door. "Thanks for the ride home and dinner, even though you didn't need to pay."

"It's not always about needs, Sam. What about your wants?" Casey asked. His voice dipped into a sultry, slow tone when he asked, "Don't you desire things instead of just needing them?"

Sam paused and looked through the open passenger door to Casey sitting in the driver's seat. His grin was so freaking sexy that it annoyed her. "Oh, I have desires, all right." She attempted to return his smolder in hopes to annoy the shit out of him too. "I have a few needs on my list before I even glimpse the desire list."

"Am I on the need list or the desire list?" Casey asked.

"Neither," Sam said before she closed the door on Casey's smirking face.

She followed the headlight beams to the 7B door. "Neither?"

she whispered to herself as she unlocked the door. "Shit. Shit. Shit," she cursed. As much as she kept trying to deny the energy she felt toward Casey, she knew it was there. She didn't even believe herself when she said neither. When she turned around and saw the beaming smile on Casey's face through the windshield, she knew he hadn't either.

She slammed the door shut on his Cheshire Cat grin. She slid the deadbolt in place before she latched the chain. She had more fun with Casey than she wanted to admit. She took a deep breath as she looked around her room. Tomorrow morning, she would head home and get to work on figuring out how she ended up wrapped up in Jeffrey's murder.

After brushing her teeth and throwing on an old band t-shirt, she crawled into bed. She had a lot of angst about Jeffrey, being accused of being a murderer, and losing her focus all day. Still, she couldn't stop smiling as she drifted off to sleep.

Chapter 9

Juan Hernandez fumbled and dropped Sam's motel room key after she handed it across the front desk. Sam redirected her gaze out the lobby window for a moment. The sun was just on the verge of rising, causing the morning sky over the motel to blush with soft pinks and purples. Juan gathered up the key off the floor and hung it in the opened key box. He turned back to Sam; his tanned cheeks blushed, mimicking the sky's pink hue. He turned to his ancient computer and clicked a few times before the equally ancient printer underneath the front desk started firing up. Sam smiled at the sweetness of Juan. His kindness often seemed out of place in a dingy motel like this.

She accepted Juan's two copies of her total bill as he slid them over with a pen. "And you're sure you have no way of knowing who dropped off that package the other night?" Sam asked as she eyed the circa 1995 security camera in the corner.

She signed both and pushed one document and pen back to him.

"No, ma'am." Juan followed her gaze to the ancient camera. "Sorry, but that is just for show. It hasn't worked in six or seven years."

"Juan," Sam said in her best teacher voice, "as someone who has worked in security for a long, long time, that pains me to no end."

He shrugged, took the document, and returned the pen to

the wired pencil holder. "People like their privacy and anonymity around here, Ms. Reeves."

"I know, Juan," Sam said as she folded her copy and shoved it into her bag. She threw the strap over her shoulder and grabbed the handle of the roller bag next to her. "Just get it up and running before I come back here next time."

Juan blushed as he went around the front lobby and opened the door for Sam. He nodded as she walked out. "Yes, Ms. Reeves, I'll see what I can do."

The air held onto the morning dew as Sam walked the few blocks to her parked car at the airport park and fly. The humidity would be thick today, she mused as she breathed in the thickening air. Her shoulders relaxed as the damp air brought a sense of relief. She'd be home shortly, all cozied up in her air-conditioned home in her favorite spot: her desk. Most people didn't find comfort in front of their computers, but that's where she did her best work. To her, delving deep into the recesses of the internet and black web was as relaxing as doing a puzzle. Well, she assumed most people found doing puzzles to be a relaxing hobby. Sam wasn't sure. Her puzzle pieces were just facts, not jagged-edge shapes. Each piece could lead her closer to solving whatever investigation she was working on. She had quite the waiting list to go through when she got home. Technically, this case was closed. Jeffrey Lindahl was gone and no longer a threat to Maggie and her family. Still, she was going to help solve the murder of Jeffrey, especially since she was wrapped up in it somehow, but the "why" was a complete mystery.

The police thought it had something to do with her current investigation into Jeffrey. Sam knew better. It was no coincidence the military police patch showed up about the same time Jeffrey was killed. Someone with a tie to the Afghanistan mission did this. It had to be. She had no clue how Jeffrey was tied to the Afghanistan mission. She would have to dig through her notes on Jeffrey to see if she missed any military connections with him. Thankfully, all her notes were backed up on the cloud, so yes, the police had her laptop, but she could access them on her home computer.

Sam dug through her purse to find her car keys as she turned into the park and fly lot. The crunching sound of tires behind her made her pause and look up. She saw a man and woman in the front having, from what she could tell, an animated conversation. The minivan slowed as it pulled beside her, and the window rolled down. The sound of a young toddler singing a made-up song about an airplane ride billowed out the van's window. "Hi," the exhausted mother shouted over the toddler's singing. "Hi. Sorry. Did we miss the shuttle to the airport?" she asked.

"I'm sorry, I don't know exactly," Sam said with kind eyes as her hands pulled out her car keys. Sam looked around and pointed back behind her where the lot's entrance was. "I believe there is an information booth just over there with a number you can call."

The mother followed Sam's gesture and saw the signage. "Of course," she sighed as she glared at her husband in the driver's seat. The woman turned back to Sam with a smile. "Thank you so much." The van pulled forward, and Sam heard the woman's fading voice as the window rolled up, "I told you so."

Sam chuckled as she watched the van make its way around a row of parked cars. She continued to her car, parked at the far end of the row. She clicked the unlock button on her key fob when she was a few cars away from her car.

She heard the familiar beep of her car unlocking and the quick flash of the headlights. Then, just after the blink of the headlights, she heard an unusual clicking sound.

A bright flash exploded as a deafening blast rocketed her backward, throwing her into the air. She landed hard against her side, her head bouncing off the rough pavement, and she skidded across the roughly paved parking lot.

She heard a few car alarms buzzing alongside ringing in her ears. Sam opened her eyes after how long, she wasn't sure. Her blurry vision pulsed in time with her racing heartbeat. The world was on its side as her head lay against the gravelly ground. Her eyes briefly focused on some movement in the distance. A dark shadow seemed to be moving toward her. She needed to move, but she was tired. "I'm so tired," Sam mumbled. The dark figure approached, but Sam didn't notice. The figure blended into the fading black as everything around her faded into complete darkness.

Chapter 10

"That fucking cunt!" Lane Norris shouted as she sat in the dented, black, late-nineties pickup truck, and she slammed her fist against the steering wheel. "No!" Lane shook her head feverishly. "That fucking minivan stopped that bitch from being blown up."

Nobody noticed the stranger in the truck parked two blocks away—but with a perfect view of the situation through binoculars. All the attention was on the burning car. The man from the minivan seemed to be the one who called 911 as he was pacing frantically, talking on the phone. The woman with him was bent over Sam. Lane couldn't see exactly, but she was certain Samantha Reeves was still alive at this point.

"Dammit," she sighed. She hadn't counted on someone distracting Reeves and wasn't expecting her to unlock her car so far away. The trigger she had planted under her car should have delayed longer before it set off. "Dammit. Dammit."

She found a pen and pad on the benched seat's passenger side. Lane peered through the binoculars and found a good angle to get a read on the minivan's license plate. She scribbled the plate number down and briefly described what the man looked like. "Fat. A dumb-ass balding loser. Dead."

"You stupid fucker," she cursed as she wrote. "You're going to pay for this." Reeves would have been blown the fuck up if they hadn't stopped her. Lane tossed the yellow notepad on the passenger seat and put the truck into drive. "First, I have to fix your fuck up," she said in the direction of the parking lot. Lane put the truck into drive and pulled into the road, blending in with the early morning commuters. "The bitch needs to blow up."

Chapter 11

Why is there so much shouting? Sam thought as voices echoed around her. The smell of gunpowder filled the cab of the truck and, in turn, filled her lungs with the thick scent. Sam counted to three, readied her rifle, and on her exhale, she shoved her shoulder into the heavily armored door. It swung open, and she moved quickly, setting up around the edge of the truck door, using it as a shield. The gunner above her had stopped firing but still scanned the hillside, watching for any signs of the ambush. "Clear, Sergeant. Move!" he hollered at her. Sam nodded and moved with caution from her position, and, for the first time, she rounded the back of the truck and saw the aftermath of the attack. The flipped Humvee was twenty yards behind her. Smoke billowed around the overturned truck. The mangled wheels and heavy armor weaved together like the mortality thread of the three Fates. Had Atropos chosen to make any cuts?

Sam was still trying to understand what happened; she hadn't seen any signs of the roadside bomb or the ambush. Perhaps she was too focused on the upcoming overpass to see the signs around them. It was just a usual security mission, and then all hell broke loose in an instant.

Sam shook it off and let her training take the lead as she moved tactically around the area. Soldiers from the other teams were already in position securing the area, and the medics were moving toward the overturned truck. Sam moved in the same direction. TJ, the team lead from the rear security, was shouting something inaudible to Sam as he moved with a medic at his side. Her youngest soldier, Private First Class Lewis, who had been in the rear passenger side of the truck, was propped up near the back of the truck. His rifle lay limp across his lap. He must have exited the vehicle and still provided return fire, trying to protect his team. Sam felt her throat tighten; tears threatened to break her training. She arrived just before the medic. She checked his pulse. It was light, but he was still alive. The medic slid in next to her and signaled her to get out of his way. As she did, Sam moved his rifle to his side and took notice of how bits of torn flesh were visible through the blood-soaked pants. His face was pale, with no color on his usual tan farmer-boy face. She had to let the medic work as she went around to the driver's door to find her other teammates. Specialist Justin Sommers had been driving. "Shit. Shit. Shit. Shit," Sam muttered as she rounded the side of the truck. The tiny, thick window of the armored door made it impossible to see in. Besides the cracked glass, it was splattered and smeared with something dark and dripping. The tightness in her throat turned to bile. She swallowed it down, for she knew, at that moment, the three Fates had weaved and measured, and Atropos had made her choice and cut the thread.

"Sam. Shhh. It's okay."

Sam's eyes fluttered open.

"You're safe, Samantha. It's okay."

As her vision cleared, she saw Chief Mark Crane's warm, soft-lined face standing over her. She felt his familiar, comforting hand resting on her forearm. She attempted to smile, but a tight pain ran across her left cheek.

"You know," the chief said softly. "I've only seen you cry one other time." He gently patted her forearm.

Sam strained to lift her head and sit.

"Just a sec." He hit the arrow on the bedside button as the bed hissed and raised so Sam could sit up. He tucked another pillow under her head.

"I was crying?" Sam hoarsely spoke as she settled into the inclined position.

"Yes, but your bandaged cheek soaked it all up." The chief patted her shoulder and whispered, "Don't worry, I won't tell anyone." He kissed the top of her forehead. "Your secret is safe." He winked as he sat back in the bedside chair.

She chuckled at the chief. "I appreciate your discretion."

She'd known Chief Crane since he was just Officer Mark Crane. Her mother wasn't always on the right side of the law, and for whatever reason, he took pity on Sam and did what he could to help her, often letting her mother go on charges she shouldn't have gotten away with. He was the one who introduced her to the idea of joining the army. Sam knew he didn't want to see her go down the same path as her mother. The military promised travel, money, education, and freedom. It gave her the opportunity to escape from home, which meant being away from her mother. That sounded like everything Samantha could ever want. Mark Crane came to her basic training graduation and supported her as Sam assumed any parent would. He became the only constant in her life.

Sam lifted her hand to her cheek and felt the stringy webbing of the gauze that covered her left cheek. She remembered the blast and feeling the heat from the explosion. If this was the only damage, she'd gotten lucky, she thought.

"Was anyone else hurt?" Sam asked, remembering the family in the van.

"No, thankfully, a family happened to be driving into the lot and saw what happened. They were able to call 911 right away." A somber tone fell over him when he said, "They said you stopped to help them with directions. If you hadn't done that..." he cut himself off as he shook his head.

Sam's mind was still a blanket of fog and haze as she began to replay the entire morning and analyze the data in her head.

After a few moments, she turned to the chief and said, "I'm starting to think that Jeffrey wasn't the main target."

"Or maybe Jeffrey was into some mess, and whoever killed him thinks you know something about it and needs to clean up some loose ends," the chief offered.

Her lips pressed into a thin line as she processed the situation. "Perhaps."

She wasn't sure that was the case, but she knew it was essential to explore every angle.

"Speaking of angles..."

The chief looked at her with a cocked eyebrow.

"I'm thinking," she said as she tapped her chin. "Whoever planted those explosives had to have seen me get close, right?"

"It could have been connected to the signal of your car fob, too. Depends on how sophisticated of a setup this was."

The chief leaned back in the bedside chair and rested his hands on his protruding belly. "We checked the surveillance camera and caught a glimpse of a black or dark blue vehicle pull up next to your car late Saturday night. Stolen plates. And the angle made it impossible to see anyone get out from the driver's side."

"So, it could have been anyone," Sam said.

Casey.

"*Shit.*" She winced. "No way."

There was no way he could have done this, she thought. Sam closed her eyes, trying to make sense of her foggy thinking.

"Shit. Shit. Shit," she cursed herself and her stupidity. Here she was, defending someone she barely even knew. She squeezed her closed eyes tighter and brought her hands up to rub her temples. How this man, Casey Parks, who wasn't even here, could send her pulse skyrocketing throughout her body was beyond comprehensible to her. She dared a glance at the heart rate monitor next to her bed. A steady fifty-four beats a minute.

Fine. See? she told herself. *You're fine.*

Sam turned her head to the other side to see the chief staring at her with confusion but patience. She always appreciated his patience. She had none.

But what if. The thought pained her beyond the reach of any pain medication. She swallowed the giant lump in her throat before whispering, "Casey Parks."

The chief leaned closer. "Huh?"

She cleared her throat. "I met Casey Parks from the golf course yesterday," Sam said as her heart sank. "He dropped me off Saturday night at the motel." Sam absentmindedly started rubbing her arm. She couldn't tell if she felt embarrassed, ashamed, or a fool for admitting this to the chief. She looked at him and caught the concerned look in his eyes. She took a deep breath. "He dropped me off after he met with me at McPaddy's." Sam turned her head toward the window, closed her eyes, and exhaled the last sentence. "He wanted to talk to me about Jeffrey Lindahl."

She wanted to bury herself under the thin hospital blanket to hide the blush of embarrassment that rose to her cheeks.

She'd been stupid and dangerous, letting this guy get under her skin like he had. She worked so hard at staying vigilant and on alert, which led to a ton of success in her career. She was well known in her private investigation world. How dare she let his stupid green eyes disarm her. Those green eyes flashed in front of her. But damn, those eyes were beautiful. They somehow looked through her like nothing she had ever experienced before.

Stop! Her eyes snapped open to stop the images of Casey's intense eyes that clouded her mind.

Sam turned and found the chief sitting silently on the couch, texting someone on his phone, completely unaware of the war she was waging within herself.

He looked up and met her gaze.

"Nothing to say, Chief?" Sam threw her hand up in surrender. "Go on, you can say it. Say what a fucking risk I took considering the investigation of Jeffrey's death. Tell me how stupid I was being."

The chief tilted his head at Sam with a soft smile and rose to his feet. He patted her shoulder. "The only one saying that about you is you." He squeezed her shoulder gently. "I'll go make a call."

Before he stepped out, he turned to Sam. "Sam, you meet

and talk with people all the time about cases." He waited until she looked at him. "Why was Casey Parks any different?"

Sam's eyes widened at the realization of what the chief had just asked. "I... I..." Sam stumbled over her words.

Sam watched as the slow smile stretched across the chief's face. Maybe he did notice her little internal war after all. But she wasn't about to let it go. She opened her mouth to argue her case some more, but a nurse and doctor walked in.

The chief nodded at the nurse and walked out.

The nurse checked Sam's chart and all her vitals as the doctor asked questions about her pain level and nausea. She answered everything with the appropriate responses, but her mind raced about why she was making a big deal over Casey.

"Everything looks great," the doctor said, "but with this head trauma, we'd like to monitor you for the next twenty-four hours unless there is someone who can stay with you overnight and monitor your concussion symptoms. If not, we'll discharge you tomorrow morning if everything still looks good."

"Twenty-four hours?" Sam asked. "Besides looking like Scarface, I feel fine. I don't need a babysitter."

The doctor and nurse eyed each other for a few moments before turning their half-smiles toward Sam. It was obvious to Sam that these two were having a full conversation about her with no words spoken. It was almost eerie to her that it seemed they both knew exactly what each other was thinking in those few moments. How could two people be so close they could communicate without speaking? she wondered.

"You're on a lot of medication right now," the nurse stated.

The doctor chimed in, "How about we check back in before we give you the next dose and see how you're doing."

It wasn't the answer Sam wanted, but she knew they were right. "Thanks, Doc."

"However," the doctor said as he put his pen in the chest pocket of his smock, "you won't get out of here any sooner than tomorrow without someone to watch over you."

She nodded her head, "I'll let you know." She already knew the answer. She didn't have anyone to call.

Sam turned away and peered out the window, wishing the curtain wasn't closed. She wanted to see the sky, a bird, or just a cloud. Anything that could offer a tiny sliver of brightness to this terrible day.

The chief was on the case. She had no close friends. She knew only one neighbor, but they weren't close enough to be considered an emergency contact friend. More of a "will you feed my fish when I'm gone" person. And she had failed at even asking for help with that.

Sam's only living relative—presuming she was still alive—was her mother, Colleen Reeves. She wasn't even sure Colleen lived in Minnesota anymore. As a child, she was told time and time again to pack up her bags. They bounced from apartment to apartment, town to town, year after year. Colleen always muttered and cursed with every move that something was wrong with the rented place or how shitty the landlord was. Sam believed her mom the first couple moves, but not after the first time a police officer came to visit was when she was around seven. She had been sent to her room, and she heard the officer's soft, muffled, rhythmic tone in the living room. And her mother's pitch getting louder and louder until she was shouting.

She remembered running out of the room, thinking her mother was being hurt. She ran out just as her mom picked up an ashtray and attempted to throw it against the wall in frustration. Colleen was at least smart enough not to aim it at the officer but not smart enough to look before throwing it—it smashed directly into Sam's head, dropping her like a swatted fly.

Sam winced at the memory of the ashes and discarded cigarettes covering her. The officer came to her as her mother stood still in her place. The officer grabbed a towel from the bathroom across the hall and helped her wipe off the ashes and tears from Sam's face. Sam never forgot the kindness of that officer's eyes and the gentleness of his hands as he comforted her. Sam also never forgot how she looked up through blurry eyes and watched her mom light a cigarette and point it at her as she held it between her two fingers and said, "I told you to stay in the damn room."

How long had it been since she talked to her mother? Years. Her last conversation with Colleen was to tell her about her life as a private investigator. As usual, the conversation became about Colleen—topped off with lies, exaggerations, and requests for money.

Maybe it was the therapy after Afghanistan or years of just being numb to her mother, but long ago, Sam accepted the fact her mother, Colleen Reeves, would never love her own daughter.

In that last visit with her mother when Sam told Colleen she wouldn't give her any money for her next business venture, Colleen was graceful enough to dismiss Sam by tossing a bowl full of cereal as she left. The entire neighborhood heard how ungrateful Sam had been to her own mother as Colleen screamed profanities at Sam. As Sam drove away, she allowed herself to cry for just a moment but then never looked back.

"Seems Casey is on the up and up, Sam," Chief Crane said as he walked back in, interrupting her darkening thoughts. Sam's heart lifted out of the pit of her stomach.

Chief Crane smiled as he watched the wave of relief wash over Sam's face. He liked Casey from the two short phone calls he'd had with him. He studied Sam for a moment as the lines around her eyes relaxed. Her lips pressed together as if she was trying to prevent herself from smiling. From the look on her face, the chief mused that Sam liked Casey, too.

When the chief had stepped into the hall, his first phone call was to the station to see if they could complete the quick background check he'd requested via text. They didn't find anything and confirmed the chief's initial assessment that Casey was clean.

The chief hung up with the station and flipped open his pad and pen, where he had written Casey's contact info from his earlier call at the golf course. He then chatted with Casey Parks about his evening with Samantha Reeves.

He liked Casey even more after he wrapped up that call as he stood in the hallway. Casey had asked if the chief thought visiting her in the hospital would be appropriate. Chief rubbed his hand against his temple as he pondered how to proceed. He wasn't into matchmaking, but he had known Samantha long enough, and she never made time for herself. She never let anyone in, and he could see she was trying hard not to let Casey in, but... He smiled to himself. But it's about time he helped change that.

Before he thought about it too hard, he replied to Casey, "Welp, she really doesn't have much family around." He cleared his throat and took a long pause. "I suppose she could use someone here besides me." The chief heard the exhaled relief in Casey's voice as he confirmed he would stop by and update the chief if anything changed.

Chief Crane worried for a moment as he walked in if he should have said anything or invited Casey to visit Sam without her permission, but his gut wasn't often wrong when it came to people, and if he read Sam's face well enough, she'd be just fine with having a visitor, he chuckled to himself. "Eventually."

"I better get back to the station. I have an officer out front and sent a team to your place to ensure it's clear." Chief Crane smiled softly at Sam. "We'll figure this out."

"I know," she said with a half-hearted smile. She put out her hand, and the chief took it and squeezed gently. "Thank you."

"Don't thank me yet," he said with a wink. He kissed Sam's hand, and then he was gone.

Yet? Sam wondered what he meant but let it go. Her eyes closed, and she took a deep breath and then let it go in a practiced exhale. With nobody to call, exhaustion took over, and the last thing Sam remembered before darkness lulled her in was how utterly alone she felt.

Chapter 12

A few hours later, she woke up and no longer had the sensation of being alone. Her eyes were still shut, but she felt someone else in the room with her. She fluttered her eyes open and turned her head to the side. She was still lying in the inclined position she fell asleep in and could connect easily with the familiar green eyes watching her from the bedside chair. "Hi," the striking face said.

"Hi," Sam whispered back.

"Will you go on a date with me?" Casey asked straight-faced, looking more concerned than anything.

"Ha." Sam's sarcasm laced her tone.

Casey's brow rose at her tone. He tilted his chin down, letting his eyes stay locked on her. "Sam." He said her name as a statement.

His voice sent pulsing energy up her cheeks, sending a surprising blush to her face.

She reached up and touched the bandage covering the left side of her face, hoping to hide her flushed cheeks.

He merely said your name. Get it together, Sam.

She squeezed her eyes shut and scolded her body for betraying her mind. She brought her arm back down and suddenly was aware she had no bra on. Only the flimsy hospital gown protected her from his penetrating gaze that hadn't let up. She tried to adjust the blankets higher, but as soon as she started fidgeting, Casey was beside her, tugging the blankets up for her.

She watched him dumbfounded as she studied his features. He was ridiculously good-looking. Even the trimmed beard couldn't hide the sharp angles of his face. His dark hair made his tanned tone soft, and she thought for a moment about reaching out and touching it. She corralled her thoughts by biting her bottom lip and forcing a frown before asking, "Why are you here?"

He smiled as he flattened the edge of the blanket. "I mean, I know it's not ideal to ask you out since you're in a bit of a situation," he said as he carefully scanned her body lying on the hospital bed. She felt her skin heat as his gaze traveled up her body.

He stopped when he connected with her eyes, his head directly above hers. Casey's mouth lingered just above hers. She bit her bottom lip to stop herself from doing anything stupid, like trying to find out if that hint of spearmint lingering on him was coming from his lips or maybe it was his skin or shampoo. She'd be willing to taste everything to find out.

"But," he said softly as his eyes wandered to her lips, and she bit down harder. "I still wanted to be here." He pulled away from her and finished tucking her in. "And I want to go on a date with you." He gently squeezed her exposed forearm before sitting back in the upright, faded, upholstered guest chair.

Sam rolled her eyes as she squeezed the brim of her nose. "I need more drugs."

"What's wrong?" Casey was back up, standing at her bedside. "Should I call the nurse?"

"Yes," Sam groaned. "I'm not drugged up enough to deal with the bullshit coming out of your mouth." She raised her forearm loosely, pointing to the IV bag beside her bed. "Open the drip line."

Casey laughed as he shook his head. "I was warned about

you." He casually sat back in the chair next to the bed. Sam flipped her head toward him a tad too fast because it clouded her head briefly before it cleared. "By who?" she asked. "And about what?" she added after a beat.

Casey leaned forward and rested his forearms against his knees, clasping his hands together. "Don't worry about it," he said with a smile lingering at the edges of his lips. "What I need to worry about is when are you out of here?"

Sam raised her eyebrows, acknowledging his redirected question, but let it slide. She'd figure it out later, anyway. Like Casey said, she had other things to worry about right now. With a heavy sigh, she told him, "Tomorrow morning. Could be sooner, but—" Sam stopped herself. He didn't need to hear her painful realization she had nobody in her life. She was not going home today. "Never mind, I'll be going home tomorrow," she said, shaking her head.

"But what?"

"I said never mind. It doesn't matter anyway."

"Samantha."

Oh my God. The way he said her name sent a ripple of heat through her body that definitely should not be happening when, less than eight hours ago, she was nearly blown up.

Sam couldn't meet his eyes. She wasn't sure if it was because of her embarrassment of not having anyone or because she was terrified of her body betraying her again if she melted just at the sound of her name coming from his lips.

"I could go home earlier, but I would need someone to monitor my concussion symptoms overnight." Sam slumped back into her pillow and picked imaginary lint from the thin blanket snugged tightly on her thighs. "My visitor log isn't exactly filling up, as you could guess. So, I'll just hang out here, enjoy the scenery and fine dining." She gestured to the space around her, still avoiding his eyes.

Casey studied Sam's face as she purposely looked around everywhere but at him. He couldn't help but notice everything else about her. Right now, her neck muscles were tense, her eyes tightened, and she was biting her lower lip. Under normal circumstances, watching her play with her lips would cause him to think of how much he wanted to play with them, too, but she was obviously in no place to think about that.

"Sam, will you look at me?"

He watched as she exhaled deeply and finally turned toward him. He was hit by her big eyes, filled with embarrassment. He already understood she wasn't a person used to needing to be taken care of. She was complicated, for sure, he thought. But simultaneously, he felt she was the easiest person to read.

"So, you can go home as long as you have a babysitter for the night?"

"I wouldn't say a babysitter, but yeah, I guess," she said, still not looking at him. "It doesn't ma—"

"Well, then, it's settled," Casey said as he cut her off.

Sam turned her head faster than she probably she have, Casey thought, as she pressed her eyelids closed for a brief moment before her brown eyes flew up to glare at him.

"What is settled?"

"I'll just stay with you."

"Absolutely not."

"Seems better than being stuck in the hospital."

Casey rose from the hospital chair and stood tall over Sam. Her eyes narrowed at him, but he kept his gaze fixed on her. He opened his eyes wide and held out his hand with formality as he asked, "Samantha Reeves, would you like me to accompany you to your home and be your twenty-four-hour head trauma babysitter?" Casey asked. "And for the record, this does not count as our first date." He grinned as he looked back at her. "And neither did McPaddy's. Just to be clear." Casey settled his hand atop hers, pleasantly surprised she didn't pull away.

"Ugh." Sam flopped her head back and closed her eyes. Casey liked watching her facial muscles flex through a swirl of emotions. Easiest book he had ever read.

"What's your deal?" Sam asked, opening her eyes and narrowing them down at him. "Are you just like"—Sam gestured round the room with a twirl of her hand—"like here now?"

He knew exactly what she meant by her "here now" question. She liked him being around; he could see that, but she wasn't willing to admit it yet. It was obvious to him she was waging a war within herself. About what, he wasn't sure. But the idea of digging deeper and learning more about the inner workings of Samantha Reeves seemed like the most exciting thing right now.

"Well, if you want to go home tonight, then yes," Casey mimicked her. "I'm 'just like here now.'"

Sam squirmed under his intense gaze. He reveled in it. He couldn't help but grin, knowing he won, even if she didn't know it yet.

"I see you're considering it." He stood, taking her hand in his. "I'll find the doctor and see if I can get you out of here." He squeezed her hand gently. He leaned over and kissed her forehead. Before she could protest, he was out the door, his footsteps fading down the pale palette hallway.

Chapter 13

Casey and Samantha sat in silence as he drove his Audi RS7 north on Interstate 35E toward her home in White Bear Lake, a quiet northern suburb. It had all the feel of a small-town community, with downtown shops owned by small business owners, but with the luxuries of city life, like franchised coffee shops and quality sushi restaurants.

With the setting sun, Sam couldn't help but admire the sharp features of Casey's silhouetted face. The passing shadows darkened his rough beard. Loose strands of his black hair wisped over his full eyebrows. She knew he was incredibly handsome before, but at this moment, she struggled to find the right word. Hot? Gorgeous? Sultry? Tempting? All of the above, she landed on.

Fresh out of the hospital, and this is where my mind goes?

Sam rubbed her temples. *I clearly must have hit my head harder than I thought*, she mused, trying to rationalize her racing mind. She attempted to distract herself from her wandering thoughts by focusing on gadgets and symbols on the hi-tech dashboard in front of her. It seemed fancy and expensive compared to her modest Toyota.

"Crap." Sam dropped her head back on the soft cream leather headrest. "I just realized I have to get a new car."

"I'm sorry, Sam," Casey said. "No bueno."

"Not your fault." Her hands came up, and she rubbed her eyes. "No car. No work. Double crap."

"Sam, you just got out of the hospital because someone blew up your car." He tilted his head toward Sam. "I don't mean to tell you what to do, but I'm guessing working isn't one of them."

Sam narrowed her eyes but kept her head forward. "You are right, Mr. Parks. You shouldn't be telling me what to do."

Sam heard Casey laugh under his breath. She liked that she made him laugh, even though she was being serious. She could manage things on her own. She'd been doing all right so far. Well, if she were being honest, she might allow him to tell her what to do in one scenario. She laughed to herself this time. But this wasn't the time.

Fucking hell. Even her high school crush and her soldiers didn't cause this much emotional turmoil. She had to pull her mind back into focus. She had some lingering brain fog. She could feel it at the front of her head, but dammit, she thought, if she could shake off the military patch she got at the motel, then she could certainly shake off Casey and his "tempting" presence that kept creeping into her mind.

"Get it together," she commanded herself.

"What was that?" Casey asked.

Sam froze as she felt the rush of embarrassment brighten her cheeks. She prayed her face was also cast in shadow, and he wasn't able to see the heat on her face. Apparently, she didn't say it to herself as much as she thought.

"Sorry, nothing. Just thinking out loud, I guess."

Sam saw her house and guided Casey to pull into her driveway. She recognized the unmarked police car sitting across the way as well. Sam gathered her bag into her lap and went for the door handle as Casey put his hand on her arm and commanded, "Wait."

His tone was so unexpected that it startled her. Was something wrong? She wondered. She hadn't noticed anything out of the ordinary, especially with the police car there. As her brain raced with panicked thoughts, she watched as Casey exited the vehicle, walked around the front of his car, and opened the door for Sam. As Sam looked up, a bit confused at first, Casey smiled at her and put out his hand. It dawned on her that nothing was wrong. He just wanted to open the door for her. "Men actually do this?"

"Real men do," he said with a wink.

She rolled her eyes but still found herself reaching for Casey's outstretched hand as she allowed him to help her out of the car. She slung her small bag over her shoulder and faced Casey, standing closer than she intended. She matched his gaze for a moment before thanking him with a brief, closed-lip smile. She heard footsteps behind her and turned toward the approaching police officer.

"Hey, Tony." She recognized him immediately. She met him in a few steps and stepped into a hug from him.

"Hey, Sam," he said with care in his voice as he pulled back. His eyes looked over her and up and down, inspecting the damage, Sam assumed.

She heard the bang of the car door being closed behind her. Within seconds, she felt the heat of Casey standing next to her.

"How are you feeling?" Tony asked. "Is there anything you need from me?"

Sam smiled at Tony; he was young and relatively new to the force. He was incredibly sweet with a rare kindness she hoped the force never dulled in him.

"I'm good. Thank you, Tony." She pointed to her bandaged face. "It's just a bump on the head and a slight abrasion on my cheek." Sam flipped her finger over and aimed it toward Casey. "Doctor said I need to have a babysitter for the night. Make sure I don't die." Tony's eyes widened, and Casey cleared his throat. She looked between the two guys that wouldn't meet her eyes. Sam's brow furrowed when she realized what she just said. "No. No. No. That's not what I meant. I meant, die from the concussion." She shook her head and rested her hand on

Tony's forearm. "Sorry. I didn't mean to sound so grim."

Tony's mouth perked to the side as he put his hand over hers. "And I'll do my best that you don't die from out here." He spun his head around from left to right before whispering, "From whoever tried to blow you up."

Sam half-heartedly laughed as she thanked him. Not only did she like Tony for his sweetness, but his dark sense of humor matched her own.

Casey stuck out his hand and directed his attention to the officer, "Yes, much appreciated, sir. Casey Parks. The babysitter and friend." He winked at Sam.

Sam grumbled an exasperated moan with an eye roll for good measure.

"Tony Pierce. Nice to meet you." Tony shook Casey's and then turned his grin to Samantha, "I'm glad to see she has someone to take care of her."

Sam repeated the same grumbled moan and eye roll and dropped her head back.

"And I'm glad to see your humor wasn't rubbed out with the rest of your cheek there," Tony finished.

Casey smiled at Tony as he stepped to the side of the car and took out Sam's overnight bag from the back seat.

"Well, they gave the all-clear on your place a while ago, and we've been watching it since with nothing unusual to report," Tony smirked. "Well, I'm assuming an empty fridge and moldy bread are not unusual for you."

"That is my norm, Tony," Sam said, walking to her door with Casey right in stride with her. "Thank you for the reminder that I'll need to go grocery shopping soon."

"Anytime." Tony looked at his watch. "I'll be on for a few more hours, then someone will come for the night shift. We'll keep here for the next forty-eight hours, reevaluate the situation, and see what the next steps are."

"Sounds good." She waved as Tony stepped away. "Have a good night."

Casey nodded in appreciation at Tony before he turned and followed Sam through the front door. Soft whites and creams greeted him. Walnuts and new woods accented the plush chairs in the main open living room with tall ceilings. The anchor of the combination living area was a magnificent mid-century velvet blue sofa that divided the living room from the small kitchen that had a white marbled island with simple wooden stools. The open staircase was on the far back wall, extending above the kitchen's dark gray cabinets and white counters.

"Your place is beautiful, Sam."

"Thanks," Sam said, acknowledging his compliment as she took in her home's beauty. She inhaled the familiar fragrance of pine, faint but lingering, which reminded her to add some more air freshener to her shopping list. A sense of peace settled over her as it always did when she walked into her sanctuary home. When she was younger, living with her mother, they jumped from apartment to apartment, and Colleen never bothered to add decorative things. What was the point of hanging art when you had to patch a hole when you moved out? Art was a waste of time and money, Sam was told.

Colleen never bought anything new. And rarely "bought" anything used. Instead, on garbage days, she would wake Sam up with her stale cigarette breath and say, "Time to dumpster dive." Which meant Colleen would point from the driver's seat, "Grab that one." Sam did all the diving and hauling it into the back of the car. Anything Colleen thought she could sell to a friend for a couple of bucks, she would.

Sam squeezed her eyes to clear her mother from her mind.

"After you stayed in some of the places I've been." She looked up at Casey. "You learn to appreciate coming home to something beautiful and safe."

Sam reached for her overnight bag that Casey was still holding. His hand stayed in place as hers tried to tug it away from his grip. Her eyes moved from their hands together on the small strap and trailed up Casey's arm, following the taunt muscles as they disappeared under the cuff of his dark gray t-shirt sleeve.

She tugged one more time, hoping to get further away from him and her vexing thoughts. Unfortunately, her plan backfired. Sam's attempt brought Casey within inches of her. His eyes shifted into a deep green as they transfixed on Sam's. She sucked in her breath as his heat rippled through her like a match burning too close to her fingertips. *How did he take up so much space?* she wondered. This close, and she wanted to inspect him more than she did in the car. Here, she could see his face fully. Her gaze drifted away from the intensity of his stare, fell down the tip of his sharp nose, and landed on his full lips. She still hadn't figured out if his spearmint smell was coming from his mouth or body. She licked her lips at the thought of finding out. She studied his beard and wanted to know if it was rough or soft and how it would feel against her skin. She watched as his jawline flexed and let her eyes wander down to his broad chest and shoulders. Her fingers twitched as she wanted to feel the softness of the t-shirt against the hardness of his chest. Sam tried to swallow down the tiny moan that escaped her throat, but she heard Casey's sharp intake and watched his chest expand. *He must have heard it*, she thought.

Did the air pressure just change? She wasn't even touching him besides her hand, and yet, it felt like he was everywhere on her. Sam considered investing in a barometer to test this theory. One more thing to the shopping list, she mentally noted.

She forced herself to look up and found Casey's eyes darkened, locked on her mouth.

She tried to step back, but Casey's free hand came around her back, and he pulled her fully against him. Now everything was touching, sending a frequency through Sam that wasn't even possible to measure. No way just a barometer was going to work; she'd need an oscilloscope or an EMF device at this point. Maybe all three.

"Don't worry, I'm having those thoughts, too." He trailed his hand up her back, over her arm, and carefully touched her bandaged cheek. He tilted his head down, impossibly close, and Sam thought he was going to kiss her. Her heart pulsed in her throat as Casey's lips brushed against her temple. "You're thinking about oscilloscopes too?" she whispered to him.

Casey laughed against her ear, his beard slightly tickling her cheek as he pulled away. "You know that's not what you were thinking about, Sam." Casey's lips brushed against her ear. "You want to know how I taste, don't you?"

Had Casey not been holding her, she wasn't sure she'd stay upright. That whisper and touch alone nearly sent her over the edge.

How is he having this effect on me? she thought. Her head felt foggy, but it wasn't because of the concussion. Casey was clouding her head. She had dated plenty of men over the years, but not frequently or recently, as she didn't have time or the patience for it. This guy, though. This man was able to make her feel like nothing before.

Sam could hear the lyrics from one of her favorite artists. It went something like, "It's funny how the warning signs can feel like they're butterflies." That's exactly how she was feeling. She couldn't tell if it was a warning feeling or a good, everything-is-roses-and-daisies feeling. Right now, it felt good—really good—probably too good.

Her body wanted nothing more than for him to keep touching her. But her rational brain was still there, although it was concerningly getting quieter around Casey. She had to call her rational brain back to the forefront of the battlefield.

She attempted to collect herself and made sure she could remain upright before she stepped backward, out of his touch. *Run away! Run away!* She heard her internal monologue shout.

"I need to shower."

"Need help?" Casey grinned.

"I think I can manage." Casey let go of her bag, and Sam threw the strap over her shoulder.

Sam did a quick half-smile before she headed toward the stairs. Sam felt the atmospheric pressure drop back to manageable levels with each step away from Casey.

"Make yourself at home," she called over her shoulder. "I would offer you some food, but as Tony alluded to"—she shrugged—"I don't have any." Without waiting for a reply, Sam ascended the stairs. She took each step with a false confidence, hoping that he couldn't see she had nearly come apart.

Casey stared after Sam as she made her way up the stairs. Her oversized sweatshirt hid the trim figure he had imprinted on his brain from when he saw her at the golf course. He scanned her house once more. A big bookcase sat against the far wall with some decorated pieces mixed among the variety of books. The TV hung above a low, modern electric fireplace with a tall black vase with pampas grass splayed out on its mantle. He noticed a lack of framed photos, which made him curious. He remembered the chief saying she didn't have much family or friends, but still, there was nothing. He meandered into the kitchen. After opening a few barren cabinets and leaning over the hollow refrigerator, he whistled. "She wasn't lying. There is no food in here." He ran his hand through his hair, then shook the dark strands out as he took out his phone. "Hey Will, it's me; listen, I have a favor to ask you."

Chapter 14

Sam was in no hurry to get back downstairs. She needed time to collect her thoughts away from the intensity that was Casey Parks. She took her time removing the bandage from her cheek and inspecting the damage in the bathroom mirror. Not so bad.

She lightly touched the bit of road rash. The laceration had two butterfly stitches holding it together.

She turned on the shower letting it warm as she undressed and stepped in. She let the stream of steamy water rain over her, and she took a few practiced breaths to help clear her head.

Ever since that police patch showed up at the Lakeside Motel, she'd been making mistake after mistake. Now, with Jeffrey dead, her car blown up, and Mr. Hottie Distraction downstairs, she was all out of sorts. She needed to reset. She had a long waiting list and was acutely aware she would need to start her next case soon. "I better knock out one or two easy ones that don't need a car this week," she said as she squeezed shampoo into her hands and began lathering the relaxing lavender scent into her hair.

All of this needed to happen, closing the Jeffrey case and trying to open a couple of others, but none of it would be easy with Casey's intense energy around her. "Seriously," she said to herself as she rinsed. "Buy that barometer or whatever to measure his energy field."

Sam emerged from the shower feeling better but still exhausted. She wiped off the mirror with a hand towel and, with a new determination, decided that Casey had to go. She nodded sharply at her reflection, confirming to herself. "I am strong and capable." She towel-dried her hair as she kept on with her mantra. "I will focus on my job and not the hottie babysitter downstairs, in my house"—Sam looked down—"while I'm naked, upstairs." She had a flash of him coming into her bathroom and her towel dropping. She smacked her forehead and made sure the lock on the door was still latched, mostly for her own sake. She tossed her head backward in frustration. After a few deep breaths, she connected with her own gaze in the mirror. "Strong. Focused. Capable. Dammit!" She'd need a few more minutes before she'd be able to see him again.

Sam finally made her way downstairs in a black tank top and loose, comfortable gray sweatpants. Her hair, blown dry, lay loose and spread across her shoulders. As she walked into the kitchen, she could smell the familiar aroma of sweet and salty fried Chinese food. Her stomach twisted and moaned as her taste buds reminded her that she hadn't eaten all day. The hospital food left a lot to be desired.

"What's going on?" she asked.

Casey was bent over the fridge, filling it with produce from a brown grocery bag.

He stood and shrugged. "Well, as your official babysitter," he formally bowed with a pint of raspberries in his hand, "I know one of my responsibilities is making sure you are fed." He cocked his head at Sam. "I think that was in one of the Babysitter's Club books my little sister read. Step one: feed the children."

Sam stood with her mouth hanging open as Casey dropped the lettuce in the crisper drawer and shut the refrigerator before he continued, "Also, having a younger sister, Nikki, who lives with me, by the way, I understand the importance of snacks." He proudly nodded to the three bags on the counter. "So, I called in a favor and voilà... snacks and food."

A protective dam of welled-up emotion had split and begun to spew out the edges. Every freed drop rushed through Sam as it spread an unfamiliar warmth through her. She had to blink rapidly a few times to stop the wave that threatened behind her eyes.

"I don't," she stuttered. "I don't know what to say."

Before Sam realized what she was doing, she walked around the kitchen island that separated Casey from her. She reached up, tangled her fingers into the hair around the back of his neck, and pulled him into a kiss. His lips didn't move at first but then pressed against hers. Reality hit just then. She was kissing Casey. She froze as Casey's hands caught her around her waist, pulling her hips into his. His hands fit like they were molded for her waist. The heat from his hands seared through her top and into her skin.

He kissed her back with an intensity Sam hadn't known; she couldn't help but kiss him back, matching the intensity as her mouth opened, letting his mouth explore hers more deeply.

A guttural moan escaped from the back of Casey's throat that reverberated throughout Sam's body. His hands drifted higher, circling her back as if he needed to feel every part of her. She wanted him to keep exploring her. She wanted to keep kissing him, taste the spearmint that she confirmed was definitely coming from his mouth.

But she hadn't expected this. *What was she doing?*

Samantha pulled back out of his kiss, breathless. Casey's hands still held her hips against him.

She brought her fingertips up, covering her flushed lips. "I'm sorry," she whispered. "I don't know what came over me."

"Don't do that." He tucked her hair behind her ears. "Don't apologize for that."

He lifted her chin to meet her eyes. He sighed, "I'm glad

you did. I've wanted to kiss you too for a long time." He brushed his lips against the outer edges of her flushed mouth. "Don't be sorry," he whispered.

"You haven't known me for a very long time," she whispered back.

"Oh, you have no idea how long time can stretch when consumed by..." Casey grinned. "...my thoughts." He flexed his eyebrows up and down at Sam.

Sam rolled her eyes and tried to hide the smile that tugged at the edge of her lips. She brought her hands up and rested them on his firm chest before she pushed against him to escape the growing heat between them.

"Well, thank you," she said as she straightened her top and ran her hands through her hair, trying to occupy her hands, unsure what to do next. She settled on peeking inside one of the grocery bags. "For all of this, it's incredibly kind of you."

"If a couple of bags of groceries and some Chinese food gets me a kiss like that, what will you do if I bring you the whole damn grocery store?"

She couldn't help but laugh. She couldn't remember the last time someone made her laugh so unrestrained. How was she so comfortable around him, yet so uncomfortable, about how she felt about him?

Casey pulled her back into an embrace and kissed her worrying thoughts away without knowing it.

"So, you're just around now, and you're kissing me now?"

"Something like that." Casey's smile was electric. She was grateful for her babysitter tonight.

She sighed as she resigned to the reality of the evening. Casey would be here. All of the willpower she gathered as she chanted her strong and focused mantra in the mirror did nothing—it was worthless.

Still, she could maybe focus. "I need to get some work done." Sam stepped out of his arms toward the food. "But first, I need food."

Sam started to dig into the greasy, stained take-out bag. She could feel him studying her as she loaded her plate with sesame chicken, rice, and steamed broccoli. She took a giant bite of a crispy fried vegetable eggroll. "What?" she asked with a mouth full of eggroll.

"Still always about what you need, huh?" Casey asked.

Sam grinned as crumbs of the crispy eggroll coated her lips. "Yup."

Chapter 15

Juan Hernandez heard the dangling bells chime over the Lakeside Motel's front door just as he was closing up the books for the evening. He checked the small desk clock in front of him and sighed. His wife would be upset once again, but hopefully, he could get this guest in and out with no problems.

His late-night guest wore a plain black sweatshirt with the hood up over their hair and oversized sunglasses blocked out their face. Juan smiled politely, as he always did. He was a professional, after all.

He was used to people coming in like this. Hiding from spouses or worried about being caught with drugs or prostitutes. Nobody came to Lakeside Motel for the view.

On rare occasions, these hooded strangers would attempt a rob the front desk, usually a druggie looking for a way to pay for his next hit, but Juan kept his gun in the desk drawer. He'd been around long enough to know who to be cautious of when they walked in. This stranger wasn't very large. The clothes were new and clean. The all-black Nike Air Force Ones told him his gun would not need to come out.

After twelve years of running this motel, he'd seen it all. There was never a shortage of scum, cheaters, and drug and sex addicts that came through, which he didn't love, but he had to make money somehow. He was fine looking the other way if it paid him for the day. But many times, there were wonderful people, like Ms. Samantha Reeves, he reminisced, thinking of the beautiful private investigator that used his motel over the years. He'd always looked forward to her walking into the office. She, too, was often dressed in black, like this stranger, but she never tried to hide from him. He looked up at the security camera, remembering their last conversation. *Yeah*, he thought, *I should get that fixed.*

He turned to the guest. "Hello and welcome. How can I help you this evening?" Juan asked with his professional smile in place.

This hooded stranger reached out and laid cash on the lobby desk.

"Room 7B, please."

Chapter 16

Samantha looked up from her laptop, noting it was just past eleven. Half-empty water glasses sat on the coffee table. Casey sat across from her on one of the plush chairs, reading a book he'd taken off her bookcase. She stretched as she stood, moaning from the ache in her back and the fuzzy, pained headache that crept back in.

"And she's back," Casey said without looking up.

"Huh?" Sam asked as it dawned on her that Casey was referring to her. "Oh, sorry." She shrugged. "I get wrapped up in my work." Sam grabbed her glass and headed into the kitchen to refill her water. She turned, taking a long swig before adding, "And truthfully, I forgot you were here."

Casey threw his hand over his heart in an exaggerated attempt at shock and hurt. Sam smiled at him as she walked back and leaned on the back corner of the sofa. "And I'm just not used to having someone, you know," she gestured her free hand wide around her, "just like... here now."

Casey smiled and held her gaze as he stood and dropped the book on the table before he stood directly in front of her. He crossed his arms. "Yes, he answered. "I am just here now." Sam rolled her eyes but said nothing. He winked at her and then changed subjects. He asked, "Have you gotten any closer to finding out what's going on?"

"Ugh. Not really."

She hated that she didn't find any answers. She spent the

majority of her evening on the social media sites of family members on her team. Everything seemed as normal as a social media account could. Nobody posted a selfie next to Sam's car and captioned, *Hey, I just planted a bomb in this car, hee hee. Let's see what happens. LOL. Live, Laugh, Boom!*

If only every bomb were that easy to see, she thought, as a wave of darkness swallowed her and she retreated into her thoughts.

※

The smell of lingering gunfire, lead, and burning metal seeped into Sam's nostrils. She was standing in front of the sand-colored armored door; its tiny, thick window cracked and speckled with blood splatters, making it impossible to see through. She knew he was dead. She didn't have to open the door to know that.

Shouting came from beside her; the medic was there. She slung her M4 over her shoulder, and they struggled together to rip the driver's door open. Sam cursed under her breath as she recalled all the roll-over training they did in simulator trucks. It was always from the inside that they practiced opening a door upside down. She never imagined having to be on the outside of an overturned truck and opening a heavily armored door upside down.

Finally, with a few steel-toe-boot stomps on the warped metal, it broke its hold. Sam's best friend, Specialist Justin Sommers, hung loose and still, gravity pulling his hands and helmet toward the ground as the seatbelt held his body in position; the medic stepped in front of Sam, and they immediately started their assessment.

Sam's eyes drifted to the shattered windshield as the foggy fumes escaped the truck's cab. The fumes also filtered through the large fractural hole blown through the truck's steel floor, which was now skyward.

"Shit."

Sam heard the medic as he stepped back. Sam could fully see Justin's face now. The once handsome, young, and full-of-life friend she had sat with every day for the past year was gone. The shards of glass, shrapnel, and blood made his face unrecognizable.

Red. Sam saw nothing but blood, but it was so brilliant. The bright red against the tans, browns, and army greens of her surroundings felt out of place. Red didn't belong here, on Justin, or on any of her guys. She'd never wear red again.

Her eyes drifted to a large piece of shrapnel as it jutted out of a small gap between his body armor and head. The red streamed from the gap of his neck. She followed the dripping blood and watched it pool on the roof below him.

"He's gone, Reeves."

"Nooo!" Sam screamed and tried to tug away from the solid, warm arms that wrapped around her.

Casey had seen the distance grow in her eyes; he guided her down the side of the couch and onto the soft velvet cushions. He wasn't sure what to do, and he wasn't even sure what was happening. He thought back on the videos he'd seen online of people sleepwalking and such. The way her face morphed into another person frightened him. His heart hammered in his chest as he worried about what was going on.

He kept his arm around her and pulled her into his chest as she mumbled in tones and pitches more than she spoke actual words.

I shouldn't have let her work so hard after the concussion, he thought. He was a terrible babysitter. He leaned back carefully to pull his phone out of his pocket and wondered if he should call the police or run and get Officer Tony or whoever was out front.

As he debated his next steps, Sam started fidgeting more and began to moan—beads of sweat formed across her forehead. "Red," she moaned. He felt her head shake back and forth against his chest. She whispered through tears, "Too much blood."

Casey put his hand into her hair and pulled her closer to his chest. "Sam, you're safe." He rocked her without knowing what else to do. "Shhh. You're safe, Sam. Shhh."

Sam's eyes snapped open, and she scrambled out of Casey's lap. Her chest heaved a few times as she looked around the room and finally back at Casey. A look of horror crossed her face.

Her hand flew up to cover her face. "Oh my God. Oh my God. I'm so sorry!"

Sam sat back down, tight against the corner, and curled up her legs in front of her, her hands still covering her face, and shook her head from side to side. "I am so so so very sorry you had to see that."

Casey wanted to ask her what *that* was, but as Sam sat there, continuing to cover her face, with her legs up, in a fetal position, he realized then that she was in a very vulnerable situation, and he intuitively knew it wasn't a place she liked to be in.

He let a minute or two pass by before he gently placed his hand on her knee. She didn't flinch like he was worried, but he felt her energy shift with his touch. He patted her knee, grabbed the glass of water off the coffee table, and held it in front of her. "Sam, here, take a drink."

She moved gingerly and used both hands to take a shaky sip. Her eyes were red and glossy, and her bruised, road-rashed cheek flushed, which reminded him she had been through a long ass day.

Sam handed the glass back to Casey. He put the glass down, and in a slow, careful swoop, he picked her curled body up and headed toward the stairs that led to Sam's bedroom.

Sam rested against his shoulder with her eyes closed. She had no fight left in her. Casey laid her down on her bed with care and pulled the covers over her. As he kissed her forehead, he could tell she was already asleep.

Chapter 17

The ombre sun crested over the horizon; the brilliant glow oddly trapped inside itself instead of filling the morning sky with light. Sam turned on her side and threw her arm over her face, away from the morning light cast into her bedroom. "Ow." She winced as the weight of her arm reminded her of her injured cheek. She rolled back, wiping her eyes with widespread hands. She moaned. *Ugh. Feels like I got hit by a dump truck.* Sam sat up. *Oh, wait.* She tossed the blankets back and kicked her legs over the edge of the bed. *I got hit by a car bomb.*

Sam's body ached with every movement. She considered rolling down to the floor to do her morning workout, but thought better of it. Her body needed rest. It was the first time in years she'd skipped her workout, but she would tell no one. The fact that she slept through her internal alarm clock was telling of itself. *When did I fall asleep?* Sam asked herself.

She flashed back to last night. She remembered the warmth of his shirt against her skin, the way her head rested on her shoulder as he... "Oh my God," Sam said as she rubbed her temples. "The poor guy. I probably traumatized him last night from my mental breakdown." It was safe to assume, Sam thought, that Casey was gone. He probably left as soon as she fell asleep. Sam squeezed her eyes shut. But dammit, part of her desperately wanted him to be there.

Sam slid out of bed and into the bathroom. She studied herself in the bathroom mirror, running her hand over her cheek. "Nobody would stay to be part of this shitshow."

Sam's toothbrush buzzed around her teeth as she thought of her dating past. She dated a few times throughout the years, but nothing ever lasted. *You're great, but...* insert any variation of excuses of why Sam was not the right one. Not that Casey and she were dating; she'd known him for just a few days. But the man already witnessed her in a hospital bed, seen a PTSD episode, and had to carry her to bed. "Yeah..." Sam shook her head as she rinsed her mouth. "Nobody is staying for that."

She tried to smile at her reflection even as an empty pit opened in her stomach. She was fine before Casey Parks. She'd be fine with him gone, too. Better, anyway. He distracted her too much. She would figure out this whole Jeffrey mess, and life could go back to normal—a life of routine and comfortable feelings—and emotions she knew how to navigate.

Her eyes focused on her cheek. She brought her hand up to the healing road rash. She sighed as she cleaned it up, just as the doctor ordered. "Maybe it won't scar." She shrugged, forcing herself to think positively. She recognized the false bravado but wanted to embrace it.

Today would be back to routine. Coffee. Work. Coffee. Work. Work. Tea. And more work. She mentally made her list as she made her way down the stairs. "Food." She snapped her fingers. "Don't forget to add food in there today."

Just as she stepped on the last stair, she saw a muscular forearm strewn across the arm of the sofa. "No fucking way," she whispered.

She tiptoed closer and saw his arm covering most of his face as he lay on his side, his limbs jutting out of the small gray throw blanket covering him. She noticed Casey had neatly folded his jeans and shirt on the coffee table—his bare back rippled with muscular definition, the small chenille throw barely covering his waist and calves.

"Holy hell," she whispered louder than she wanted to. She threw her hand over her mouth. Casey was very much naked on her couch. She was acutely aware of how her body responded to this news. Not fully naked, she hoped. *Or did she?* She assumed he was in his underwear, and thankfully, the throw covered his mid-section.

She used her hand to close her jaw which still hung open, before she spun around into the kitchen to make some coffee.

She had just finished pouring her cup when he stirred on the couch. His head popped over the back of the sofa as he propped up on one of his elbows.

"Morning," he said, eyes still half closed.

"Hi."

She smiled at him as she sipped her black coffee with both hands wrapped around the oversized mug. "Coffee?" She hoped her voice sounded stable as her mind certainly was not—Casey had stayed.

He grunted and nodded yes as he sat himself up. As Sam turned to grab a mug for him, she caught him from the corner of her eye standing up as he pulled on his jeans over his black athletic boxer briefs. *My God, that ass,* she thought.

He turned and caught her staring at him. "I like mine black," he said as he buttoned his jeans, grinning. He went to the kitchen stool without bothering to put his shirt on.

Knowing she had been caught, she thought she better play along to stop the blush. "Your coffee or your drawers?" she raised her eyebrows, challenging him over her mug.

"Both," he said as he took a seat.

She poured him a cup and sat on the stool beside him with her mug.

Casey took a sip. "I didn't hear any snoring from down here last night," Casey said with a wink.

Sam giggled behind her mug and just took a sip with a shrug.

"Interesting. Neither did I."

They both sipped their coffee in a comforting silence. Sam kept her eyes trained forward, trying to ignore the fact he sat shirtless next to her. She didn't last long.

"Can you put a shirt on?" she asked.

Casey looked down at his chest. "Oh, ha. Sorry. I didn't realize I hadn't put it on yet." He looked over at Sam. "I'm not used to waking up in other people's houses." He said with a wink.

"Oh. I just," Sam fumbled. "No. it's okay." She cleared her throat, which suddenly had gone dry. She took a long sip of her coffee before saying, "Thanks for staying last night. You really didn't have to, though. I was just fine."

Casey sat momentarily, looking at his coffee before turning to meet Sam's dark eyes. "You know, Sam, people can do things for you because they want to, not because they have to." He leaned over and kissed her cheek before he whispered in her ear, "I stayed because I wanted to."

Sam blinked back a wave of strange emotions. *He stayed because he wanted to.* How was that possible? He saw the worst sides of her in less than three days, and yet he still wanted to stay. Sam had to pause for a moment to let this wave settle down. And as it did, a new wave washed over her. Sam knew this one, but she never let it take control over her logical brain, but it was too late. Sam felt only one thing—desire.

Her hands left her coffee mug as she slid closer to Casey. She wrapped her hands into his unraveled hair, and she pulled his mouth to hers. A frantic energy had come over her, and she couldn't help herself. She had to touch him. Her hands found their way to his broad shoulders and bare chest.

Casey matched her frenzied need as his mouth moved from her lips to her neck, still careful to avoid her healing cheek. Casey moaned with need, melting her insides. Casey's hands cupped her ass as he lifted her onto the countertop. Her arm flung back, which sent his coffee mug crashing to the floor, the coffee splattering on the lower white cabinets and polished floor.

"Shit, sorry," Casey said breathlessly.

"I don't fucking care," Sam responded as she dipped her mouth into his neck, drinking in his scent. He groaned, found the edges of her shirt, and pulled the shirt off. Casey did a once over and found her eyes hazy with passion and need. "You're gorgeous." Casey's mouth found hers again, completely forgetting about the shattered mug.

His hands roamed her breasts as she moaned into his mouth. She cried out his name as his mouth left her lips and followed his hands. She arched under his touch, his tongue teasing her nipples until flashes of light began to form behind her eyes. It was pointless to try and think at this moment. She would usually be worried about her coffee breath, her scarred body, or whether he was enjoying himself. It was nearly impossible to be in the moment when it came to sex for Sam. But with Casey, at this moment, she didn't think about anything but how the desire she felt was a need she had to experience. Casey's hand circled her waist and slipped under her sweatpants. His touch left a trail of sensation. *Yeah.* She thought she'd never felt better about giving in to desire. She had no control right now, and it was sublime.

Sam noticed Casey's hand stopped moving. He rested his forehead against hers, breathing heavily. "Sam..."

She could hear the protectiveness in his voice, yet yearning in the same tone. He was trying to control himself, too, she thought. But if she wasn't going to, there was no reason he should either.

"Sam, you're still recovering. I don't want to hurt you."

"You won't."

She tilted her head up to find his lips and kissed him. She wrapped her legs around his hips, pulling him in closer. Sam felt something inside her lift, then felt every guard of hers fall. She found his green eyes matching the intensity in hers. "I need you, Casey."

With a husky growl, he moved his hands quickly and pulled her sweatpants down. The cold air against the wetness of her center brought colors to the back of her eyes. He crushed his mouth against hers and let his hands fall between her legs.

"Fuck, Sam," he moaned as he found her wet and swollen for him. He teased along her edges, and Sam's fingers dug into Casey's shoulder, and her other hand squeezed the counter's edge. Her breath was increasing rapidly, and she knew she'd be done in mere moments.

He muttered something under his breath that she didn't quite hear over her racing heart, but then he slipped his fingers inside her and circled her clit, and it didn't matter what he said. She threw both her arms around his neck as her body bucked against his hand. Within moments, she said his name again, but this time, she screamed it as her body arched and tightened around him. The world ceased to exist as she was elevated to another universe. Her body rebelled coming down, but eventually, it did, and she collapsed forward onto his shoulder, letting her sweat-soaked forehead rest against his shirtless collarbone.

They sat still, both trying to catch their breath. Sam felt Casey smile against the top of her head. She looked up and met his gaze. He had a goofy grin on his face that Sam couldn't read. "What?"

He cocked his head to the side with one end of his mouth raised in a grin. "I knew I was on the need list." She laughed as his mouth found hers.

Chapter 18

When Casey walked in to work at the country club, he found Will pouring himself a presumed second cup of coffee from the coffee bar.

Will caught sight of Casey and took an exaggerated glance at his watch, then up at Casey with an arched eyebrow. "Ladies and gentlemen." He gestured to the empty breakroom. "Let it be known that on this very day, Mr. Casey Parks is late to work for the first time, maybe ever?" Will looked around, pretending to expect a round of applause.

"Hardy, har, har," Casey said as he set a mug under the coffee drip and pushed the orange lever for the stream of hot coffee to fuel him.

"Seems like my grocery run worked out well for you last night." Will eyed Casey over the rim of his coffee mug.

"Thank you for that. I had no idea what address I was at, and you could ping my iPhone much faster than I could figure the shit out." Casey took a sip of coffee and let out an appreciative moan. "Uber-Eats-Will: Five out of five stars. Highly recommend. Timely service."

"Are you going to explain to me why you were buying groceries and take-out instead of wine or champagne?" Will asked as he leaned against the coffee bar.

"Give me a minute, man. I haven't had any coffee yet." He took another sip as his mind flashed back to the coffee mug he sent crashing to the ground in the sexy, hazed energy of this morning with Sam. He hadn't expected her to respond like that or to have her let go like that, but God... He wanted to see that side of Sam all that he could. He wanted to spend all morning with Sam. He wanted to hear her scream his name like that again and again. He swore it was the best sound he'd ever heard.

"Holy shit." Will grinned, bringing Casey back to the present. "I wish you could see your face right now."

Casey sipped from his coffee and lingered, avoiding Will's interrogative look.

"No, man." He laughed. "Tell me it wasn't that bombshell in the pink dress from this weekend?"

Casey took another sip of his coffee. He appreciated his friend's ability to read him like a book. It was a blessing and, on some days, a curse. Casey dipped his head in acknowledgment. "Yes, sir. It was."

"Well, that explains the stupid-ass look on your face."

Casey punched Will in the shoulder.

"Hey, man, don't spill my coffee. I need every drop for our meeting, that is in..." he looked at his watch "...ten minutes."

"Finalize the agenda for the Tee It Up For The Troops Tournament next week?"

"Right indeed. And besides the veteran congressman being here, they are bringing in some bigwig decorated colonel that served overseas when all of this Afghanistan shit started. They want to make sure the red carpet is ready for this guy."

Casey nodded as he sipped his coffee before saying, "Then it shall be."

"Don't think you're getting out of telling me about this girl," Will said as they made their way to their morning meeting.

"I'll find some time, but it's a long story."

"How?! It's been like three days," Will questioned.

"I don't know, man, but we'll catch up this week, okay?" Casey raised his coffee mug as a promise.

"You better," Will said as he returned the gesture, and they stepped into the conference room.

Chapter 19

"Yes, more towels right away." Juan hung up as he hurried his morning motel checks along. Once again, his housekeeper had not shown up this morning, so he had to cover the basics until he could get someone to come in. Juan went to the back closet and grabbed a stack of fresh towels. He left the front office and made his way across the parking lot. Juan was about to knock on 7B when he noticed the door was slightly ajar. "Hello?" he called out. "Housekeeping. I have your towels." The room was dark, with the shades drawn and no lights on. "Hello?" Juan called out again as he stepped in. "I'll just put your towels on the bed."

Juan placed the towels on the foot of the bed. Without warning, the door he had left open slammed shut. He let out a surprised gasp and clenched his hand over his chest as he spun around. Initially, he thought it was the wind, but he watched as a shadow emerged from the corner from behind the door.

"Oh, you almost gave me a heart attack," he said as he watched the person come toward him.

"No, I'm about to give you a headache."

His eyes adjusted just in time to see the blunt end of the gun smashing toward his head—cracking his temple as he collapsed, knocking the towels off the edge of the bed and leaving his body to lay limp across the well-worn carpeted floor.

The heavy weight of his eyelids made them impossible to open. Juan squinted and moved his jaw around, noticing that his face felt crusted with something like dried food or that he had been drooling in his sleep. He tried to bring his hands up to clear his face, but his arms were immobilized; he twisted them left and right, up and down, but they didn't budge.

Juan flashed back to the time when he was just maybe five or six, and he was playing cops and robbers with his older brother. Adolfo tied him up to a dining room chair out in the half-collapsed garage that they used as a fort most of the time. Adolfo tied him up so tight he cried as the hemp rope cut into his wrists and ankles. Adolfo told him to stop being a baby and that he wouldn't come back until Juan stopped crying and ruining the game. Adolfo left Juan alone for what felt like hours. A terror ran through him that he would be forgotten and he'd die for sure before his parents found them. They never came out to the garage. Juan remembered the dread he felt being tied up by his brother. Eventually, Adolfo came back, and Juan refused to ever be the robber again.

Juan knew it wasn't his brother who'd tied him up today, but the same dread filled him. This time, it felt more like terror.

With fear-filled adrenaline, Juan found the strength to open his eyes. After a few moments of adjusting and letting the pulsing behind his eyes cease, he saw a faint light glowing around the closed curtain. His head buzzed as his surroundings cleared, and he realized he was in one of his motel rooms. "Oh, gracias a Dios."

"I wouldn't thank your God quite yet."

Juan turned his head to the sound of the voice. He saw a small figure outlined in shadows standing between the two beds. It was still very dark, with only the faint light from the window, but he could see a bulky figure sitting on the bed in front of him. He tried to move his arms again and concluded it was pointless. He looked over his other shoulder and noticed the chair was in front of the small thirty-two-inch TV that boasted free HBO but rarely seemed to work.

The small lamp above the bed flipped on, momentarily blinding him. After his eyes focused, he recognized the person in the dark sunglasses who had checked in the night before. A woman, for sure, who was in the same clothes as the previous night. Black on black. Her hood was down now, and her hair was pulled back tightly in a low ponytail. It was too dark to make out a hair color, but for a petite-sized woman, her eyes pierced with blackness and an evil gleam. She was packing or unpacking a sizeable black gym bag; he couldn't tell—he was too distracted by all of the wires and cords that lay across the bed. He followed the wires off the bed onto the ground, and as they neared his body, he noticed for the first time they connected to a vest or harness of some sort with two small boxes wrapped in black tape around his chest.

"What's going on?" he asked sounding braver than he expected.

"Well, it seems you have become part of the plan."

"Plan? What plan? I don't even know you." He looked down at his chest again. "What is this?"

"Both things are irrelevant to you," she said as she zipped up the black gym bag, confirming to Juan that she was, in fact, packing up. Hopefully, she was leaving, and he would be able to get out of whatever mess this was.

"What is relevant is that I need to get a message across to someone." She walked over to Juan and stood in front of him. "And since you did such a good job delivering my package to this very room to Ms. Samantha Reeves, I thought it would be great if you could do it again."

"Yes. Yes. I can do that. I will do whatever you want. Please don't hurt me," Juan pleaded. He realized he no longer sounded brave. "Let me go, and I will call Ms. Reeves right now for you. Just untie me, please."

"Oh, that won't be necessary, Juan, my dear." The strange woman placed her hand on Juan's cheek as she bent over and looked into his face. "I am glad you are willing to do whatever I want, though."

Juan flinched as she patted him on the cheek. He averted his eyes from her soulless eyes and focused on her hand as it tapped on a phone that had appeared in her hands.

"Now, let's record our message, shall we dear?"

Juan shook his head rapidly, wanting to get this done so he could get home to his wife. He missed her dearly at this moment. He wanted nothing more than to hear her berate him for being late.

"You just say, 'I have a message for Ms. Reeves.' That's all for now. Can you do that, Juan?"

"Yes, of course. Anything. Yes. Please. I need to get home to my family."

"Okay. And... 3... 2... 1..." She hit record, and Juan watched the gun come up and rest between his eyes; the cold metal barrel against his damp skin sent shivers down his spine.

Juan swallowed his fear and leaned over into the phone's speaker. "Yes, hello. I have a message for Ms. Reeves." He paused and looked up at the shadowed face in front of him, waiting for direction.

Her eyes narrowed as her pink-plumped lips curled up to one side. "No, Juan. You are the message."

Her gloved finger tapped on the screen once more, and she stood tall before grabbing the duffle bag off the bed and walking toward the door.

"I... I... don't understand." Juan's wide filled with tears as panic took over.

"Juan. Ms. Reeves killed the love of my life. And Ms. Reeves has killed many others. You have no idea," She snapped. "And now... poor, poor Juan. She's going to kill you."

"What do you mean? Ms. Reeves would never hurt anyone!"

Juan watched her body stiffened before she jerked her towards him. Her nostrils flared. "Ms. Reeves is a MURDERER!" She leaped forward and wrapped her hand around Juan's throat, squeezing until he gasped for air. "Death without suffering is a luxury she does not deserve." He gasped for air as the woman stuck a piece of duct tape over his mouth. Juan desperately tried to calm his breathing, but it came in heaves as he watched the woman throw her hood up, put on the oversized sunglasses, and walk out the door.

Juan scanned the room, looking for a way out. He tried to slide his chair to try to reach the door, but the cords pulled at his chest, and he froze. He looked again at all the scattered wires, cables, and small bricks attached to his chest. It was pointless to try and move. Juan didn't watch much television but had seen enough to realize he was strapped to a bomb.

Chapter 20

Sam pulled up to the police precinct in her newly rented Prius just as a response team rushed out. Standing to the side, she waited for them to pass as she made her way to Chief Crane's office. He was rushing out as she approached, meeting him in the hallway.

"Monday morning rush hour around here?" she asked.

Chief Crane kept his pace and Sam joined him in stride. "I just heard about a bomb threat called in at some dingy motel. I didn't get much more details than that."

"That's quite a statement for a cheating spouse or snitching gang banger."

"Who knows these days."

A police officer fell in step with the chief as he read from a clipboard. "Chief, the tip came from an anonymous call. The transcript read, 'Someone needs to pay since she didn't last time.' It was followed by another voice that said. 'Yes, hello. I have a message for Ms. Reeves.'"

Sam froze in place. The chief paused with her.

"What's the name of the motel?" Sam asked the officer.

"Lakeside Motel," he said, looking at his notes.

"That is near where your car was blown up, isn't it?" Chief asked.

She nodded, eyes wide, as terror slithered through her veins.

Chapter 21

Lane laughed as she peered at the Lakeside Motel through her binoculars. It was amusing to watch the chaos around the motel as soon as the bomb squad arrived. The motel had been evacuated, which was only mildly irritating. Taking down more than one person would have been more fun, but she felt her message was pretty straightforward this time. "It's her fault the sweet Juan will die," she said through gritted teeth. Lane's hands balled into fists. "And it was her fault that…" Her fisted hands smashed against the wall next to the window, causing the pane to rattle. Even after ten years, it was too painful to say out loud.

"She took away everything possible from me." Sam needed to understand that. And she would. Ever since Sam snuck back into her life, it had consumed Lane. She leaned into the binoculars, waiting for the perfect moment. It was risky to do an in-person detonation, but the remote timer didn't work last time… She sat back in her chair. "That reminds me to track that family down." She let out a sigh and leaned back in. She couldn't risk another mistake and have to do another cleanup.

She should have thought more carefully about framing Reeves for Jeffrey. She was the last person to see him alive and was following him around. It should have been easy. Lane thought about it more clearly and realized she had let her emotions get the best of her. She couldn't help it. The world needed to know Reeves killed people before. Why would her killing Jeffrey have been any different?

The bomb squad was about to breach the door when another police car came ripping up to the motel.

Odd. They usually don't let other officers get close once the area has been secured, she thought.

Lane watched as a head of dark, bouncy hair pulled back in a high ponytail jumped out of the passenger side as another officer stepped out of the driver's seat.

She saw the exchange between the bomb squad's team leader and the police officer, but only in the peripheral. She was laser-focused on the woman.

"Why the fuck is that bitch here!" She sat back and pulled the chair closer to the window, bashing her knees against the wall with fury and confusion.

"Wait a minute." After a few moments, a smile crept across her face. "I guess this could work." She shrugged. "Nothing like delivering my message in person."

Peering back through the lens of the binoculars, she watched as the door of 7B was breached by the bomb tech in his bomb attire. "Hope the suit helps," she said as she triggered the bomb.

Chapter 22

Sam watched as the medic moved back and away from Justin. There was nothing he could do to save him; he had to prioritize those he could save. She nodded at him as he left, and she was left there kneeling in front of Justin, hanging upside down. She inhaled through her nose, trying to take a cleansing breath, but nothing but diesel fumes and dusty sand filled her lungs.

JT from rear security appeared beside her. He nodded as she grabbed her knife clipped on the front of her body vest. He squeezed in beside her in front of the open driver door. They both braced themselves as Sam cut the seat belt that was holding Justin in place. His weight was immediate; his large six-foot frame weighed nearly two hundred pounds of pure muscle, and his body armor and gear added an additional forty pounds. Her lower back screamed against the weight as she and JT twisted and stood, pulling Justin out and laying against him alongside the truck on the ground. She looked back in the truck as the filtered sunlight beamed through the floor of the overturned truck. There wasn't much of a floor, or anything, or anyone left on the passenger side. "The IED was underneath the road," she said as she assessed the damage.

The world slowed down as Sam took in the surroundings. Soldiers were securing the perimeter; medics knelt over the other team members. Two soldiers lay motionless as others readied litters next to them. She could see people shouting, speaking, gesturing wildly, weapons at the ready, but it didn't feel real. The world was silent as chaos spun through it.

"I did this." She looked down at her gloved hands soaked through with blood, her tan boots now mudded. "I'm so sorry." A deep shadow set *inside her. Her chest burned as it felt as if this deepening darkness was trying to consume her. She closed her eyes and tried to stop.*

"Sergeant Reeves! Sergeant Reeves! We gotta go..."

Sam's eyes flew open and she caught site of chaos as everyone rushed around.. She tried to shake away the odd feeling that now settled in. "Get it together." She told herself. Sam shook her head, slung her rifle back around, readied herself, and carried on.

"Where are my gloves?" Sam wondered as she rotated her hands in front of her, seeing nothing but dirt and gravel embedded into the palms of her hands. "Why am I not wearing my gloves?"

"Sam."

She lifted her head at the soft whisper of her name. After a moment, her vision cleared, and she saw Chief Crane kneeling in front of her. Sam pressed back against the discomfort of the hard metal on her back as she realized she was seated against the side of the police car.

She dropped her hands and looked up at the chief.

"Who was it?" Sam met Chief's eyes. "Who was strapped to the bomb, Chief?"

"The motel manager." The chief pulled out his notepad. "Juan..."

"Juan Hernandez," Sam said, finishing his sentence.

She choked back a cry as her eyes began to burn with tears. "Not Juan." She shook her head. "Why Juan?" she asked no one.

She turned her head away from the chief as she wiped the tears that had fallen down her cheeks.

"I did this," she whispered.

"Now, don't go saying crazy stuff like that, Sam. Of course, you didn't." He rested his hand on her foot. "Sam, I need you to really look at me." Sam obliged. "None of this is your fault."

Sam nodded as she rose into a standing position, not quite hearing the chief. He stood cautiously, standing alongside her. Sam looked around and saw all the chaos around her.

It's happening again, she said to herself as she watched the fire department work on controlling the flames from the blast. She noticed that the bomb tech who went in was being assisted on the side of the bomb tech truck. She gasped a sigh of relief. He was okay. But Juan was gone.

"His family." She whispered. A single warm tear ran down her cheek.

Her eyes trained back on the room she stayed at just a few nights ago. It was gone. The surrounding rooms were also burning, but it was obvious that 7B was targeted.

A familiar darkness started to threaten again. She felt it seep into the edge of her vision. She inhaled and forced it down. She was on a mission here. She wasn't allowed to process emotions right now. She had to get to the safety of her home.

"Chief, I think I've been almost blown up enough times for one week." The chief nodded with a brief smile of relief passing his face.

"Sam, I have to stay here, but we'll get you home." He called out to the officer who was standing nearby. He turned and stood beside Chief Crane. "Go with Officer Yuusuf; he'll take you back to your car or home, whatever you want."

"Thank you, but I'll just need a ride back to the station to get my car." She followed the officer away from the burning motel to the police cruiser. She stopped as she opened the door and looked back at the chief, who was still watching her.

Not many people in her life ever took care of Sam, but looking at the chief, she knew he did. "Thank you," she mouthed as she put her hand on her heart before she slid into the car.

Chapter 23

Sam sat on the edge of her bed, in the position of attention, without acknowledging her straight ramrod stiffness. She had been transfixed on the small indent in the drywall for an unfathomable amount of time. She remembered it happened a few years ago. It was when the movers had brought the dresser into the room. It took her nearly a week to notice it for the first time. She had been putting her neatly rolled socks away in the upper drawer of the dresser when the sun seemed to be shining a spotlight on the tiny infraction for her. "What the hell?" she remembered thinking; she noticed everything. How had she not noticed it right away?

She spoke to her therapist back then and she had recommended that she leave it. She said, your mind isn't designed to notice everything. Give it a break and watch as your brain chooses to let go of the tiny dent. Sam had to force herself every day for a month not to look at it and did a lot of self-talk, but eventually, it did disappear.

But not today. Sam honed in on the dent in the wall. She had let her brain tell her that this was of no importance long enough. She needed to regain control over her brain and emotions. She had missed too many details the past few days and look where it got her—a dead subject and nearly blown up twice.

Sam forced herself out of her mental paralysis. She stood and shook her shoulders loose and decided she'd had enough.

She hurried down the stairs and dug into the back of her closet by the front hall, where she kept all of the household repair things and a tool kit. She found a small wall patch and a pint of crusty-edged spackling with a pink label and made quick work of the next twenty minutes repairing the damaged wall.

After another few hours, she repaired four other minor defects in the walls, replaced two light bulbs with the proper wattage bulb, and tightened the screws on the loose toilet seat.

She returned everything to the front closet, ready to be done, when she caught sight of the vacuum tucked in the corner.

"Well, all the dust and spackle need to be cleaned up."

By the time the sun started to set, nothing in Sam's house was left untouched.

She cleaned up all the spackling mess, but that led to every floor, shelf, and surface being cleaned, dusted, mopped, and polished.

Sam clicked off the vacuum and moaned as she stretched her back and reached her arm overhead. Her stomach clenched, forcing her to fold forward and balance herself on her vacuum, which was now acting as a cane.

"Crap." She'd spent all day focusing on her tasks at hand, but she never stopped to think about eating. "I really need to stop doing this to myself."

She forced herself to stand up, tucked the vacuum away along with the rest of the cleaning supplies into the closet, and made her way to the kitchen.

As she opened the fridge and found the fresh stock of groceries that Casey had bought her, it dawned on her that she had never once stopped to check her phone. Casey could have called. She was so wrapped up in her need to regain control that she hadn't stopped to think. She looked down at her watch and saw that she'd had it on silent mode.

Shit. She had a fridge full of food all because of him and she hadn't stopped to reach out to him once. "But what would

I have said?" she shrugged. "Hey, sorry, I experienced another explosion today. Or maybe, hey, someone died because of me... How was your day, dear?" Sam stuck her tongue out in disgust.

Sam's hands smothered her face as she stood before the open fridge door. She wasn't used to someone in her life. *How the fuck am I supposed to do this?*

She slammed the fridge shut. This is why she didn't have friends or relationships. She'd already let her guard down with Casey when she had her flashback episode with him. She couldn't let him see another time when she lost herself or when she let her emotions control her actions.

Part of her wanted to believe he cared and would stick around. Casey stayed once that first night but that must have been a fluke. It was probably because of the doctor's orders. How likely would it happen again? Sam sighed with heaviness. Eventually, they would *see* her, and just like everyone else, they would go.

Sam closed her eyes and sat for a few moments. She forced herself to smile and get out of the negative thoughts of being alone. She was fine.

She opened her eyes, looked back at the fridge, and rubbed her aching, empty belly. She had cleaned her entire house today; you think she would have learned how to feed herself by now, too.

"For Christ's sake," she scolded. "Fix yourself."

Her stomach lurched again, reminding her she still hadn't finished what she came into the kitchen to do. Eat. She was incredibly grateful for Casey. "Argh, dammit."

She needed to call him.

"Is it the food I need, or is it Casey?" She threw her arms up and shook her head, exasperated. "Bloody hell, I can't think straight."

She pulled out sparkling water and a leftover take-out container from the fridge. As the microwave spun the cold noodles around in slow, even circles, Sam dug in her back pocket and found her phone. Thirteen messages. Two missed calls. All from Casey. The last message was about twenty minutes ago. The microwave chimed as she walked back over, removed the container, and set it on the center island as she read the last message she received.

> Casey: I'm worried now. I'm coming over. Be there soon. Hope you are okay.

As if almost on cue, Sam saw the headlights sweep across her living room and shut off as the car stopped in her driveway. She left the microwaved noodles on the counter and headed to the front door. Every conflicting emotion and feeling she had experienced in the past hour settled into her chest, leaving her with an ache she wasn't sure what to do with.

Sam opened the front door just as Casey strode up the three front steps. He was inside before Sam could say anything. He shut the door behind him and locked it before he turned and wrapped Sam in a heavy embrace. Every ounce of control she thought she had gained today immediately dissipated into his arms.

She inhaled his earthy scent and let it soothe the ache she had in her chest. Casey's silent embrace annihilated every guard Sam had built throughout the day. Sam felt the wells behind her eyes fill, and she tried to control them and regain some sense of self and strength. Casey kissed the top of her head. Nothing was said, but Sam cried. She hated herself at first, but Casey's hand ran softly over her back, and the embarrassment lessened. When Casey pulled her in tighter, something released in her, and she let go and cried.

Chapter 24

Sam sat on the sofa with the chenille throw covering her tucked legs as Casey cleared the empty food boxes from the coffee table. Sam had just finished explaining everything that happened at the motel over their "leftovers" dinner. She watched from the sofa as he poured two glasses of wine and brought them over, handing one to Sam. "Thank you." She wasn't used to someone doing things for her, but if it was cleaning up after dinner and wine delivery, she could get used to it pretty easily.

"What I don't understand Sam, is why are they targeting you?"

"Well…" Sam stumbled for words. She had never told anyone about the IED explosion in Afghanistan besides Chief Crane, her mom (big mistake), and her therapist. Of course, people heard about it when it happened. It was reported all over the news. American soldiers died, so people read about it that day and then waited for the next headlining attack or death tally update. She was grateful her name was never mentioned in any articles she ever read. The media mentioned only those who died, never the ones who survived. Those soldiers live with their fallen soldiers deaths every day.

"Hey, Sam." Casey gently rested his hand on her leg. He waited for her to look up at him. "It's okay. Tell me or don't tell me; totally up to you."

His warm hand seared through the thin blanket; she hadn't

realized she was shaking. His touch and words calmed her so much that they made her laugh. "You're annoyingly good at knowing how to say the right things."

"Give it time. I'll fuck it up eventually." He smiled.

Sam rolled her eyes and took a long, slow sip of her wine. The warm cabernet soothed her into a comfortable space, giving her some liquid encouragement.

"You still haven't answered my question." Casey squeezed her leg before leaning back. "Why do you think someone would target you?"

Sam took a deep breath and uttered her unspoken truth. "Because I failed."

She paused and looked up at Casey, waiting for the judgmental expression to cross his beautiful, lush green eyes, but none came. She saw only patience in them.

Patience for now, she thought. As soon as she shared with him what was really going on, he would get up and leave. She knew it. There was no way he would stay after she told him the truth. She inhaled a deep breath and took one more drink of wine before she decided just to tell him and get it over with.

"I failed to do my job, and four men died because of it. My team and I led a security mission through Afghanistan about ten years ago. I was the lead vehicle observer. I didn't see the telltale signs of a planted IED."

Casey tilted his head inquisitively.

"Sorry, a roadside bomb. Anyway, I didn't see any signs of one, but there was one. It was buried in the road and blew up the truck behind us, killing the four men inside. My men. My team. Not only have I blamed myself all these years, but apparently, someone else does, too."

Sam took a deep breath, realizing she had forgotten to breathe as she spoke. Casey sat patiently listening.

"Whoever that someone is, hates me enough to try to kill not me but people around me for some unknown reason. It makes no sense why they killed Jeffrey and Juan. I never had any relationship with any of them."

Sam paused but kept her eyes locked on her hands holding her glass. She just confessed to causing the death of three people and that someone was trying to kill her on top of people dying around her. Those are three pretty big red flags.

"I know nothing in my life is normal, and I totally understand why you wouldn't want to stay." Sam played with the fringe of the chenille blanket, not meeting his eyes.

Casey was silent for a moment before he cleared his throat. It made Sam flinch,

This is it. This is when he leaves. She slumped further into the sofa as Casey leaned forward to put down his wine glass on the coffee table. Sam sipped a bit more of her wine before she left her eyes fall closed. *It's fine. Totally fine. I knew he would leave.* Even as she said it to herself, the pain still seared through her heart and dropped into her stomach.

She felt's warmth against her hand as Casey sandwiched her free hand between his. Her eyes opened and she found his gaze on her. He brought up her hand to his lips, and tapped a light kiss on her knuckles. "I know this has probably been said to you a hundred times, and it won't erase the years of guilt, but I still wanted to say it." He slowed his pace as he said, "It is not your fault those men died. That bomb killed them. Not you." He kissed her hand again and then rested it back onto her tucked-up legs.

Sam felt her throat constrain as years of repressed guilt rose from the pit of her stomach. Chief Crane had said it to her earlier too. So had many others, She knew it, but right now, she felt it. She was not going to cry again, so instead of attempting to say anything, she just looked at her hand with his on top of it.

"It's okay to be not okay," Casey said softly as he squeezed her hand, pulled her chin up, and placed a feather-light kiss against her lips. He pulled back just enough to meet her gaze. "I'm here. I want to be here. And I'm fine with you not being okay all the time." His lip twitched up in a half grin as he said, "The most normal thing is to be not okay all the time."

Casey let go of her hand and grabbed his own wine glass off the table before leaning back, throwing his arm over the back of the sofa toward Sam, acting as if what he just said was the most casual thing in the entire world, when all it did was turn her world upside down. "Everyone is fucked up, Sam."

"Oh, how are you fucked up?"

"Well, once upon a time, I met this girl, and within two seconds of meeting her, I was fully captivated by her brown eyes, wit, and obvious disdain for me." He emphasized with a wink, and Sam added an eye roll. "And I asked her out on a date as she lay in a hospital bed, and then I inserted myself into her life fully." He took a sip of his wine. "Nothing about that, Sam, is normal."

Sam turned her head as she watched Casey in awe. She was losing control emotionally with him—she literally just cried nonstop because of a fucking hug. Now she told him about her guilt of getting three men killed. Sam threw back the rest of her wine in a giant gulp, trying to swallow down her guilt for sharing her feelings with him.

"So, we're just two fucked up people, I guess," Sam said as she tipped her wine glass toward his, and they clinked glasses in agreement.

She put her glass down a bit harsher than intended on the table. "But for real, why are you still here?" She crossed her arms across her chest.

Casey's eyebrow arched up at her questions and seemingly cross-question. "What do you mean?"

"I just shared all of these," Sam threw her hands up in quotes as she said, "feelings, and you're still here. Men usually run after that."

Casey shrugged. "Remember, I'm 'just like here now,'" he said with a wink. "And men don't run from"—he mimicked her gesture—"feelings." He added, "Cowards do."

"I'm so confused by you," Sam confessed.

Casey grinned.

"Give it time." He looked at her for a long moment, and then Sam could feel him studying her, making her feel more vulnerable than she expected. "It'll all make sense when you allow it to."

Sam scrunched up her face at him. "What the hell is that supposed to mean?"

Casey just laughed and said, "You'll see."

Sam shook her head. "Thanks for the clarification, dillhole."

"You're welcome."

He stood and held his hand out to her, "Now, you've had a long day," Casey nudged his hand forward, indicating with his eyes that Sam should grab it. She eyed him suspiciously before taking it. He carefully pulled her up, and they stood chest to chest. He held both her hands down at their sides.

"I'm going to head home now because you've had another incredibly difficult day." He tucked a piece of hair behind her ear. "But know that I very much want to repeat what we did this morning." Casey kissed her and whispered against her lips, "And so, so, much more."

Sam closed her eyes, and before she overthought, she said, "Then stay." She looked into his eyes before she moved her gaze down to his mouth, licking her own, tasting the wine mixed with the taste of his lingering kiss.

"Sam," Casey groaned her name as he watched her tongue flick over her lips.

He pushed his hips forward, letting her feel what she was doing to him.

"You understand how hard it is for me to leave you tonight, right?" he said through gritted teeth.

Her eyebrows raised as she pushed back into him. "I certainly can see how hard it is."

His hands let go of hers and were around her face, carefully avoiding her injured cheek. He frantically devoured her mouth like he could not live another minute without her breath on his. She melted under his touch, and her arms moved over his chest and around his neck, pulling him impossibly closer. He couldn't get close enough to her.

Casey moaned and pulled his mouth off Sam's as he stepped back.

"Fucking hell, Sam." He rubbed his hands over his face. "I'm going to go home so you can get some rest."

"I don't need rest, Casey." She stepped toward him. "I need you."

He shook his head as he grabbed her shoulders and kissed her once more. "I love being on that list still." He grinned. "But I need to be sure you're okay, and hell, I need to be okay, too."

He backed away and went to the front door, leaving Sam frozen by the sofa.

"Sam," he said with his hand on the doorknob. He turned to Sam with a devilish grin that made her insides flip over. "Next time I come over, I'm not leaving until the next day."

"You better not." She smiled as he stepped out the door. She closed the door, locked it, and watched as he approached the police car outside. The men chatted briefly, and he gestured his hand over his shoulder. They both turned toward the house and caught Sam watching them out the window. Casey grinned, and the officer waved as she leaned back from the front window.

Sam picked up the wine glasses and tidied up as she shut off the lights and made her way up to bed. She laughed to herself as she realized she just had another insane day of being blamed for a murder, a complete loss of the illusion of control and still, she found herself smiling as she made her way to bed.

Chapter 25

The rest of the week went by with Sam burrowed away in her townhome under the surveillance of a police officer. She dove deep into each one of her team members' lives, hoping to find a connection to the picture that was left at Jeffrey's house. She listed every known relationship and struggled to find any evidence or red flags of a murderer.

She reviewed her list of pending cases she needed to act on. She had to do what she hated and started sending them to another PI in town she worked well with. He was good, but she had no choice. How do you do surveillance on someone when you are being surveilled? Jeffrey died under her watch, and Juan died while she was on a case, too. She couldn't risk involving someone else by taking on a case right now. She had enough guilt for a lifetime.

Sam wasn't sure how, but the week went fast. There had been no messages or bomb incidents since earlier in the week. It was almost a normal week, minus the part that Casey had come over every night. She'd be researching until she heard her phone buzz, which signaled that Casey was on his way over after work.

He made good on his word. The next night he came over; he didn't leave until the morning. She smiled at the memory of seeing his overnight bag in his grip as she walked in the door with a devilish grin. "I warned you," he said as he tossed his bag on one of the chairs. He unzipped the bag and pulled out a black and golden box of condoms. He held them up and grinned.

Sam's mouth dropped open. "Aren't you presumptuous?" she teased.

"I will always presume safety and no babies."

Sam laughed, "I'm clean and on birth control."

Casey's face flashed with heat. He let the box drop back into his bag. "Can I presume we are fine without?" he asked cautiously.

Sam closed the few steps between them, jumped up, and wrapped her legs around him. "Yes."

Casey groaned, "Fuck yes," and carried her up the stairs.

Now, Sam She stared blindly at her computer screen, not getting any work done because her mind kept replaying the guttural way he moaned for her that first night and nearly every night this week. "Casey," she hummed. Into her cup of now cold green tea.

He had spent every evening with her since she came home from the hospital. She thought having to share her space with someone would be uncomfortable. She lived alone the majority of her life, even as a kid; her mother left her alone so much she never experienced being dependent on someone. It was crazy to think that Casey would fit into her life in just one week. He was "just like here now."

All week, Sam struggled to find the word to describe what Casey was.

The only thing she could land on was *natural*. It felt natural being around him.

Every other "feeling" word she put around him made her queasy. He unknowingly forced her to explore emotions she'd avoided for so long that the only way her body knew to respond was to become nauseous.

But she melted into his charm every time she was around him. Her worries vanished.

Worry crept in only when she was alone, and she worried she might be putting him in danger. Each time, she thought about what it would be like to lose Casey, like how in Afghanistan she lost...

Sam felt the black shadows swoop in from the corner of her eyes but shook them away. "No, dammit. Not now," she shouted as she slammed her hands flat against the natural wood desk. Sam shook away the thoughts by taking a drink of the cold tea and shaking her shoulders.

She wasn't sure why she was having more flashbacks than usual. Before Casey and Jeffrey, she had barely had any episodes in years.

Sam snapped her fingers. "That stupid patch."

She couldn't let a four-inch piece of fabric ruin her life. It was still buried in her bag, but maybe she needed to put another bag on top of it or a few hundred pounds of dirt to ensure it was buried as far away as possible. She considered tossing it but couldn't bring herself to do it. Even burning it felt sacrilegious even though, religion wasn't something she participated in. Between Jeffrey's death, meeting Casey, and the resurfacing PTSD, she had some work to do to regain some control that she had lost. If she was being honest with herself, she felt emotionally unchecked while she was around Casey.

"Not that it was all bad." She grinned. "Wait a minute," Sam said, cocking her head to the side. "Shit. Maybe I haven't had a breakthrough with the case because *of* Casey." Sure, they brought up the case and talked through some things, but deep down, she knew he was a distraction. Her focus was split between work and Mr. It's Not Fair To Be That Good Looking And Funny. "Dammit." With her hands still flat on the desk, she flopped her forehead between them and sighed. "But it feels so good being around him."

She heard the familiar sound of Casey's car pulling up and

the check-in with the posted officer out front. She had to move to unlock the door for him, but she didn't want to disrupt the pity party she was throwing for her emotional turmoil.

"I should just give him a key," she said to herself as she pulled herself out of her chair and stretched. "What the fuck did I just say?" She rubbed her hands over her face, shook her head, and walked to the door. "Get it together, Sam. It's only been a week."

She opened the door to find Casey grinning wide as he held up a bag of takeout. Casey nodded as he walked in, pressed a light kiss, and breezed by making his way to the kitchen. *Natural.* Sam thought as she watched him walk in like he'd been in her home a hundred times.

After a quick wave at the police officer, she locked the front door and made her way to the kitchen. The smell of food permeated Sam's nostrils as he set the bags on the counter.

"Oh my God, That smells amazing. I think I may have forgotten to eat today."

Sam rounded the kitchen island, where Casey pulled out the overfilled and leaking food containers. "Thank you for dinner once again," she hummed into his chest as he hugged her.

"You're welcome." Casey kissed the top of her head as her face was snuggled into his chest. "And if I were to guess, you forgot to shower too."

Sam pushed him away playfully. "Rude." She cracked open the food containers. "But accurate."

Sam plucked up a crispy egg roll, skipped the dipping sauce, and moaned as she bit into the crunchy exterior. "Oh my God, this is heaven right now." But she pointed the other half at Casey, who could not peel his eyes away from Sam while she devoured the egg roll. "You're going to make me fat if you keep bringing me takeout every night." She shoved the last half of the egg roll in her mouth, moaned again, and closed her eyes with an appreciation of the food.

"That's it." Casey grabbed Sam by the waist, spun her around, and pushed her up the stairs. Her mouth was still full of eggroll, so she couldn't do anything but mumble her protest. By the time he got her into the bathroom, she was able to spin around to face him. She stood in front of the walk-in shower and put her hands on her hips, eyes narrowed. Sam felt as if his pulse echoed through the tiled bathroom. "Clothes off. Now." Casey's voice darkened with every word.

Samantha glared for a second before deciding to play along. She threw her hands straight up into the air, and a challenging smile reached her eyes as she looked up to match Casey's demand. He reached down teased along the hem of her shirt. Instead of lifting it, he tightened his grip around her waist and, like she weighed nothing, picked her up like a candlestick and moved her ninety degrees to his left—never breaking eye contact. He stepped to the shower, opened the door, and turned on the rain shower head, filling the room with rolling steam. He stepped back in front of Sam, whose arms were still stretched above her head. She licked her lips, clearing away any of the lingering eggroll crumbs.

Casey's hands lightly circled her waist and flat stomach, teasing with slow movements, with his eyes locked on hers. He could see her chest rise and fall in time with his movements. He liked the seductive catch in her breath with each of his touches. For Sam, it seemed like hours before Casey finally pulled her t-shirt above her head, revealing a simple but sexy black push-up bra. Her arms dropped to her sides as he dropped her shirt on the floor; he lightly traced the lines of the bra, making her breath come quicker as he rounded the form of her breasts. He leaned in close and kissed the edge of her mouth as his hand went behind her back, unclasping the bra with a single motion. He leaned over further, tracing her neckline with his mouth down to her bra strap; his hands met his mouth there as he pulled the straps down over her shoulders, letting the bra tumble to the floor between them. He trailed kisses down her front, cupping her breasts as he kissed and teased them, continuing down lower. He moved to his knees, his mouth hovering over her stomach. He pulled her hips closer, knocking her slightly off balance and into him. He lightly bit the soft skin on her stomach. She moaned louder as she braced her hands against his broad shoulders. He laughed as his tongue ran just above the hem of the black running shorts she had been wearing all day.

"You taste delicious." He kissed her skin as he pulled the shorts lower. "Salty." Lower. More licks and kisses. "Sweet." He whispered into her skin. "Sexy." He let the shorts fall to her ankles. "Perfect." He looked up to meet her eyes, which were rolled back and closed. He paused and waited for her to look at him. Noticing his movements had stopped, Sam looked down to find Casey searching for her eyes. "Even un-showered for how many days?" He raised an eyebrow. "You're still perfect."

His hand found her then, wet and swollen, and she would have toppled over if she had not been braced against him. Casey stood, his hand moving inside her; he matched the rhythm of her body as she rode against his hand. His mouth found her neck, a delicious sensitive spot that made her lurch forward into him. "Casey, fuck." He felt her tighten as she shouted his name once again as she came.

"Good girl." His voice was husky with possessiveness. She moaned softly as he held her up, letting her rest against him for a few moments as she recovered. She could feel the soft cotton of his t-shirt against her cheek and realized she was very much naked, and he was very much fully clothed. She pushed her palms against his chest to stand on her own, even though her legs were still quite shaky.

"God dammit. You are good." Sam did a slow once over him, appreciating his tanned skin and the bulge pushing against his pants. "You have too many clothes on." She smiled gleefully as she grabbed the hem of his shirt and pulled it up and over his head—having to stand up on her tippy toes to get it over his head of unruly hair. Her hands went to his jeans and worked on freeing his erection. "Sorry, I don't have the patience to undress you slowly."

She unzipped and found his boxer brief hemline and followed it around his waist as she pulled his underwear and jeans down, squeezing his firm ass along the way. Once he was free of his clothes, Casey moved in one quick motion, and both were under the hot water spray, soaking them as their mouths found each other's, and their frenzied hands could no longer restrain themselves. Sam couldn't think of anything but the hot stream of water and the searing heat coming off Casey. No room to worry about solving a murder, feelings, or how she was letting go of control being around him. Her hands glided over his broad shoulders and down his flexed arms. His hard body pressed against hers, forcing the water to river around their bodies. Casey carefully turned Sam's body, making sure not to slip, pushing her against the chilled, wet tiles. Casey stepped back slightly to let his green eyes connect with hers as he took her in fully, and Sam couldn't think of anything but this unbridled pleasure right now.

After their extended shower, Sam and Casey ate their lukewarm takeout dinner. Again, Sam felt that juxtaposition of feeling so natural around him, yet the thoughts of him as a distraction crept back into her mind. She knew someone was watching her every move, which meant they probably knew about Casey too. And Casey could become a target. Given her past and current circumstances, the possibility of Casey being hurt or even killed was real. And it would be her fault.

Oh my God, stop it, she thought. She had to do something to stop from going down that dark path.

Sam looked around and decided she'd just focus on work to prove to herself that Casey wasn't a distraction. She could focus on her job and do it well, even with him around. She grabbed her laptop, sat on the sofa, and dove into her work.

Chapter 26

Casey noticed a shift in Sam halfway through dinner. He noticed she was getting lost in her thoughts. She would stare at nothing, her fork hovering above her food for longer than necessary. He watched her face's features go rigid and then soften after a moment. He ate the rest of his dinner in silence, unsure if he should interrupt her. When she got up and announced she needed to get some work done, he just nodded and let her go as he took his final bites and cleaned up the kitchen, putting the leftovers in the fridge. By the time he was done, she was consumed by the light of her laptop while she sat on the sofa.

Casey found some herbal tea and an electric kettle in the cupboard. He brewed a cup of herbal tea and brought it into the living room for her. He gently put his hand under her chin, tilting her head in his direction. He waited for her eyes to focus and kissed her forehead. He smiled and handed her the tea, and she returned the smile, wrapping her hands around the steaming mug.

"Thank you. You don't have to stay; I want to work just a little bit longer," Sam said, her eyes already returning to the laptop.

Casey thought about going home tonight but knew his sister would be home and would probably lean hard into him since he hadn't been home all week. She was already blowing up his phone with text messages, asking where he had been and why his mail had been stacking up. But he wasn't ready to explain the situation with Sam to her, mostly because he didn't know himself. He also wasn't thrilled about leaving Sam alone. He didn't want to find her again in a hospital. It was only the third time he saw her, but it burned something into his heart. He recalled seeing her there, sleeping with the machine beeping around her and her face bandaged. His stomach dropped, and a sense of helplessness ripped through him. He wasn't sure what possessed him to show up at the hospital that day, yet there he was, asking a woman he had met twice to go on a date with him. He just couldn't imagine never seeing her again for some reason. And seeing her there, sleeping soundly on that hospital bed, he knew he needed her in his life.

Casey looked over at her. She held her mug with one hand and worked the mouse pad with the other, scrolling through newspaper articles on her laptop. But now, he thought, he wasn't sure he could handle it if it happened again.

Casey flipped on the TV, which cast the living room in a soft glow alongside the modern glass table lamp. He found a replay of an old hockey game, let his mind go of worries, and enjoyed his comfortable evening with Sam.

Chapter 27

Sam tried to focus on the file that she had been ignoring for the better part of ten years, but it was the last place she hadn't looked through yet, and she knew it could maybe help her investigation. But it would also trigger her trauma, and up to this point, she wasn't sure if she could handle it with everything that was going on. Sam wasn't looking to get back into therapy sessions but maybe, she thought. She would probably need to.

Someone had tried to kill her, killed two other people, was stalking her, and knew all her moves. She was anything but safe.

Sam looked up from her laptop and over at Casey. She studied him as he sat relaxed next to her at the other end of the sofa. He wasn't completely tucked in the corner, but far enough to give her space, but it didn't feel like he was avoiding touching her anything. It just seemed he knew what to do, what she needed. Sam tried to understand how it was possible but couldn't. She just felt safe with him around. Again, in reality, she was not even close to being safe, nor was he, but he was someone who just fit into her life. She'd been avoiding talking to him about her issues with PTSD ever since the first night he stayed over, but no time felt right. And she was terrified of what happens after she does.

Time to be brave, she told herself.

She inhaled before clearing her throat. "I need to explain something to you."

Sam saw the surprise cross Casey's face. He muted the TV but kept it on, which kept a soft glow over the room. He turned toward Sam as he sat, readjusting his leg by tucking it under his bottom and leaving the other still stretched out on the ground; he rested his elbow on the top edge of the sofa and leaned on it. "I'm listening."

"Oh, God," Sam said as she moved her laptop from her lap and onto the coffee table before mimicking Casey's position, except she tucked both legs underneath her. She watched as Casey sat with patient eyes studying hers.

Sam took a deep breath and began. "I have PTSD—posttraumatic stress disorder. If you want to get technical, it's called complex PTSD, family trauma mixed with military trauma." Sam waved her hands in front of her, dismissing her train of thought. "Anyway, I struggled with it for a long time. Mostly it's uneventful and unnoticeable to everyone. It's generally not as bad as you have seen."

She dared a glance at Casey, and seeing him still listening, she continued. "I'm not crazy or anything. Think of it as like a high-functioning PTSD. I still function. Just differently than others." She shrugged. "It's not like I want to kill myself. Although suicidal thoughts are common with PTSD, for some reason, that's not me. I love life. I just get..." Sam paused before thinking how to say it. "I just get dark. Like I have this dark fog that rolls over me, and I can't always stop it. Sometimes I feel it coming, but it comes out of nowhere too, like that first night here with you."

Sam started playing with the edge of her blanket on her lap, her head down, watching the fringe of the blanket slide through her fingers. She inhaled, "I just detach from life, when I get dark." Sam let a sad laugh escape as she shrugged. "I don't know if I'm doing a good job of explaining this, especially because it's different for everyone, but for me, it's just a dark fog that I can't see through. It haunts me, but oddly, it also comforts me." Sam whispered so low that she wasn't sure if she meant for Casey to hear it or not. "My darkness often feels like the only thing that can protect me."

Sam paused and took another deep breath. She had already shared more with Casey this week than with anyone else. She dared to look up into his eyes. Sincerity and concern were arched in his eyes.

"Protect you from what?" he asked carefully.

"I don't know. Everything," she shrugged. "Being hurt or vulnerable, hurt others. Having to deal with emotions and feelings of all of that.

Sam tucked her legs in tighter, bringing her knees up toward her chin, not realizing she had curled into a fetal position. "My dark fog feels like it protected me from the guilt I feel for failing to see the IED that killed my team. It prevented the flashbacks from being so harsh, as well as the nightmares." Sam shook her head. "Those visions will never escape me, but in my mind, the darkness softens the blow."

Sam stared unfocused on Casey's leg as she processed her thoughts for a few more moments. Still feeling that safety net Casey provided, she decided to keep sharing.

"That night after the hospital when you saw my 'episode' is just a small example of how trauma is constantly part of my life. I'm hypervigilant, to the point of insanity at times. You mentioned my minimal décor, and it is lovely, but it's so strategic. It's so I can easily notice if something was disturbed or moved while I was gone."

Sam looked around her clean and tidy living room. These were just a few personal pieces from some travels and some things she picked from a home décor store to bring life to her bookcase. She loved her home, but truly, it was barren of personality and life. Much like herself, she thought. She sighed, "I'm emotionally detached because of my fear and anxiety around losing people I care about. It's just too much to bear sometimes." Sam unconsciously stretched her arm on the back of the couch toward Casey, and he did the same, lightly laying his hand on her forearm.

"All week, I've spent an immeasurable amount of time trying to decide whether you being around me is a good idea or not." She furrowed her brow as she looked at Casey. "Someone tried to kill me. They have killed people that have been around me, Casey." She put her free hand on his knee. "That makes you a target now, too."

Sam choked on the lump in her throat that leaped from the bottom of her stomach. "It's really too dangerous to be around me. I've somehow brought you into this world of murder and chaos when a week ago, your life was much better without me and my shitshow." Sam pulled her arms back and into herself, away from Casey's touch. "I'm not worth this, Casey."

She curled her knees up entirely and hugged her ankles while lowering her forehead to her knees, trying to regain herself.

After a few moments, Sam felt Casey inch closer, his hands rubbing her calves. They slowly moved to her shoulders and gently lifted her chin. "You are worth everything," Casey said softly.

She shook her head and dropped it back onto her knees. "No. No. You're wrong."

She took a few composing breaths before she continued, "I don't have friends." She lifted her head and connected with Casey again. "I don't date. I don't have a family. Because it's just not possible, I can't." Sam shrugged as she sunk into herself. "I struggle to connect with anyone, and when I do…" Sam barely whispered the words so as not to cry. "They get hurt, Casey." A few tears found their way out of Sam's brown eyes and down her cheeks. "They always do."

Casey reached out and wiped his thumb across Samantha's cheek, wiping away tears she didn't realize were falling. "They get hurt?" he asked.

Sam leaned into his hand, comforted by his touch, and inhaled his scent; he always seemed to have a woodsy scent matched with the light spearmint that permeated her senses. She felt so safe, but she knew he wasn't—not with her. It pained her, but she pulled her head back from his warm hand, which embraced her cheek.

"They. Me. People. Doesn't matter. Someone gets hurt. You. You'll get hurt, Casey."

"I'm fine, Sam. I really am. I'm going to be fine." She lifted her chin once again. "And so are you."

Sam sighed, "I'm fucked up. I know that." She said with a half attempt at a smile. "I hear myself say these crazy things, and I know how fucked up it all sounds. But the other part of me can't let go of it." Sam shook her head. "I may seem cool, calm, and collected on the outside, but that is because I have no choice but to be that." She sighed deeply before saying, "But underneath it all, I'm a hot fucking mess."

Casey reached out, pulled Sam toward him, and forced her body to squeeze next to his. He brushed back loose strands of her hair. "I mean this in the best way possible, but I haven't seen you as the cool, calm, or collected Sam yet."

Samantha laughed through her tears, "Geez, thanks."

"Yeah, sorry. That sounded terrible." He shrugged. "See? I told you I'd fuck it up and not say the right thing at some point."

He smiled and was grateful she returned it. "I mean that I see you. Even at the golf course, when you were looking for Jeffrey, I could see that you presented as cool and calm, but I don't know; I could just see you. Even in that dress, I knew you were not being you." He nudged her with a wink.

"Even when you are undercover as a PI, Sam," he continued as he gestured quotation signs as he said undercover. "Nothing feels ingenuine with you. When you are cool and calm, I see that. When you're a hot fucking mess, I see that.

Especially the hot part," he said out of the corner of his mouth.

Sam looked up and watched Casey's face as he seemed to process what he was saying. "I don't know," he said. "I can't explain it any better." He shrugged and waved his hand around. "It just feels natural being around you."

"Seriously?" Sam shook her head in disbelief as she tried to understand how he used the same word she had landed on earlier to describe how it felt to be around him. "How do you do that? Just when I think you finally said something stupid, you go and turn it into something perfectly articulated and needed."

"It's a gift, apparently."

Sam leaned forward, resting her forehead on Casey's chest. She spoke into his lap as she said, "I did some therapy right when I got home from Afghanistan, which helped tremendously." She sat up. "But somehow, in one week, you've made me feel safer and more understood than anyone ever has."

"I guess that's a gift, too." Casey smiled. "But one that I have reserved just for you."

Sam kissed him then. She curled her hands around the sides of his head and pulled him into her with an intensity that seemed to overwhelm her senses. She had no choice but to kiss him to try and relieve the feeling, but it just seemed to amplify the longer their lips touched. Tears fell from her eyes, but this time, it wasn't because of any trauma; it was something that hit deeper than before.

She exhaled deeply after the kiss. "You can't be real." She sat back and looked into the green depths of his eyes. "You can't be real." She shook her head. "No. There is no way someone sees all this and stays."

"I am real." Casey took her hands and placed them on his face. "Look at me."

It took Sam quite a few moments to refocus on him.

"Sam, I'm here. I'm real. And I want to stay. My life is better with you." Casey pulled her into an embrace and rested his cheek on her head.

Fuck me, he whispered to himself at his own admission. He actually did want to stay. He couldn't remember the last time he wanted to be around someone this much. He shook his head as he grasped Sam tightly. He didn't know how he would feel without her. This week, he had a sense of fulfillment like he hadn't experienced before. He wiped his hand down his face. There were so many red flags he shouldn't overlook, but he couldn't help but be blind to them. Plus he knew Will and Nikki would point them all out. He had to admit Sam was sort of fucked up and obviously had some mental health issues to work through. And to top it off, someone was trying to kill her.

Casey could feel Sam's body relax against him and sink further into his. He inhaled the fresh, citrusy scent of her hair. It sent a velvety wave of peace through his whole body. Through all of Sam's supposed red flags, he still couldn't imagine being anywhere else than right here, with Sam in his arms. He needed to be here. She didn't seem to believe that. He planned to keep telling her as long as it took to get it through her stubborn head. He chuckled at himself. Hell, it was only a week; he wouldn't believe himself either.

Feeling her body soften, he pulled her back and looked into her eyes again. "You can have all the good and then some." He made sure she was focused on him, "You are worth it, Samantha Reeves." Casey moved a hand under her chin, forcing her to look at him and see him clearly. "Are you okay?"

Sam sighed and then laughed. "No." She kissed him, though. "But I will be. Thank you." Another kiss. "For everything." She leaned against his shoulder and curled up against the heat of his body, firm, safe, and comforting.

Chapter 28

Sam was asleep when her phone buzzed on the coffee table, waking her. She hadn't realized she had fallen asleep in Casey's arms on the sofa. Sharing feelings was exhausting, she thought as she yawned and picked up her phone to see who had sent her a text. She sat up straighter when she saw it was a text from Maggie Lindahl.

> Maggie: Hello, Sam. This is Maggie Lindahl. Sorry for the late response to your text from last week. Planning Jeffrey's funeral and dealing with the kids and all. Can we meet tomorrow for coffee?

"What does she want?" Casey asked.

"Meet for coffee, I guess."

"Are you sure that is a good idea, with everything you've been through and, you know... the sociopathic murderer that killed her ex-husband is now after you?"

Sam cocked her eyebrow at Casey. She paused before she replied to Casey with a sarcastic comment but realized Casey had a point.

"True," she said as she studied the text on her phone. "However, Jeffrey was murdered by that sociopath while I was on the case. So, to be fair, the killer probably thinks I know something and is trying to tie up loose ends." Sam shrugged.

"That's my current working theory. I can't figure out how this is all tied to Afghanistan yet, but I will. Someone is obviously upset about that, but I can't seem to figure out how Jeffrey is connected."

"Seems all bit of a stretch theory and very confusing."

"I know that," Sam said as she stared back at her phone. "I guess, maybe I feel like I owe Maggie an in-person apology for the loss of her ex-husband she didn't even like?" Sam said slowly as it dawned on her. "That sounds absolutely insane as I say it out loud."

Casey stared with narrowed eyes with questioning concern.

"I'm not saying I am responsible for his death," she paused and playfully slapped his shoulder. "See. Look at me learning and growing." She looked back at her phone and began thumbing the screen. "But I do have a responsibility to my client, and I need to see that through, no matter how it ends."

> Sam: No worries. I'd be happy to connect over coffee with you. Does 10 tomorrow morning work?

> Maggie: Perfect. See you then.

Sam put her phone down after they finalized the location details. She looked up at Casey as he watched the muted television, his hand resting on her knees.

She shook her head in disbelief. Here she was, just having an emotional breakdown, and Casey was there and still here, just chilling like it was no big deal. He didn't seem phased at all. He kept her safe and pulled her out of it faster than she probably would have recovered on her own.

And lately, her past trauma came floating up out of the

depths of the darkness more often than she cared for. It kept bobbing up out of the deep water, trying to breathe and live in the present. For years, she tried to keep it in the darkest depths of her past, but studying Casey, his stubbled jawline in the shadows of the softly lit room, Sam thought, maybe, just maybe, if the past kept surfacing, she'd be okay with him here. She wasn't always going to be okay; she recognized that. But for whatever reason, Casey gave her a space to be not okay, too.

A warmth spread across her chest as she put her hand on Casey's and squeezed. He met her eyes. "Thank you. Truly." Sam leaned over to grab her laptop off the coffee table as she said. "I think I feel good enough to open a folder I keep..."

Casey's hand wrapped around her wrist, stopping her, and he said, "I think..." He paused, looking at her. "...we're done with work for tonight." She leaned back, moved out of his grasp, and crossed her arms with a pouting expression.

"What?! Why? I feel good. I have a second wind!"

"We're done because of two reasons. One, you've dealt with a lot today, Sam." Casey stood.

He peeled her arms from her chest, grasped her hands, and pulled her up next to him; the chenille throw blanket fell between them. "And two, we need to go to bed now if you want to make it on time for coffee tomorrow."

Sam looked at her watch. "It's nine-thirty," she said warily. "I have coffee at ten in the morning."

"Well, shit. We better hurry." Casey started dragging her behind him as he made his way to the stairs.

"What in the hell are you talking about?" Sam asked.

He turned and winked. "That doesn't leave us much time for sleeping." He laughed as he watched Sam's confusion melt into a sultry grin as she began to laugh with him.

Chapter 29

The next morning, Sam stood waiting for her craft coffee. The barista called her name just as she caught sight of Maggie walking into the coffee shop. She'd only met Maggie once before, which was at that fundraiser dinner she had met Jeffrey as well. In both instances, Sam observed that Maggie knew how to walk into a room. Her carefully styled bright red hair made both men's and women's eyes turn. A classic shoulder-length bob with beach waves sculpted her narrow jawline and over-plumped lips. Lululemon gray capris paired with a brilliant blue top reminded Sam of all the women who go to the gym and leave, never breaking a sweat. Maggie was the type who brought coffee on the treadmill instead of a water bottle. Sam didn't love the vibes she got from Maggie when she'd hired her to trail Jeffrey, but that didn't matter. It was a job.

"Hi, Maggie. Do you need coffee or anything?"

"I'm fine, dear. Please," Maggie gestured to a table. "This won't take long."

Sam followed her to a corner table. She made sure she could see her car from the corner and could watch all the entries and exits as she sat. Sam had already surveyed all the patrons as soon as she walked into the coffee shop. None looked familiar, and no alarms were going off in her head. She was certain whoever it was knew she was there or nearby. She just had to keep up her diligence and all her senses up and firing.

She met Maggie's eyes and wasn't sure if she realized

how oddly dark they were, considering how brightly her hair shined. Maggie sat with a straight back and clasped her hand in front of her.

Sam smiled. "I'm glad you wanted to meet up. I've been meaning to reach out, but it has been a hectic week with everything going on."

Maggie made a scuffing sound from the back of her throat.

Was she about to roll her eyes at me? Sam thought. *No,* she reconsidered. *Why would Maggie do that?*

Ignoring the odd behavior, Sam continued.

"I'm so sorry about what happened to Jeffrey. I know the police are doing everything possible to solve this case and find out who would have killed Jeffrey."

"And no thanks to you, dear," Maggie said, even-toned and with an expressionless face.

Sam, taken aback, responded, "I'm sorry, what?"

"Well, it's no secret that you were the last to see him and had been watching his every move for the last several weeks. Were you not?" Maggie paused and looked Sam squarely in the eyes.

"Well, yes... but..." Sam stammered.

"No buts, dear," Maggie said with an edge as sharp as steel. "He died because of you."

Sam flinched internally and prayed her face didn't do the same. Her throat constricted as she attempted to swallow back the guilt rising up with the familiar sting of bile.

Breathe, Sam, she told herself.

Maggie continued with a coldness that kept Sam frozen in place.

"I was told you were one of the best investigators, yet you let a man you were investigating die on your watch." She kept her eyes locked on Sam's as she continued in her matter-of-fact tone. "It seems to me that you didn't do your job." Maggie stood to leave. "I will not be paying the final installment of our agreement."

Maggie threw her bag over her shoulder and hovered over Sam. "Jeffrey died because you didn't do your job. You failed, Ms. Reeves. I owe you nothing."

Maggie donned her oversized sunglasses and strolled out of the glass-paned door as if she was just leaving a casual lunch. Sam watched as she left and stared even as she lost sight of Maggie around the corner. At that moment, she was not okay.

Chapter 30

Casey left Sam's place and headed home to take care of things around his house that he neglected all week. He pulled up to the small rambler in Mendota Heights he had bought when he got the job with Will at the golf course. It was modest but built with quality wood and nice furnishings. His mother came for a short visit when he first bought it. She wanted to ensure their Cuban heritage was displayed throughout his house with brilliant colors mixed with rich textures of brown leather and rustic woods. His sister Nikki had moved in with him, too. She was a nurse at the local emergency room. Completely dedicated to her profession and working through her doctorate program, she had no spare time to take care of a place of her own.

Casey smiled at his sister as he walked in, tossing his overnight bag on the sofa. Nikki sat in her scrubs with a morning newspaper and a coffee cake in front of her at their small round table surrounded by yellow walls, the mid-morning sun echoing the soft tones of the walls. She insisted on still getting an actual newspaper. She was barely thirty but had old lady tendencies he liked to give her grief about.

She eyed him through her lashes without moving her head from the paper. "Did you move out and forget to tell me?" she asked as he kissed the top of her head.

Casey sat on the wooden chair beside her. "Ah, you missed your big brother?"

He tried to pick up her fork, but she batted his hand away

without averting her eyes. Casey grunted at her but went to the kitchen, grabbed a fork in the drawer, returned to his chair, and dug into the coffee cake, chewing a mouthful before continuing. "No. I have not moved out." He took another forkful before speaking carefully. "I've been needed elsewhere."

Nikki finally looked at Casey. "Needed?"

Casey felt the weight of her stare.

Nikki raised one eyebrow. "Who is she?" She emphasized the last word.

Damn his sister for knowing how to read him so well, he thought. There's no point hiding it. He resigned. "Yeah, well, I met this woman last week at the golf course, and it's been the most amazing but also the strangest week of my life."

Nikki laid the paper down and eyed her brother. "You've been staying with the same woman every night this week?!" She gestured her hand at Casey. "And here I thought you and Will finally confessed your love for each other and left me the house while you moved into his momma's mansion."

"First off," Casey took another bite of food, "why is it shocking news it's the same woman? I'm not a man whore." He shook his fork at Nikki. "And second, be nice to Will. He lost his mom not even a year ago, and she left him that house. He really didn't have a choice in the matter."

"You always have a choice," Nikki said coldly with a shrug. "And Will chooses to be an ass."

Casey shook his head. "You know, someday, you guys will have to settle whatever this discontent is between you two."

Nikki huffed, "The less I have to see of that man, the better. He can get lost in his momma's big ass mansion, and the world would be better." She averted her attention back to the paper in her hand.

Casey just shook his head. Will and Nikki dated briefly in college, but it ended just as quickly as it started. Neither of them explained what happened between them. It bothered him initially since his sister and best friend were so tight-lipped about it, but he never pushed it. They tolerated each other for him, and that was enough.

"Seriously though, Nikki, this woman, Samantha. She is... Sam is amazing."

"But..." Nikki prodded.

Casey sighed. "She is involved with some really crazy shit right now, like pretty certain someone is trying to kill her type of crazy shit."

"Casey!" Nikki dropped the paper in her lap and turned her whole body to face her brother. "If I've ever seen a red flag about a woman—that is a giant, flaming red flag!"

"It's not like that, Nikki. I can't quite explain everything happening because I'm not even sure what is happening, but I'm there every night because I can't imagine not being there for her if she needs me."

"And putting yourself next to her, you could get yourself killed, estúpido." She smacked the paper against Casey's head.

"Ow!"

"Momma would smack you across the room if she knew how stupid you were being over a woman you barely know."

"But I do know her. I can't explain it, Nikki, but she isn't like any other woman I've met before."

Nikki straightened her newspaper, preparing to read again, but looked Casey square in the eyes. "You love too hard and too soon, brother. It seems like you're ready to die for this woman, and you've known her for a week." Nikki turned back to the paper. "Don't be stupid, Casey; nobody is worth dying for."

Casey smiled as he took the last bite of the coffee cake. "Oh, Nikki, Nikki, Nikki." He grabbed the crumb-filled plate and his fork, putting it in the sink. He stood behind her and patted her head before giving her a big hug from behind. "I can't wait for you to get 'it.' Some people are worth everything."

"Ha," she laughed sarcastically. "You'll be waiting forever."

"I'm sure I won't."

Casey cleaned up the table as Nikki gathered her stuff to head to work. She paused as she stood in front of the door. "Casey," she said with a serious tone. "You met this girl a week ago and barely left her side." She shook her head. "Some people are broken and can't be put back together. Are you really needed, Casey? Or are you just trying to fix someone that can't be fixed?"

The door shut softly behind her as Casey stood in his kitchen. This week had been amazing, but maybe Nikki had a point. He did love too hard and too soon. He married way too soon the first time, and he had a habit of being the friend who took care of others. Nikki yelled at him quite regularly about putting others needs above his own.

But was he trying to fix Sam?

He was pretty confident Sam wanted to be with him, but maybe he was being too strong and forward with her. He recognized she needed her own space, too. She was used to being alone. She admitted she'd struggled this week. He realized he was causing stress for her even though things were going so well.

Casey changed into his ratted t-shirt and grass-stained, torn jeans to get started on the lawn. "Distractions today," he said to himself. "Give her and myself some space today. I won't even think about her today." He heard her voice in his head, *I need you*. He smiled to himself. "Okay, maybe for a little bit, I will."

Chapter 31

Sam pulled into her garage, barely noticing the still-present unmarked police car.

He died because of you.

Her surroundings blurred into wisps of shadows and lights as she made her way inside her home.

You failed, Sam.

She repeated Maggie's words as she sat on the edge of her bed and stared mindlessly at the bi-fold closet doors slightly ajar in front of her.

He died because of you.

They died because of you, her inner voice corrected.

She dropped her head into her hands. Her past demons had broken through her protective fog and taken hold of her. She sucked in her breath as she tried to stop the swell of emotions carried in through this broken barrier. She swayed her head back and forth, holding the sides of her head. "I can't keep doing this."

The heaviness sat on her chest and started to burn into her throat. Her breathing quickened, and the burning morphed into a tightness, which forced her breaths to come in short and shallow heaves. "I can't." She exhaled as tears streamed down her face, spotting her black leggings with tiny blotches.

She wasn't sure how long she sat there and cried. Her throat burned, her face felt swollen, and her cheeks had dried as the tears had stopped falling. Her breathing evened out as she finally inhaled fully and regained rhythmic, controlled breathing.

Finally, her inner demon voices quieted, and she heard a familiar deep tone through the thinning haze surrounding her. *It's okay not to be okay.*

Just hearing his voice, even in her head, spread a warmth across her skin that settled deep into her soul. She picked her head up with a newfound feeling that she wasn't sure what it was, but it felt lighter, warmer, like Casey's arms wrapped around her.

Her vision cleared, no longer blurred from the salty tears, when she caught a glimpse of her suitcase sitting on the floor of her closet. She stood, stretching her shoulders back before she slid the folding doors open and took out the suitcase. She kneeled, dug deep into the bottom of the bag, and pulled out the envelope labeled with her name and her room at Lakeside Motel—7B. She ripped it open and pulled the tape and tissue paper away. She let the military police patch fall into her open hand.

She heard Maggie's stern voice in her head. *You failed, Sam.*

Sam thought her tears had dried up. She had no more left, but as she studied the patch closer, her flushed cheeks began to streak with tears once again. Sam ran her thumb across the stitching. "I'm sorry, Justin, but I'm... I'm..." she whispered, not sure what she was trying to articulate. The patch weighed nothing, yet it was the heaviest thing she had ever carried. It was a weight she could no longer carry.

"I have failed." Sam pressed the patch to her chest. "But I need to let go." Sam inhaled sharply. "I need to be okay with not being okay."

The shock and adrenaline from this morning's encounter with Maggie finally crashed into Sam's system. Her heart hammered as she lay on her bed and let the tears soak her pillow as she fell into a deep sleep.

Chapter 32

Maggie Lindahl barely kept a straight face as she walked out of the coffee shop, leaving Sam open-jawed and immobile. She popped into her Mercedes and laughed until her sides hurt. "Oh my God, that felt so good," she exclaimed as she regained her composure. Maggie replayed the conversation in her head. She wished she would have recorded it. It was truly priceless to witness. She would have loved to relive that moment as much as possible—that moment when Sam felt small and worthless. It was a dream come true.

Maggie fixed her makeup in the rearview mirror just as she watched Sam walk like a brainless zombie out of the coffee shop.

Maggie's fit of laughter flipped over to anger at the site of Sam. "God, Reeves, you're the worst."

Maggie eventually pulled up to her Edina home. Its massive four-car garage made the ten-thousand-square-foot home feel small. Jeffrey wanted the garage to be fully stocked with all the red metal tool chests, vintage car signs, bar stools, and a custom bar at the back of one of the stalls even though he never worked on these vintage cars. He just pretended he was a significant and vital part of the car society. She hated the big house and everything about it, but taking it away from

Jeffrey out of pure spite and watching his gray eyes burn with anger and hatred pleased her more. All of his hot-shot attorney skills couldn't save him from her.

She looked around at all the stuff in the garage that Jeffrey loved. He must have known she never loved him since he spent his time on things and his friends and never her, which she was okay with. Since day one, Jeffrey had been just a pawn. Maggie knew she'd never love again.

The sun never seemed to warm her skin after her true love died. He died, and so did her light; the only thing that brought comfort was letting darkness fill the void. There, in the darkness, she thought of nothing but how to avenge the unnecessary death of the love of her life.

And it wasn't until a couple of years ago that the darkened void changed. She and Jeffrey had been out for a fundraising dinner when she laid eyes on Samantha Reeves, and as soon as Maggie noticed her, she knew instantly who it was.

She had managed to move on after Sam ruined her life the first time. She was fine living in the sunless void, but then fucking Reeves reappeared. Hate seeped out of every pore and was only amplified by the fact that Samantha Reeves had no idea who she was, but then again, why would she? It didn't matter; what mattered to Maggie was that this bitch responsible for ruining her happy life was right in front of her, smiling and laughing and acting like life was just peachy and bright.

"Fuck that!" Maggie shouted as her memories of seeing Samantha again flooded her mind.

Maggie checked her reflection in the rearview mirror as she sat seething in her car in the garage. Maggie tried. She tried to be the perfect wife—cook, clean, and raise children. She even controlled her impulsive side. She convinced Jeffrey a monthly gun range club was a good idea for a woman to keep up with safety in the big, scary city. "Idiot."

Every once in a while, she'd get a familiar pulse of excitement course through her from a firework display or a news story about some accidental explosion, but she convinced herself she was fine. She was handling herself well. She didn't need all that therapy they tried to make her do. She managed just fine.

It wasn't until she was face to face with Reeves that something changed inside her. The void felt like it was morphing from nothing into something. It took some time, but Maggie understood it had morphed into—revenge. The more she thought about ending Reeves, the more she felt whole.

She let out her breath and let the anger melt away as she slid out of her care and shut the door. She looked across the the garage at the last stall. She couldn't help but laugh as the anger melted into something more sinister.

Jeffrey would turn over in his grave if he saw that truck in his pristine garage. Sitting there, it seemed so out of place with the fire-engine red chests and glossy floors, but her fifteen-hundred-dollar, beat-up black truck was a solid investment. And soon, it would pay off tenfold.

Chapter 33

Samantha awoke sweaty and stiff. She blinked a few times to clear her vision and saw that the sun was still high in the window. As she went to stretch, she realized something was in her hand. She unclenched her palm to see the military police patch lay wrinkled there. Sam smoothed the crunched edges with her other hand, letting her fingers scroll over the embroidered surface.

This patch used to symbolize so much to her. She had taken an oath when she enlisted as a military police officer. For the first time, she felt she was where she was supposed to be. And when she recited the words, "no higher calling than to assist, protect and defend fellow soldiers..." she did not take it lightly.

Now, this patch was a symbol of suffering and guilt over her fellow soldiers.

Sam closed her eyes. "I have to stop doing this."

Her fingertips caressed the patch as if it were a delicate piece of silk. "This patch needs to mean more."

She pressed the patch to her chest, inhaling the fresh linen smell that floated from her bedding. As she exhaled, she relaxed her shoulders and stood. She lay the patch on the bed and made her way to the bathroom.

The woman reflected back at her looked like hell, with a fading pinkish slash across her cheek and swollen, red-veined eyes from the unfamiliar burn of so many tears shed. Sam laughed at herself. Considering how terrible she looked, she felt lighter than she had in a long time.

A few hours ago, she was accosted by a "Can I see the manager" suburban housewife. Add on top that she was being targeted by a murderer and nearly blown up twice in one week. Sam's little chuckle became an all-engrossing laugh. Her life was nothing but absurdity right now. "And I feel... lighter."

After catching her breath, she turned on the tap and splashed cold water on her face.

Sam studied her reflection as she patted her skin dry with a terry cloth towel.

Maggie's words echoed in her mind. *You failed, Samantha.*

This time, however, she heard those words and it didn't seem to hit as deep as it did before her she fell asleep.

She hung the towel and stepped back into her room beside her bed.

"I failed."

Sam picked up the patch from the bed. She walked over to her dresser and propped the patch against the emerald green vase with white-flowered branches streaming out the top. "Failure suck. but I have to stop letting failure control me."

She made her way downstairs. "I sound like a freaking inspirational meme." She laughed as she made herself a cup of coffee before sitting in front of her laptop. She relaxed her shoulders and took a cleansing breath. "I need to nap more often."

Chapter 34

It was almost dinner time, and Sam had checked her phone for the hundredth time since she had woken up. She felt ridiculous expecting Casey to reach out by now. Since the first day she met Casey, they had talked or texted every day multiple times. She hadn't heard from him since he left this morning. Didn't he want to know how it went with Maggie? She wanted to tell him, but she wanted to wait to say to him in person.

She looked forward to talking about her day with Casey, which was a strange, new concept for her. She never had someone to come home to and just talk about their day with. But she liked it, and it was scary to think she could get used to it even though it threatened her self-proclaimed loner status.

When she realized he hadn't sent her a text or called all day, she tried not to let the annoyance sit in her stomach and churn. But after another fifteen minutes of fluttering and staring at the same webpage, she scolded herself. "Stop being ridiculous."

She unlocked her phone and texted him.

> Sam: Did you plan to come over tonight? Trying to decide on dinner plans.

It took just a minute or two before the three dots in the bubble appeared. Sam's fluttering stomach turned once, not sure what to expect.

> Casey: Are you good with me coming over? I absolutely want to, but I recognize I've been there a lot, so if you need space, that's okay. 😊

Even through a text message, he seemed to say the right things. Double checking with her if she wanted her own space or not. "Damn," she said out loud. "He's just a walking green flag, while I'm a red flag the size of the moon."

Sam was still feeling that lightness from her nap, and the angst in her stomach was dissipating. She thought how excited she was to see him. Even though she did want and love her own space, she wanted and loved the way Casey's mouth found hers, the way his hands explored her body, finding every sensitive spot that sent shivers of heat through her body. Sam felt an ache in her center, and she knew she definitely wanted him over.

> Sam: I wouldn't have asked if I didn't want you to come over. Besides, I've had my space all day I'm good with my alone time. I need you tonight. 😈

Sam hit send as heat flushed her cheeks as she imagined his emerald eyes filling with intensity just as they did when he fixated on her. She grinned devilishly, too. If he could play into this "need thing," she could too. The three dots appeared almost instantly.

> Casey: Good God, woman. Let me shower first, and I'll head over. I've been doing yard work all day, so I need to clean up.

> Sam: LOL. Sounds good. I'll make dinner tonight to honor your hard work all day.

> Casey: You know how to cook?! 😏

> Sam: Haha. I know how to use a knife, if that's what you mean.

> Casey: I have no doubt about your knife skills. And thank you. I'll be over around 7. I have to get naked and wet now.

Sam rolled her eyes but still felt her body tighten at the image of Casey naked. "This guy," she said. She typed a quick reply with just a fire emoji before putting her phone down, steepled her hands together in front of her, and pressed them to her lips.

Sam breathed a sigh of relief. He was coming over. She never had someone outside of her military deployments to share about her day with. And now it was Casey, and she liked it, despite her initial efforts of trying to avoid it.

Her mother, Colleen, on the days she did come home between "jobs," never asked Sam how school went or what she had been up to. Sam learned quickly to assess her mom's behavior as soon as she walked in. Most days, a quick analysis provided enough evidence to Sam that it was best to stay out of Colleen's way. Colleen didn't bother her daughter much as long as bologna, bread, and whiskey were stocked in the house. Samantha had been an oops baby, and Colleen made sure she knew that.

Sam stood, not letting herself get too far along on that negative freight train and found herself standing in the middle of the kitchen. "Now," she exclaimed, "to figure out what the fuck to do for dinner."

Sam had just put the frozen tilapia in the oven when her smart watch binged with a text from Casey saying he was there but chatting with Tony outside. "Of course, he is." Sam rolled her eyes as she went and unlocked the front door and returned to making dinner.

A few minutes later, Casey walked into mellow music paired with a pleasant garlicky aroma. His heart twisted with such force at the sight of Sam standing in the kitchen he stopped mid step and just watched her. Her dark hair was pulled back in a disheveled loose bun high on her head, strands dancing against her cheeks. She had just finished slicing something on the wooden cutting board and was adding it to a glass salad bowl filled with leafy greens.

She seemed to fill the space with energy he'd never felt before. Even as he attempted to distract himself all day, Samantha never left his thoughts. He knew she was strong and could kick the ass out of any situation she faced, but he was still overwhelmed with an unprecedented need to be there for her. It wasn't how Nikki made it seem earlier, he decided. He wasn't trying to fix Sam; he wanted to protect her. He wanted to protect her because he wanted her in his life. And that was it. He shouldn't have to justify more than that, he thought.

He spun Sam around, pulling her into his chest. "Hi."

"Hi."

Casey kissed the top of her head as it became his usual hello. "You are the most beautiful woman in the world." Casey pulled back to look into Sam's brown eyes. He watched her eyes expand and try to hide her surprise and appreciation of his compliment. He saw the edge of her mouth perk into a smile before she pulled it back down. He loved reading her so well. He knew she was about to protest the compliment, so before she could, he dropped his mouth to cover hers, stopping any words from forming. Instead, a light moan escaped her lips, which melted Casey deeper into her. Only when he needed air did he finally break free of her lips. He watched her reddening lips relax into a soft smile. His hands came under her chin as her eyes fluttered open to meet his. "Don't tell my mother or my sister I said that." He quirked his brow up. "They can get very jealous, these ladies." His words were warning, but the smile said otherwise.

"No." Sam shook her head. "I would never." She kissed his cheek and whispered, "Your secret is safe with me." She laughed as she turned her attention back to making the salad.

"And because I haven't met them." Sam froze at her realization, stared at her hands, and decided how to process this information. Why did it feel like a big deal?

"I love my family, and I'm sure you will too, but Cuban women..." Casey whistled and left the sentence unfinished. "What can I do to help with dinner?" he asked.

Casey didn't seem bothered by it as he carried on while Sam's mini freak-out subsided.

"Just pour yourself a glass of wine. I'm good," Sam replied.

He pulled a wine glass from the open shelf and poured himself some of the open sauvignon blanc sitting on the counter. He topped off Sam's half-empty glass. He leaned back on the counter behind her.

"After getting married fresh out of college, Nikki, my sister, assumes I'm ready to propose to any woman that I date longer than a week. And my momma wants me to propose to any woman that I date longer than a week. I can't win."

"Do you propose to women often after just a week?"

Sam asked, looking at her watch, screwing up her face as she looked down at it. "Cause we've known each other for a week, so should I expect a ring soon?"

Sam's mind fired into panic mode. Did she really just ask if Casey was going to propose to her? No wonder she kept away from relationships. She was freaking herself out. She was about to apologize for making thingss weird when she caught Casey smiling at her.

"I mean, I did ask you out on a date in a hospital bed."

"Technically, we still haven't gone on a date," Sam responded.

"Well, there is this tiny thing about something trying to kill you that makes going out on a date a little precarious at the moment."

"Fair point," Sam agreed. Okay, she got out of that awkward comment unscathed. Sam took a big gulp of her wine before returning to the cutting board with freshly washed vegetables of bright yellows and greens waiting to be sliced.

They fell into a comfortable silence as she chopped, and he sipped a few more times on his wine.

"Just one time, and it was a mistake." He took a sip.

Sam spun her head to look at Casey with a look of confusion on her face.

"Proposing after a week," he clarified. "I did it one time, and it was a mistake," he said.

"Ahhh," Sam said. She didn't love talking about his past love life, but she listened as she worked with the food.

"And one, apparently, that my sister can't let go of, even though that was a long time ago." Casey took a swig of wine. "My buddy Will and I have just stuck together, really. After my divorce, we just sort of..." Casey stammered, looking for the right words. "We just..."

"Used each other as a wingman and never actually dated to avoid falling in love?" Sam asked with an eye raised.

"No!" Casey immediately replied. "Well..." Casey rubbed

the back of his neck. "Maybe, a little." He winced with a shrug. "I mean, I'd go on dates, but I haven't really dated." Casey shrugged. "After my very short marriage, I realized I married for my family's sake, not myself. Nikki is always on my ass about caring too much for other people, so I guess I get cautious when it comes to women."

Sam stopped and looked at Casey. "Are you trying to sell yourself here? Because you're doing a terrible job."

Casey slapped his hand on his forehead. "Sorry." He dropped his hand and looked at Sam. "Wait, how did we get here? Why are we talking about my dating past? This isn't where I expected this conversation to go."

"You wanted me to lie to your sister and mother," Sam stated.

"I didn't say lie. I said don't tell them. They will fly off the handle in a hundred different ways."

Sam accepted the strange pivot with a sigh. Discussing Casey's previous love life left an odd feeling in the pit of her stomach, and she'd rather move on from it.

"Between a protective sister and a watch-your-back best friend, it seems like I will have to do some serious impressing to make the cut and be accepted by both."

"So, you want to impress my friends and family?" Casey asked.

Sam paused, slicing the zucchini she was preparing to crisp up on the stove. She looked up toward the end of the counter, appreciating the light gray marbling cascading over the edge. "At the hospital, you said, 'You're just like here, now.'" She waved her knife. "I like you here now."

Sam felt muscular arms wrap around her waist from behind. She felt his breath against her ear. "I like being here with you," Casey said, brushing his nose along the edge of her ear.

Sam leaned back in his embrace and let his mouth graze her ear and neck down across her collarbone. She playfully held the knife up to eye level. "If you make me mess up dinner, the one time I'm cooking, I'll have to rethink you being around here."

Laughing, Casey backed away slowly, waving his hands in front in surrender before picking up his wine and taking a drink. "Now that's settled, how was your day? How did your coffee date with Maggie go?"

Sam put down the knife abruptly on the cutting board. Casey jumped at her sharp movement, his wine nearly sloshing over. She moved the cut veggies to the cast iron skillet and dropped them in with a sizzle. "Let me tell you a story…"

Chapter 35

"So let me get this straight." Casey poured the last of the bottle into Samantha's glass as she hit start on the dishwasher, and they made their way to the open living room to relax on the sofa and finish their glasses of wine. "A crazy client says you killed Jeffrey and then refuses to pay you for weeks of work. You have a mental breakdown. Nap. Then wake up, refreshed, work, and make a fabulous dinner for a guy you're dating. All while being stalked by a sociopath murderer who has killed at least two people and tried to blow you up multiple times."

Sam took a long sip of her wine and nodded.

"Did I get that all right?"

"Most men would have run after the first murder attempt. They would have run far, far away."

"I thought I told you earlier this week I'm just like here now," he teased. "And besides." Casey shrugged. "You're pretty fucking hot."

Sam smiled with a tilt of her head, "Well, thank you, and I'm sorry. I'm just not used to someone sticking around." She took a drink. "I'm going to be a skeptic for a while. Is that okay?"

"Of course," he said as he gently squeezed her arm.

"And you must really think I'm hot to put up with all this crazy bullshit." Sam gestured in circles around herself.

"I do think so." Casey smiled before he took a drink. "And

you looked great in that golf dress." He smirked. "Are you excited to wear it again for the Tee It Up For The Troops Tournament?"

Sam raised an eyebrow. Casey asked her to go earlier this week and she still hadn't given him a solid answer but Sam knew she'd say yes, and apparently, Casey knew it too.

"Should I be excited to go?" Sam held her hand up and counted on her fingers. "One. I don't golf. Two. Hanging out with old veterans doesn't exactly elicit the word 'exciting' in my book. And three..."

Casey cut her off by tapping his finger on her outstretched finger. "Because you get to relive the moment you first met me."

Sam grabbed his finger and twisted it down with a smirk.

"Ow!" he said as he pulled his hand away overdramatically.

"So, you really are annoying and full of yourself," Sam said with a smile.

Casey took the hand that had just hit him and wrapped his hands around hers. "Well, another plus is that Will and Nikki will be there, so you can meet them."

"Great. Dig up old trauma with strangers and meet the approval squad. Sounds like a great time." Sam rolled her eyes.

"I knew you'd be excited."

"Elated." Sam pulled her hands away from Casey's and held up a thumb sarcastically before grabbing her glass of wine. She tipped the glass straight up, ensuring the last drops rolled down the edges and onto her tongue.

"Welp," she said, putting her glass down as she stood. "It's been a day. I'm heading up to bed."

"Really?!" Casey looked at his watch. "It's barely nine."

"I didn't say I was tired."

"I feel like this is déjà vu, only reversed."

"Oh, it is." Sam smiled wickedly. "And reverse... sounds fun."

And with that, Casey sprung over the couch and, in three long strides, hit the bottom steps and bounded to the top. Sam heard the bounce of the bed as he landed. She wholeheartedly laughed as she reached the top of the stairs and saw he was already naked and ready. "Damn, you are quick."

"Trust me, Sam." He leaned over, grabbed her shirt, and pulled her on top of him. "I won't be."

Chapter 36

The silky soft fabric of Maggie's robe didn't do anything to soften her mood.

She had grown tired of watching Reeves frolic about with this new dark-haired man. She'd seen them together constantly. Ever since they left the hospital together. Maggie had followed them to a north suburb and into a townhome drive. She was careful not to stare as she continued past, even though she wanted to scream and pull out the pistol in her Hermes bag and light everyone up who stood in the driveway.

She took a sip of her coffee before sitting down in front of her laptop. She had to formulate a new plan. The hospital had been too busy to be unseen, and now Sam's house was not an option with a parked police cruiser out front.

She followed Reeves's Romeo that first morning after the hospital to find out who this mystery man was. She nearly lost him through downtown but managed to catch up at the Mississippi River.

Maggie smiled into her coffee now, remembering the moment he turned to the private country club she and Jeffrey had been members at before their divorce.

"It seems almost too perfect."

She hadn't been there since their divorce and cared never to go back, but when she read the electric sign on the corner boasting of the upcoming event, "Tee it up for the Troops," an idea from deep in her darkness came to light.

"'Tee it up for the Troops,' huh?" She mused as she opened up laptop. "Looks like I will have to do some research."

To help our veterans Heal, Transition, Grow, and Thrive. The Tee It Up For The Troops Tournament supports programs that deliver critical services to help veterans transition from the battlefront to the home front.

Maggie glared as she read the mission statement from the website that boasted of helping veterans through golfing.

"Ha," she scoffed with zero humor in her tone. She scrolled, seeing smiling men and women with golf clubs swinging with prosthetic limbs, bulky tattoos, and veteran proud hats. "My veteran never left Afghanistan because of that stupid fucking bitch." Her manicured fingers turned white around her near-empty coffee mug. Maggie slammed the laptop closed and stared out the window.

A vision of a young soldier with green eyes, firm lips with a killer smile filled the window.

Justin. The love of her life.

She last time she felt alive was when she was with Justin in Afghanistan.

She knew the moment she saw him he was the one. He smiled at her, and that was it. Their time together was mostly great. He did talk about Reeves too much and she tried not to get jealous. He assured her they were just friends, but still, Maggie hated Reeves from the moment her name crossed his lips. She should have been the only woman in Justin's life. He should have only been smiling when he said her name, not fucking Reeves's name.

Maggie shook her head, trying to control the anger building.

Reeves ruined things from the start, but Maggie was willing to wait until they got home from Afghanstan.. She and Justin would have moved far away from her; he'd forget all about her, and then it would be just her. Only her and Justin.

Traces of the early morning sun skimmed across the dark canvas of her expansive wooded backyard. Insomnia, once again, stole another night of sleep from her. She hadn't slept properly since she had seen Sam at the fundraiser two years ago.

Well, she thought, besides the night after she killed Jeffrey. That was an amazing night of sleep. She slept well after killing Juan, too.

But now sleep eluded her again. She had a medication that used to help, but not anymore. She knew sleep would only come when Sergeant Samantha Reeves was dead. Maggie stood, making her way to the coffee pot.

The day her life fell into shadows was one she'd never forget. She showed up at Justin's bunk one night. They had planned to watch a movie together, snuggled in his bed. But when she showed up, he wasn't there. None of his personal belongings were there. It's like he was just wiped away and forgotten. Nobody was around for her to get any answers.

She returned to her own unit that night and, the next morning, heard about the blast that killed him and a few others. It was a buried IED that got them. How did their lead vehicle miss a buried IED. Those were the easiest to find. All of Maggie's anger fixated on the person who was supposed to see it. At the memorial service for the fallen soldiers, Maggie discovered it was Justin's team lead that got him killed. A Sergeant Samantha Reeves was to blame. Maggie at one-point, overheard Reeves saying it was her fault her team was dead.

"Yes, yes, it was."

With her refilled mug, Maggie walked to the floor-to-ceiling window of the breakfast nook that she liked to set up in. She watched the sun reach across the outstretched swaying branches of the trees. "Just a few more days," Maggie whispered as she raised her mug to her mouth. "Then I can sleep."

Chapter 37

Samantha's phone buzzed on her nightstand just as she finished her last set of pushups on the yoga mat covering the walnut floors of her bedside. She checked her watch; it was just past six. She heard Casey rustle in his sleep as she hopped up from the floor and sat on the edge of the bed. She felt him roll closer and snuggle around her back. His hand slid around her waist. She felt her body immediately respond to his touch. Her body recalled all the ways he touched her last night and craved more, but the buzzing phone was louder than her body. Reluctantly, she picked up. "Hey, Chief, what's going on?"

Casey ran his thumb along her lower back, feeling the beads of sweat that formed from her interrupted morning routine. All week Casey had woken to the sounds of her heavy breathing and quieted grunts as she did her morning workout. He thought all alarm clocks in the world should sound like Samantha Reeves's moaning. Casey smiled, but then a wave of jealousy washed over him. He didn't want other people to know those precious sounds. They were just for him now.

He scolded himself at the obsessive thought. His hand had paused on her hip, and he dominantly squeezed, wanting to stake his claim on her. He knew it seemed stupid, but fuck. The thought of another man with Sam startled Casey, who wasn't used to experiencing intense emotions.

He knew everything she had been through this past week. And yet, this woman still rolled out of bed and worked out. She was unbelievably dedicated to it. He worked out three or four days a week at the gym, but still, Samantha Reeves could kick his ass if she wanted.

Casey's hand rounded her lower back toward her soft, flat stomach. His feather-light fingers crossed her belly button as it continued down, and he smirked as he slid further down under the fabric of the shorts.

"Yeah, that is strange. I'll see what I can come up with." Sam wrapped her free hand around Casey's thick wrist to stop further progress. But Casey's hand overpowered hers, and it found its way to her thigh, caressing it and inching down the crease of her hip and thigh. Sam turned her head to glare at Casey lying on his side. He feigned an expression of innocence, but his hand did not stop.

"I'll stop by the station later this morning and update you on anything I can find. Thanks for the info, Chief." Sam ended the call and returned her phone to the nightstand, still glowering at Casey.

"What?!"

"What do you mean what?!" Sam looked down at his hand under her shorts and then back at him.

"Oh, you mean this?" Casey pulled her hips back into his hard erection, pressing into her back as he plunged his fingers into her sex, finding her wet and ready despite the protesting glare on her face.

Sam exhaled as she squirmed against his hard cock against her back and his fingers inside her. "Maybe annoying isn't the right word to describe you," Sam moaned, despite her insides swelling around Casey, aching against him. "Distracting seems to fit better."

"Hmmm... I'll take it."

"Right now..." Sam exhaled as she began to pull herself away from his expertly playing fingers. "...you won't."

She shouldn't be so swollen and ready for him. *Geez.* She should have been plenty satisfied with him last night, but here she was, wanting nothing more than for his hands to continue to fuck her and his mouth to explore even more.

But she couldn't. She had a job.

After the chief's call, she had a new focus, one that would give her a break on this case. She begrudgingly stood up. He protested with a groan and tried to hold her in place, but loosened his grip as she slithered out of his hands.

"Nooo," he moaned.

"I know, Mr. Parks, but I have to work." Sam straightened her shorts. "And so do you."

Sam sauntered to the bathroom and looked back at the naked man on her bed. He brought his wet fingers to his mouth. Sam watched his tongue move around his fingers, tasting her. He took his fingers out, and his tongue grazed across his lips. "Delicious."

"There is no reason I should find that sexy as hell, but fuck." Sam gave him the middle finger as Casey laughed. She turned into the bathroom, sliding the door partially shut.

She looked in the mirror as she finger-combed her dark hair and willed her body to calm down. Sam forced herself to shift focus and brought the phone conversation with the chief to the front of her mind.

"Remember my strange encounter with my former client, Maggie Lindahl?" she shouted over her shoulder through the door. Casey stretched onto his back with the thin sheet barely covering his towering erection. He yawned an incoherent confirmation to her question.

"Well, apparently, the police have been curious about her, and she has been doing other strange things. Mind you, people grieve in all sorts of strange ways..." Sam continued to fuss with her hair as she thought aloud. "She hated Jeffrey, but still, it's odd."

"What is odd?" Casey asked from the bed.

"They can't find much information on her before she was twenty. Chief Crane said it was like she didn't exist. He asked me to see what I could come up with since their means weren't finding anything." Sam added, "I'm trying to figure out how she would be involved. I can't imagine her doing anything that would mess up her Lululemon clothes or manicured nails."

Sam did a quick sniff check of her armpits and decided between the mess of her hair and the smell of sex and sweat, it was enough to require a shower. She was about to pull her t-shirt over her head when she caught sight of Casey through the slit of the door, watching her with his intense needing gaze.

Sam stopped and smiled ruefully at him as she turned toward him. She slowly pulled her t-shirt off over her head. As she dropped it in the basket by the door, her smile grew to a full grin. Sam walked a few steps to the door.

She held his gaze and shook her head from side to side as she slid the door intentionally and painfully slowly closed.

She heard him moan a sad and lonely grunt. "Fine. I'll take care of myself this morning," he called from the other side of the door.

Sam covered her laugh. "I take quick showers; better hurry."

"Oh, I have plenty of visuals to help me."

Sam laughed as she stepped into the shower and let the steaming water roll down her neck and shoulders, forcing her mind and body to calm down and let go of the visual of Casey lying naked in her bed—thinking of her.

After a couple of minutes, she was able to relax, let go, and switch her mind over to Maggie Lindahl. She needed to figure out where to go with Maggie. She did her usual background check on her when she took her on as a client, but no red flags had come up. She recalled not seeing much information about her childhood, but it wasn't relevant as it pertained to her case on investigating Jeffrey. Maggie, on the surface, seemed like your typical suburban trophy wife.

Most importantly, she couldn't figure out how Maggie would have any connection to her outside of her investigating Jeffrey. Besides that night a few years ago and then only when Maggie contacted her about investigating Jeffrey, she was certain that she had never met Maggie before. Or had she? Whatever it was, Sam was determined she could find it.

Chapter 38

Casey made Sam's bed as he listened to Sam's methodical daily routine. He knew a soft pastel-blue towel would be donned around her strong yet feminine body as soon as she stepped out of the shower. Within a minute or two, the hair dryer would cast the dark locks around her head in a frenzied dance. A simple facial care routine would be followed by a simple makeup application. Then, a quick dash to the other side of the bedroom to her walk-in closet dominated by dark hues, old t-shirts, and activewear, and she was done. She never seemed to linger long on what to wear. She would be dressed and brewing coffee within minutes of stepping out of the shower.

He would make his way into the bathroom as she dressed. He liked to keep the door open and sneak peeks of her changing. Every time he was caught, he was greeted with a headshake or eye roll, which just made his grin spread and his eyes darken.

If living with his sister taught him anything, it was not to mess with a woman's morning routine. And this morning, he'd already seen the fuck you gesture, so he danced carefully, even though he thought Sam for sure loved the banter. He certainly did.

Casey was showered and ready for work as he walked down the stairs with his overnight bag in tow. Sam was hunched in front of her computer with a coffee mug in clasped hands.

Casey poured himself a cup and sipped on it while he

scanned his phone with the daily headlines and his email briefly to know what the day would bring. A few red notification bubbles indicated he had missed calls and text messages, but knowing they were all likely from his sister or Will, he didn't bother reading them. He knew Nikki was on high alert now that she knew the highlights of what was going on with him and Sam. And unfortunately, he had been keeping Will totally in the dark about everything. He had been ignoring both of them for most of the week.

He just didn't know how to explain what was going on. He lifted his eyes from his phone and met the back of Sam's messy dark hair twisted on top of her head. How was he supposed to explain this when he didn't know how to explain this to himself?

Sam was focused on her laptop, moving every so often to drink her coffee or scribble notes on the notepad next to the computer. He wasn't sure what to do. He had been downstairs for about ten minutes, and Sam hadn't stopped once to look up or even say good morning. He wasn't sure Sam even registered him there.

How could someone who less than an hour ago was so turned on and ready for him be completely oblivious to his presence now? He tried hard not to take it personally. Casey knew she liked him, but she still seemed to pull away whenever he there was an emotional shift between them. He knew something was happening between them, but as he studied her, he questioned if it was just him or if she felt it too.

He shook his head. Maybe Nikki was right; he really did fall too hard. He was getting upset because she was at her own home and working while he waited for her to acknowledge him.

Casey finished his coffee and watched Sam feverishly type at her computer with a fixed gaze.

He put the cup in the dishwasher and approached Sam from behind her chair.

He breathed in her fresh essence, the scent of her shampoo lingering above her top bun. She sat at the clean-lined white desk in black joggers and a faded maroon t-shirt with a large print on the back that read "Bunny's" across the top.

He cleared his throat, careful not to scare her. "I'll see you after work?" he asked as he leaned over and kissed her cheek.

"Mmmm," was all he got in reply.

"Sam," he said with a pointed tone.

Casey slowly spun the office chair around as he knelt to get eye level with her. He waited for her eyes to adjust and focus on him. When he saw her erratic brown eyes soften and connect with his, he smiled gently at her.

Sam returned the smile. "Hi."

She leaned forward and pecked him on the lips gently. She leaned back and asked, "Did you need something?"

"How do you do that?"

Sam frowned. "Do what?"

"You told me you were always in observation mode and always watching your back." Casey put his hand over his chest as he leaned on his heel. "I have been downstairs here for quite some time, and you haven't acknowledged me." Casey's eyes flashed concern, but he noticed a widening of her eyes as a gentle smile crossed her lips before a small giggle escaped.

"You came down the stairs at six forty-two. Your shower was shorter than usual, maybe because I wasn't in it or..." She grinned. "You had less to do in there. That's why you've had extra time down here with your coffee and busying yourself over your phone. It's now..."—Sam glanced down at her watch—"seven-o-one, so I expect you'll leave within the next five minutes." Sam pointed her finger up to emphasize her montage. "And since it is midweek, traffic will likely be heavy through downtown, so you'll arrive at work about seven"—she paused and tapped her index finger in the air on an invisible calculator—"forty-nine." She grinned confidently at him.

Casey sat perplexed entirely by her. She threw her hands

up into a shrug. "I'm always on, Casey. Whether you notice or not." Sam softened as a new thought crossed her mind. "But I will say, when you are around, I'm not on-on if that makes sense. It's like my on isn't switched on high; it's more at a medium alert level."

Casey stared at her from his one knee. "That's a medium level?"

"You don't want to see a high alert level." Sam teased.

She squeezed his knee. "What I mean is that I *feel* you in the room, if that makes sense." I feel you with *all* my senses."

When she finally looked up and met his eyes, they lingered there for a few moments before she said, "I feel safe around you. Safe enough to drop my alert level." Sam blushed. Casey noticed she tried to hide her embarrassment by shrugging it off.

"I think," Sam said carefully, "maybe I'm not use to being in a safe space, And I've still trying to figure out how to act in it. How to be in those lower alert levels."

Casey caught her upper arms and pulled her up from the chair as he rose from his knee. He lifted her chin and met her eyes full of vulnerability. "You are something else, Samantha Reeves."

How he had doubted anything moments ago was foreign and then forgotten.

Samantha Reeves was complicated, driven, beautiful, sexy, and selfless, and he realized he was in deep with her. He kissed her, and she melted against him. He wanted to wrap his hands into her hair, tug out the bun, and pull her into bed for the day, but he let her mouth go and stepped back.

Sam put her hand on his chest. "I'm sorry I didn't acknowledge you this morning. I mean, I thought I did plenty of that last night."

"No, it's me being a shit. Don't apologize for being you," Casey said as he put his hand over hers.

"It's just that I'm not used to someone else being around. I like it, though." Sam smiled. "So don't stress about it."

She dropped her hand and placed both hands on her hips. "Now, was there something you need, or can I get back to work?" she said with a wink.

"You and that damn word—need. I only like it when it's under a certain context, and that context is when you... are under me... naked." She laughed as warmth crept into her cheeks. Casey's large hands framed Sam's face as he pulled her close to his and said before kissing her, "And no, I don't need or want anything more than this."

Chapter 39

Casey threw his overnight bag into his car and pulled out of Sam's driveway for work.

What the actual fuck?

There was nothing ordinary about this woman, and he couldn't help but let her consume his entire life. When did it happen? How did it happen? Then, the image of her standing in front of the window in that body-hugging golf dress came into vision. He moved to her like a moth drawn to a flame—unaware of the danger the bright beauty held. There was no thought or plan as he approached her. He just floated toward her, and words started pouring out.

How did this woman change his life so much in such a short time? He was knee-deep in murders and bombs, yet still, he couldn't shake the compulsion to be around her—a private investigator, an army veteran with PTSD who is currently being targeted by a murderer? Out of all the women in the world, that's who he...?

"No! Don't say it. Don't let Nikki be right again." His chest constricted as his stomach twisted inside itself. He had to wait to get through all of this drama with this Lindahl case and then he could figure out his emotions and feelings for Sam.

The light turned green, and Casey turned off the highway and went up a hilly curved road before turning into the golf course. He needed to focus on his work. The past week, he'd found excuses to work from home or run errands instead of going into the office. He knew he had to face Will and give him some answers.

The tournament was this upcoming weekend. He couldn't avoid the topic anymore. He pulled into Mendakota Country Club and looked at the dashboard.

The time was 7:49.

"That fucking woman."

He saw the regular morning golfers heading out for their tee times. From the end of May to October, the course was steady. Minnesota golfers are a breed of their own. They will golf in freezing weather and wait out thunderstorms to get a round or two in. Even when the greens were blanketed in white, the club was still busy with weddings and a plethora of galas, fundraisers, and other social events.

This morning was brisk for a early fall as Casey entered the clubhouse, but it would heat up by noon. The lush gardens were full of vibrant impatiens and pansies in patriotic colors of red, white, and blue for the tournament, and the interior decorating was just underway as he walked in.

He found Will at the coffee bar, where he was filling a second mug of coffee. He turned and handed it to Casey. "Glad to see you're still alive." He said as he raised his cup in salute.

Casey eyed him carefully as he took the cup of coffee. "I've been busy."

"Busy?" Will scoffed. "Not with work because you've barely been here at the club." He shook his head. "You're doing the same thing you did with Lucinda. You disappear, man."

Casey's eyes narrowed. "I disappeared? You did, Will."

"I didn't disappear. I just hated being around your bitchy wife," he said with a wink. "And speaking of bitchy..." Will sipped his coffee. "Because I couldn't get a hold of you, I had to talk to your sister."

"You called Nikki? Ha. I bet that was interesting." Casey started walking down the hall toward their offices. "What did she say?"

"She didn't answer. So, I had to go over to your place." Will kept up with his casual pace. "She answered the door with her normal bitchy ass..." Will caught Casey's cautious look and rephrased. "But before I could even say anything, Nikki shrieked at me." Will donned a high pitch and waved his hand flamboyantly in front of himself. "You better not be here to tell me my brother is dead."

Back in his normal voice, Will continued, "I asked why the fuck would she think that." Will paused again and took another drink of coffee. "And then she enlightened me." His eyes were straight on Casey's. "She enlightened me on your shenanigans with this new girl who is about to get you killed."

A zing of guilt shot through Casey as they approached their office doors across the hall from each other. Will jabbed Casey's shoulder. "Bombs, man? Seriously, a murderer on the loose?!"

"I know," Casey said. He had been keeping his best friend in the dark about it all. And he had to hear all about it from Nikki, who undoubtedly embellished the story.

Will turned and faced Casey straight on. "How could you not tell me about this shit, man?"

"I'm sorry, Will. There's just a lot happening, and I don't know how to explain everything." Casey hung his head and thought for a minute. "I know on the surface level there seems to be a lot of red flags..."

Will interrupted, "You think?"

"Part of me knew that you would tell me to leave her alone."

"I would. And I am."

Casey shook his head. "You don't get it. Let me try to explain everything after work. Let's get some drinks, and I'll update you on everything."

Will looked at Casey carefully after a long pause. "Fine, but your sorry ass is buying." Will turned and walked into his office. He called behind his shoulder. "And no cheap ass shit either. I'm drinking the blue label tonight."

Casey smiled after his buddy and knew he would be soon forgiven. He still owed him the whole story and then some, but things would be okay. Albeit the mess of murderers and bombs needed to come to an end, but things were going to be all right.

Chapter 40

Maggie muttered in nonsensical disgust as she drove to the Mendakota clubhouse. She had to donate more money than she would have liked for the golf tournament, but it would all be worth it in the end. She thought she had forgotten her skills from when she was young, but these past few weeks, they all came back. She was forced to dig them out of her forgotten memories when Samantha Reeves dug herself out of her dark hole and back into Maggie's life, ruining everything once again.

Maggie pulled into the roundabout drive of the clubhouse in front of the main doors at midmorning.

She stepped out into the drive and patted down her cream linen skirt that rested just below her knees. She tugged her sage green cropped blouse to ensure it sat properly against her body before she reached back in and grabbed her Hermes tote from the seat. She popped the trunk of the car and saw the newly purchased golf bag there, along with a signed Arnold Palmer framed photo she'd found in Jeffrey's old stuff.

"Do you need help with anything, Mrs. Lindahl?"

Maggie turned and was face to face with a tall man with unruly dark hair, broad shoulders, and a what he believed was a charming grin.

So, this was the man she had seen with Reeves. It sent shivers through her body. She had to shake off the urge to vomit and get herself together. She still had to play nice.

She must have been judging him long enough because he stuck out this hand. "Casey Parks."

"Ahh, yes." With a bit of disdain, Maggie ignored the handshake gesture and pointed to a canvas bag in the trunk of the car. "That bag and the golf bag are for this weekend's silent auction."

Casey grabbed the tote bag from the truck and set it on the curb before grabbing the plastic-wrapped golf bag.

"Be careful with that golf bag, dear. It's expensive." She stepped back and gestured to the golf bag as Casey set it on the curb. Maggie eyed Casey as she warned, "Keep it wrapped up during the auction. No sense risking it getting stained or dirty." She dug in her purse with a perfectly manicured hand until she pulled out a crisp white envelope. "And this is a donation on behalf of my late husband, as he was a member here as I'm sure you know."

"We'll make sure these items are taken care of." Casey took the envelope. "On behalf of the Mendakota Country Club and the Tee It Up For The Troops, we appreciate this donation too, Mrs. Lindahl."

He added almost as an afterthought, "And I am sorry for your loss."

Maggie ignored the condolences. She could barely handle them anymore. People need to move on from his death. Don't they know they have more deaths to worry about? That made the edge of her mouth curve lightly, but she pressed her lips together to prevent it from spreading further. "Please do make sure you get these to someone who knows what to do with them?"

She pointed her finger at the envelope. "And that is a large sum check in there, so don't go losing it."

Casey blinked a few times at her. She watched his lips form a line under that hideous beard before he confirmed, "I'll make sure everything gets added to the auction and donor list accordingly."

"Good." Maggie stood statue-like as she watched Casey lean over to grab the tote and golf bag by its handle.

Maggie noticed Casey's eyes lingered over her sculpted legs. *Men*, she thought as she rolled her eyes. All were the same sleazy, disgusting type. All they were good for was sex, and they were barely good enough for that. They were just a waste of space, except for one, and he wasn't here anymore. Because of fucking Samantha Reeves.

Maggie cleared her throat to get his attention. "I'm not interested in your type, Mr. Parks."

"Oh no," he stumbled. "I wasn't... I didn't intend. I just noticed..."

"Hush, dear." Maggie threw up her hand to stop him. "I understand what your intentions were." Maggie feigned a flirtatious smile. She knew he wanted to fuck her. All men did. As fun as it would be to take him away from Sam, Maggie was confident she wouldn't have the stomach for it.

Instead, she imagined pulling her gun out of her bag and putting a bullet straight into his sleazy smile and watching his teeth shatter across the drive. Maybe bits of blood and brain would speckle the potted pansies nearby. That thought made her body twitch with excitement. She put her hand in her tote and closed it tightly around her gun. Maggie took a deep breath. She needed to leave before she lost her composure and killed him right now without Sam here to see it.

Maggie turned and started toward her driver's door as Casey called after her.

"My apologies, Maggie. Were you planning on attending this Saturday? We'd love to be able to acknowledge you as a donor." Maggie paused with her hand on the open-door frame.

She twisted her head around to look directly at Casey. "Of course," she said as she eyed him up and down and smiled. "I hear it will be a blast."

She dropped her grin as she slid onto the leathered seats and pulled away.

Maggie could barely keep her mind on driving. She smashed her fist on the dashboard in delight. "Yes." She had been face-to-face with the two people she hated the most in the world and handled it like a pro.

Sam, who ruined the best thing, and then this Casey guy, who clearly wanted to have his way with her.

Ha!

The fact this guy wanted her more than Sam sent a feeling of victory through her whole body. She was going to take away both and love every minute of it. She could find a way to use Casey in some way before she killed Sam, maybe force her to watch him die. Then Sam could feel the tiniest bit of what she felt so long ago.

Her body vibrated again at the thought of killing Casey. Maggie let a yearning sigh release from her lips. "Damn, this feeling is better than sex." She remembered the orgasmic rush as she shot Jeffrey in the head. The incredible wave of energy that pulsed through her as the click of the gun sent the bullet through his skull was unmatched. It rippled an intensely satisfying rush that she had never experienced before. Jeffrey's dick never provided that level of emotional release. Maggie unclutched her fist from the wheel and let her hand run under her linen skirt. She found her center swollen and wet with excitement under her lace thong. She smiled in delight as she teased herself. She imagined Sam screaming in deep pain as she watched Casey being ripped away from her grasp. She wanted Sam to look her in the eyes as she put a bullet into Casey's head. "Yes! Yes!" Maggie climaxed behind the wheel as she imagined the look on Reeves's face right before she set off the one last explosion.

Chapter 41

Sam's limbs snapped and creaked like old abandoned stairs as she unfurled her body from her office chair. She looked down at her watch and realized it was after four. Besides a bathroom break and coffee refill, she hadn't moved all day.

Her mind, for better or worse, could pull her out of her body to focus on the task at hand. Hours would go by in wisps of articles, emails, and text messages. She used to laugh at those who spent hours addicted and unwavering in their need to play that candy match game or to thumb and swipe through videos and profiles. But as she stretched and leaned over her outstretched right leg, she realized she does the same. Addicted and unwavering in her need to finish tasks.

"Needs," she mused out loud, shaking her head. *When you are under me, naked.*

Those words warmed her cheeks again, just as they did when he said them to her this morning. Casey was right about her needs, though. Her list of needs was extremely long, and most of these so-called needs weren't healthy or actual needs. She needed to finish everything. Never leaving a job undone topped her list.

That was the part of her that knew why she couldn't let go of Afghanistan. She needed to finish their mission, but she couldn't. Her men. Her team. Her friends. They couldn't finish.

Dark fog threatened the corners of her vision, and bits of her team flashed through the thick cloud, but a strange sound seemed to pop into her mind, dissipating the darkness. The pop sound turned into a loud rhythmic noise.

It took a moment of refocusing to understand that the pounding was actually someone knocking at the front door.

She peeped through the door before opening it to see Chief Crane standing in his uniform, stretched tightly across his midsection. She stepped clear of the door and said, "Chief, come on in." She closed and locked the door as she followed him into the kitchen. She pulled two bottles of water from the fridge and sat them on the countertop as he bellied up to the kitchen island, resting his forearms against the marble top. "I hope you got further than we did today."

"I'm not sure about that," Samantha said as she took a swig from her water. "The only thing I've been able to confirm is that you were right. She just appeared out of nowhere. It doesn't make sense."

Chief fiddled with the soft flex of the plastic bottle. "People start over and get new lives. But we can usually find a thread to sew this case together. Lindahl's death—you're blamed through a picture. Your car is blown up—with you intended to be in it. Juan's death—in the same hotel room you stayed at."

"And the unit patch," Sam added quietly.

He looked up at Sam. "What patch, Sam?"

"Shit. I know. I tried to forget about it."

"Sam," Chief warned.

"Okay." Sam took a big gulp of water and jumped off the counter. "First off, I'm sorry I didn't tell you sooner." Sam hung her head. "I felt I needed to keep the patch safe. I know it sounds dumb, but I didn't want to just hand it over to your guys."

The chief responded by clasping his hands together in front of him and waiting for her to continue.

"Okay, fine." She took another drink of water before crushing the flimsy plastic and dropping it in the recycle bin. She popped herself up on the counter and began.

She explained the whole story about the patch being delivered to her motel room with her name on it and how it was from the unit she served with overseas when her teammates were killed. Chief Crane listened as Sam talked about it, never once interrupted her. After her wrap up for the Chief, she said with finality. "And that's where I'm at."

"Sam." Chief stood and walked around the kitchen island to stand next to her. "You realize what the thread is?"

Sam shook her head. "What do you mean? I've spent all day trying to learn more about the Lindahls, and I can't see a thread at all."

He gently put his hands on her shoulders. "The thread is you. You found nothing today because you were investigating the wrong people." Chief saw the realization set in as Sam's eyes widened. "You need to investigate your past to find the connection."

"Chief, I have no past. I have a mother—who knows where the hell she is. And a few years in the army. That's it."

"Well, sounds like those are the two places to start."

He walked over to the trash bin and threw the plastic bottle into the recycle bin before he turned and continued. "Look. I know it's not pretty. But something or someone in your army past has crept into the present. Hell, it seems like an army thing, but maybe check in with your mother if she is still around. Who knows what she has been up to or what she is involved in now? She could have gotten caught up with the wrong people, and they are going after you for her wrongdoings."

Sam listened as he spoke and made his way to the door. She followed behind, and they both stood at the front entry of her townhome.

"I know it's going to be very difficult to go back and revisit things you would much rather leave buried." He hooked his thumbs into his worn belt. He kicked his foot around the floor at some imaginary dirt and exhaled deep before finally looking up at Sam.

"Difficult is better than dead."

"I know," Sam softly said as she watched the chief struggle with worry over her. He went to grab the door handle, but Sam moved to sweep him into a hug. "I appreciate your concern. I'll do it, Chief." She pulled back and looked at him. "I'll be fine."

He smiled at her and took a step out the door. Sam grabbed the door to shut it behind him when he turned and said, "You know, this is one of the first times you've said you'll be fine, and I actually believe it."

Sam's brows furrowed together. "What does that mean?"

He laughed lightly. "He's good for you, Reeves. Keep him around."

And he strolled back to his car, leaving Sam without a word to say.

Chapter 42

"I'll meet you there," Casey called across the parking lot to Will as he slid into his car and dialed Sam's number. "Hey, how was your day?" he said when she picked up.

"Ugh."

"That great, huh?" he said, smiling into the phone. "Want to tell me about it?"

"Yes and no."

"Okay. Should I be concerned? Do you need me to change my plans with Will?"

"No," Sam said quickly. "Absolutely not. You've been a shit friend; you better spend time with him."

Casey laughed. "Okay, well, give me a quick overview of what happened," he said as he put his car in drive and connected his phone to his Audi hands-free audio system.

"Chief stopped by and told me I'm the thread through all of these cases and that I need to stop digging into Maggie and Jeffrey's past and focus on my own," she said in almost a single breath.

"Sooooo..." she said, holding the "o" far too long. "This is why I'm on my way to meet my mother."

"You're what?" Casey blurted out. "I thought you didn't know where your mother was."

"I didn't. But Chief tracked her last known address to a small apartment in Hastings."

A wave of protectiveness washed over him. He knew Sam

could take care of herself, but he couldn't help but want to cover her with a shield and block the shots he knew she was about to take.

"Are you sure you are going to be okay? I can come with you."

"Absolutely not." Casey could hear the stubbornness dig in deep with every word. "She'll have too many questions, and I'm not going to answer any of them."

Sam heard the exhalation of defeat from Casey. His concern for her was evident, but Sam didn't know what to do with that. "Look, she knows I'm a private investigator, so I'm just going to talk to her like any other person I would interview, okay?"

"Sam," he pleaded.

"I'll call you when I'm on my way back."

After a few beats, Casey relented. "Fine, call me as soon as you are done, and I'll meet you at your place, okay?"

"It's going to be fine, Casey. I'll talk to you soon." Sam ended the call and exhaled the breath she hadn't realized she was holding. As vulnerable as she has been with Casey, she had to be careful. So far, she had created this safe space with Casey in it. And it happened with alarming ease. But to involve him in a life outside of her safe space, she wasn't sure.

She feared losing her independence. All she had ever known was doing things alone. If she were to give that up, what would become of her?

Sam spotted the red-tinted arches of the four-lane bridge that crossed the Mississippi River and opened up to the heart of downtown Hastings. Just below the bridge, along the river's edge, were several breweries, shops, and restaurants. The city hung flowerpots from the light posts filled with fragrant cascading pansies in the summertime, and the sidewalks were full of patio seats, drinks, and lively conversations. The antique shops roll out their rusty and dented antique wagons alongside their vintage garden statues in front of the shops to prop open their doors. They rely on the summer breeze to skim the river and carry the cooled air into their old historical buildings. If one were to exit to the right off the bridge, they would drive along a lush green open park overlooking the lock and dam on the Mississippi.

Most summer weekends, the lawns were filled with some fair or festival with the white pop-up tents lining the Riverwalk. Last year, an investigation brought her down during their Annual Rivertown days. Carnival rides and live music were at every corner of the downtown area.

It was quite a helpful cover-up, keeping her blended in the crowd so she could keep her eye on her subject. And the amount of alcohol he consumed there was a big help in providing enough evidence of his adultery and lies.

Sam didn't turn either way off the bridge, though. She kept straight on Highway 61, following the guided GPS directions to the address Chief Crane gave her. After a few turns and a drive through a residential neighborhood, Sam pulled up to a one-and-half-story brick apartment building. Sam parked next to an older white Taurus with rust-eaten wheel wells, which conveniently matched the wrought iron spindles on the decks of the main floor apartments.

She looked up for her spot and noted the terrace in front her her. It had a dented brown folding chair next to a weather-worn side table with an ashtray as its centerpiece surrounded by scattered cigarette butts and ashes. Looking down at her phone, she saw the apartment number for her mother was 2C. Sam quickly calculated and deduced that the terrace was likely where her mother lived.

"It's just an interview," Sam reminded herself as she grabbed the bag on the passenger seat with her notebook and recorder. Sam closed the driver's door and caught her reflection in the window. "Just do your job. And then get out."

She cracked her neck side to side and approached the entrance. A rolled-up newspaper was jammed in the door frame, holding the door open. Her Spidey senses went off, silently scolding the idiot who left it there. Anyone would have access to this entire place. Seeing the patio doors were secured by a wooden rod across the bottom of the doors; she was certain the front door locks weren't any better.

She pulled open the oversized glass door and kicked the paper out. "Sorry if I just locked your ass out." She said to no one in particular.

The door loudly slammed shut behind her. Sam's heart jumped as she spun around. "Dammit." She scolded herself for allowing the loud noise to get to her. She collected herself, climbed the worn, carpeted half-stairs, and found herself in front of her mother's door.

She heard the muffled sounds of the television as she raised her hand to knock. Then, the familiar scent of stale cigarettes and outdated perfume sent her back to a vision of her coming home from school on a Friday with her torn backpack dangling from her hand when she was eight. She had planned to make some macaroni and cheese and dive into her new books all weekend. It was library day at school, and the latest *Baby-Sitters Club* she had on hold was finally hers to read. Instead, she found her mother was home, muttering through her menthol lights in the kitchen with the cupboard open, newspapers wrinkled up, and cardboard boxes scattered across the cabinets. "Mom!" Sam cried. "We just got here!"

Without turning around, Colleen gruffly replied, "Then you don't have any reason to be upset, now do you?!"

"Where are we going?" Sam brought her backpack to her chest, hugging it close. "Do I have to change schools again?"

"It's not always about you, you know!" Colleen turned and pulled the cigarette from her mouth, pointing it at Sam as she leaned on the counter. "You'll get your precious books no matter where you go," she mocked with a roll of her eyes.

"Mom! It's not fair!"

"Go pack your room, Samantha!" Colleen dismissed her with a wave of her hand. "We'll end up wherever we end up."

That wherever ended up at "Cousin Tim's" house for almost a year. Tim was no relation. She was sure of that. He smelled of patchouli and body odor, and every shirt he owned had a hole torn along the hem. He was kind enough, but she heard her mother and Tim argue enough to know they wouldn't stay long. Sam wasn't happy sharing a room with her mother, but resolved she would make the best of it since staying at Tim's meant she didn't have to change schools.

Before Sam chickened out, she knocked on the door. "You have a mission," she encouraged herself. She heard some muttering, and the television went silent. Slippered feet scuffled across the presumed linoleum floor, and she heard the sliding sound of the chain lock being undone.

The door opened to an underweight graying woman with oversized sunken eyes nestled in leathered skin and narrowed lips that half snarled as recognition of her daughter set in.

"Huh," Colleen Reeves said as she stepped back and waved her only daughter in. "Wasn't expecting to see you again."

"Same."

Sam stepped into the small, sparsely furnished apartment with smoke-stained walls. The kitchen opened to a long, narrow, combined living and dining space. A round, heavy wood table sat covered with an overflowing stack of unopened mail surrounded by unmatched chairs. A bulk package of paper plates sat as the centerpiece. A brown sunken love seat backed against the wall next to a worn pastel blue recliner, with a side table that had an ashtray and a half-drunk Diet Coke nestled on top.

Nothing was familiar in the space, no family heirlooms or

childhood mementos. With every move, Colleen left more and more behind, never caring enough to bring along anything. Everything was used, borrowed, or found during those garage bulk pick-up days. The only consistent thing from her past was her mother.

Sam took a deep, cleansing breath. She couldn't imagine her mother could help her find the missing connection to her past when she never carried the past with her.

Chapter 43

Maggie kept her eyes glued on Sam as she pulled the old truck to the opposite side of the road and put the truck in park, killing the engine. She watched Sam walk into the apartment building and disappear behind the glass door. "What are you doing here?" she asked out loud. After a few minutes, Maggie pulled her hoodie over her head, carefully crawled out of the truck, and darted across the street to the front of the building.

She quickly read the names on the buzzer call list. About a third of the way down, she saw a handwritten name: C. Reeves. "C. Reeves? How intriguing?" She quickly popped back across the road and into her truck. Obviously, it was someone related to Sam. And with that thought, Maggie grew excited. She just found another way to send a final message to Sam to let her know her time was coming soon.

Chapter 44

Colleen shuffled to the recliner and folded down into the chair as she reached for her cigarettes, lighting a new one. Sam followed her into the space and sat on the faded sofa. Sam reached out and pulled out her notebook and some papers. "Mom, I'm here to ask you some questions about a case I'm working on."

"Of course, you come here because you want something from me." Colleen took a long drag. "Can't even pretend to have any appreciation for your mother," she scoffed. "Just want this. Need that. Me. Me. Me."

"I see your charm and maternal instincts are still intact after all these years," Sam said, unable to keep the sarcasm from tumbling out. She pressed her lips in a tight line. She was being baited into an argument and wouldn't get anywhere doing that. Sam opened her notebook, pulled out a picture of Maggie and Jeffrey, and handed it to her mother. "Do you recognize either of these people?"

With a disgruntled huff, Colleen took the photo and eyed the picture, holding it with an outstretched hand to see it clearly. "Nope. Never seen them before." She handed the photo back to Sam. "What do those people have to do with me?"

"I don't think they do, but that's what I'm trying to figure out." Sam studied the photo in her hand. It was a photo Casey had gotten from the clubhouse. Maggie's red hair was longer than when she saw her last. It hung in loose curls over her shoulders, and a black silk evening dress seemed to hug every curve on her body. She held a champagne flute while Jeffrey, next to her, held a whiskey tumbler in his hand. He wore a black suit with a black silk tie that seemed to be the exact fabric of Maggie's dress. They stood close but not touching. They had been posing with another couple, but they had been cropped out. With just these two isolated in the photo, Sam noticed that neither of their smiles reached their eyes.

"Are you sure that you don't know them? Could one of them have been a neighbor, friend, or babysitter in the past?"

"I told you I don't know them, Sam. Did you not hear me the first time?"

Sam shook the rudeness off. "I did, yes."

"I don't know what kind of glamorous life you're living, but I don't run around with people like that," Colleen said with disgust, emphasizing the last phrase.

Sam thought back to a rare evening when she was invited over to play with a friend and have dinner with them. Sam said it was fine and her mother wouldn't mind. But this friend's mother insisted she speak to Colleen first. When she finally got Colleen on the phone, Sam could hear her mother through the phone, berating this parent for thinking she wasn't capable of feeding her own kid. She ended up being sent home right away, and that girl never spoke another word to Sam. Anyone who had any means more than Colleen was viewed as an evil threat that was trying to tell her how to live and Colleen had zero patience for that.

"You done, or you have more questions to bother me with?" Colleen asked, pulling Sam out of her past.

It took every bit of energy for Sam not to roll her eyes at her mother. "Just one more," she said, looking down at her notepad. "Has anyone in the past few months asked you about me or my time in the service?"

Colleen scoffed a laugh before she took another drag from her cigarette. "You really think the world revolves around you, don't you?"

"Can you just answer the question?" Sam said in a clipped tone.

Colleen took another drag before she ground out the cigarette in the ashtray.

"Ain't nobody asked about you because nobody cares about you."

"Well then," Sam said as she stood. "I can see what a mistake this was."

Colleen looked directly at Sam with her brow furrowed. "Same," she said without tearing her eyes away from Sam.

Sam stared back, waiting for her mother to show any signs of remorse for her words or any kindness, but nothing flashed across Colleen's worn face. Sam broke the staring contest first as she bent down to grab her things off the couch. Colleen grabbed the remote and clicked on the television. "If that is all you need, you can see yourself out."

Sam watched as her mother locked onto the television and ignored her daughter's pain. It was a familiar feeling and one she experienced throughout her childhood. She knew her mother would not have changed, but the little girl inside still wanted to be seen by her mother.

Sam pulled one of her cards out and dropped it on the kitchen counter. "In case anything comes to mind later, here's my number, Mom, in case you don't have it anymore."

Sam went to the door and looked back as she opened it to see if her mother would at least look up before she walked out. Colleen Reeves just puffed a fresh cigarette and kept her eyes on the television.

A heavy wave of numbness filled Sam as she crossed the arched bridge with the lights illuminating the rusty reds against the dark, moonless sky. After less than ten minutes with her mom, she felt pulled into that deep, isolating fog. Just as she made a step ahead in her mental health, she got pulled back. It seemed to be a never-ending cycle. One thing for sure though, was Sam was done with the cycle with her mother. If she never saw her mother again, it would be for the best.

The drive home was a quiet blur. She got nothing from her mom for the case. She wasted the entire evening. The only thing she was walking away with was utter exhaustion. Sam dropped everything by the front door as soon as she got home, went straight up the stairs, and collapsed on her bed.

Chapter 45

Casey found Will at the end of the long marble bar with a few empty barstools around. Casey walked behind him and claimed the seat around the corner closest to Will. Two whiskey tumblers clanked down just as he settled in. Will held his drink up to Casey. "To blue label." Casey returned the toast with a head nod and let the smooth, smoky whiskey soak into every tastebud before he put his glass down. "Delicioso."

"Si de hecho," agreed Will. He took another drink from his tumbler, then slid it out in front of him, half across the bartop. "Now." He leaned over, crossing his arms up on the bar top, and looked expectantly at Casey. "Start talking."

The bartender cleared the remnants of chicken wings and steak tacos as Casey wrapped up telling Will everything that had happened since he met Sam.

"I know it sounds crazy, but I can't stand the thought of someone trying to hurt her." Casey shrugged in defeat. "The moral of the story, Will, I think this girl is the one."

Will shook his head, "I swear to God, if you pull a ring out of your pocket…"

"No. No! It's not like that. I mean, maybe eventually, but not now. We need to get through this whole 'someone trying to murder her' thing first."

They both took a drink from their tumblers and sat in silence as the premium whiskey played with the flavors of the food in their mouths.

Casey broke the silence. "I just can't imagine a day without her."

Will hummed an indescribable sound in the back of his throat. Casey studied his friend as he took a long and slow drink. "Yeah," he finally said. "Seems quite obvious to me the way you talk about her." Will covered his mouth and pretended to gag. "It's disgusting."

Casey half laughed at his best friend. He knew his friend well enough to know there was pain behind his disgust for romance. He had a feeling it involved his sister, but he figured that was why Will never talked to him about it—he didn't want him to have to pick between his sister and his best friend. Not that he ever would.

"Romance and wanting to be with someone every day isn't all bad, Will," Casey said.

Will just grunted a reply before downing the last of his drink.

Casey pulled out his phone to check to see if Sam had texted him yet—no new notifications.

The bartender brought the check over. "He's got it." Will nodded in Casey's direction as the bartender slid the black leathered folder in front of Casey.

Casey signed the receipt with finality. "My penance has been paid." Casey pushed himself back from the bar and stood. "I know I should have told you sooner about Sam and everything going on. I just knew you would have told me to walk away. Cut ties before it was too late."

Will grasped Casey's shoulder. "I probably would have." He briefly searched his buddy's face before adding, "But I can tell she is different."

"She is."

"I just need to know if I need to worry about you getting yourself killed," Will said. And in a more hushed tone, he added, "I just lost my mom, Casey. I can't lose my best friend, too."

"I'm sorry. Fuck. I truly am sorry, Will. I wasn't thinking about that." He brought Will in for a hug. "Nothing bad is going to happen, okay?" Casey turned and began walking out; he pulled out his phone and saw he still had no missed messages or calls from Sam. He cursed under his breath as he shoved the phone back into his pocket. His stomach clenched as he hoped he didn't just lie to his best friend.

Chapter 46

Small arms fire was flying overhead as Sam ducked out of the truck and ran for a secure area to lay down suppressive fire.

Sweat ran along the rim of her protective eyewear and streamed into her eyes, blurring her vision. She heard the familiar pops of gunfire better than she could see them. She blinked as rapidly as she could to clear her vision for just a few seconds to see where the muzzle blasts were coming from. Pop! Pop Pop! Her vision blurred again as the salty sweat continued to flow into her eyes. Another muzzle flash slightly to her eleven o'clock. Pop! Pop Pop! Sam wasn't squeezing the trigger anymore, but she continued to hear the rifle firing. She listened carefully and realized it wasn't the sound of a rifle. Sweat drenched her, and the pounding continued to get louder. Sam looked around her, and something wasn't right; this wasn't how it happened. Where was everyone? Her team wasn't there. Fuck! Fuck! Fuck! What was happening, she wondered as the blasting continued. Pop! Pop Pop!

Sam woke and realized the pounding was real, just not in her dream. She raced down the stairs towards the rapping that was coming from the front door. She stepped over her bag that she had dropped, looked through the side window, and saw it was Casey, one hand pounding against the door and the other with his phone in hand.

"I'm here!" Sam yelled through the door. "Hold on."

As soon as Sam opened the door, Casey flew in and wrapped her tight into a hug. He kicked his foot back to close the door and, in one motion, locked the door while keeping his embrace tight against Sam. Casey had a million things running through his head that he wanted to say. How worried he was. How pissed he was at her for not answering. What was she doing? Why didn't she respond to him? The only thing that came out when he pulled back to look at her was, "Why are you so sweaty?"

Sam half-heartedly laughed and shrugged. "Bad dream."

"Seeing your mom went that well, huh?"

Sam just shook her head and cast her eyes down and away. She didn't know how to explain her mother to him and what a waste of time it was. Casey was already deep into the mess of her life. She didn't want to bring him further down with her relationship issues with her mother. She sighed and attempted to smile up at Casey. "I didn't walk away with anything helpful; let's just say that."

Casey grabbed Sam's hand and led her upstairs into her bathroom. He turned on the shower and let the steam build around the tiles as he carefully peeled off the sweaty, damp clothes that clung to her body. She had no energy to protest. Casey studied Sam's blank expression and kissed her gently on the fading scar on her cheek. It seemed he saw her lying in the hospital bed with that same cheek bandaged forever ago. But it was just a barely two weeks ago, and his life hadn't been the same.

He removed his clothes in a few swift movements and pulled Sam under the spray in the shower with him. Casey lathered up the soap as the water softened Sam's body. He began washing her shoulders, and their eyes found each other.

"Casey, I..." Sam couldn't finish her sentence. She didn't know what she was trying to say. Being cared for by someone was a new experience. Seeing her mother today reminded her of how little she had growing up. Now, standing here, under the shower, was a man who seemed to understand her. He saw her and yet, he still was here. He didn't just quit and leave when she knew he probably should. Casey saw through her walls even though she had grown blind to them.

Sam closed her eyes, rested her forehead on Casey's broad chest, and breathed in his scent mixed with her almond butter body wash.

Before she knew it, she was wrapped up in a clean towel. She met his eyes in the mirror. The words *I love you* were on the tip of her tongue. Casey leaned over her shoulder, kissed her cheek, and locked eyes in the mirror again. "I know." He lightly squeezed her biceps, kissed the top of her collarbone, and left her alone in the bathroom.

She stood perplexed as he walked away. *Did I say it out loud?* she asked herself. She leaned closer to her reflection. *I didn't, did I?* She brought her hand to her flushed cheek and shook her head with finality. *No. No way I did.* Sam felt better about the situation for a split second before realizing that if she didn't say it, what did he mean by *I know*, or could he really read her that well? She was the observant one. Her job is to read people. She was the one who was supposed to know people better than they did. Sam stood tall in the mirror and decided to accept her new reality; she had finally met her match in Casey Parks.

Chapter 47

The beat-up black truck was too old for a Bluetooth connection, so Maggie sat in the truck with one air pod in her ear, streaming alt-rock music from her phone while she waited. An overweight woman with her hair wrapped high in a towel and a big robe stepped out in front of the apartment complex. She held the door with one hand as she kicked a piece of trash into the door frame to prop it open. She pulled out a phone and cigarette, chirped into the phone, and puffed animatedly on a slim cigarette.

A gleeful smile reached Maggie's eyes as she checked herself in the mirror to ensure the blonde wig and black beanie covered her red hair. "What luck," she said as she grabbed the two paper grocery bags on the truck's passenger side and crawled out of the truck. Maggie acted quite casually as she walked up to the door and saw the shameless woman was paying no attention. Maggie rebalanced the bags, opened the door, and walked right in. The door slammed against the careless door prop as Maggie passed through. She was in. It was hard to contain the exhilaration with every step toward Colleen Reeves's apartment door.

Colleen turned off the television as she stood, deciding to crawl into bed. There was an early bingo game at the hall tomorrow, and she hadn't won in a couple of weeks, so she knew her time was due tomorrow. She tossed the Diet Coke can in the over-filled trash can and cursed as it rolled off the top onto the ground. She'd deal with that in the morning. She made her way around her small apartment as she shut off the lights for the night.

She saw Sam's card sitting on the counter. She picked it up and looked at the plain, simple card. Like always, Sam was focused on herself and never considerate of her own mother. The sacrifices she had to make. Now, she showed up after years away, and there it was again, always about her. "Ungrateful child. Thank God I only had one," Colleen muttered as she tossed the card into the bin, and it stayed. She reached to shut off the kitchen light.

Knock. Knock. Knock.

"What the hell?" she said as she paused before she flipped off the light. Colleen shuffled to the door and peeped through. She saw a figure of a person with two grocery-style bags blocking most of their face. Colleen kept the chain on the door as she opened it.

"Yeah?" she asked warily.

The figure shuffled the bags. "Do you mind? These are kind of heavy."

"I didn't order anything."

"I have a Shipt grocery order here for Colleen Reeves," the stranger read from a stapled white receipt on the bag.

"I didn't order anything. Didn't you hear me?" Colleen stepped back to shut the door when the stranger asked,

"Can you just let me put these down, and we can figure it out then? It says Colleen Reeves, Apartment C2, right here."

"Ah, for Chrissakes, fine." Colleen shut the door and unlocked the chain. She opened the door, let the stranger in, and gestured to the counter for the groceries. "Two unannounced visitors in one day." Colleen shook her head in disgust as she shut the door. As she turned back around, the stranger's back was to her as she shuffled around in the paper bags.

"Now, what on earth is going on with this late-night grocery delivery that I didn't order?"

Maggie heard Colleen shuffle toward her. Her hand found the grip of the 9mm pistol just in time. She turned around with the gun aimed square into Colleen's forehead. Colleen froze at the site of the gun.

"That's a good girl, Colleen." Maggie stepped closer and pushed the barrel of the gun on her forehead. "If you would have screamed, I would have had to put the bullet in your head right away, and that wouldn't have been any fun."

"I don't have any money; what do you want?" Colleen whispered in a cracked voice.

"Oh, I don't want money, dear. I have plenty of that." She used the gun to tap the side of Colleen's head. "Go have a seat, why don't you?"

Colleen carefully walked over to her usual chair with the stranger close behind and the gun fixated on her head.

"You're doing great, Colleen." Maggie grabbed the back of one of the mismatched dining chairs and set it backward between Colleen and the TV. She sat on the chair, using the back of it to rest her arms, with her hand still gripping the gun. "Let's have a little chat about that bitch of a daughter of yours, shall we?"

"Figures something like this would involve her." Colleen looked up at the stranger. "Huh. I think I saw a picture of you today. Your hair was red, though."

"Oh my, Sam asked if you knew me?" Maggie shrugged with the gun. "Well, did you?"

"I ain't seen you before now."

"And don't worry. You won't ever see me again in a bit. I

don't like your daughter," Maggie said flatly.

"Ha. Get in line," Colleen said.

"Don't you love your daughter, Colleen?" Maggie asked, sounding concerned, but was anything but.

"Love?! I don't even like my daughter. Never wanted kids. Shits don't think of anything but themselves." Colleen shook her head in disgust.

"Oh well, that's disappointing to hear," Maggie said. "At least we both have that in common. We both wish she were never born."

"I tried to abort her by starving myself and other ways, but nothing worked." Colleen stared at the blackened television screen. "Biggest mistake I ever made was keeping that kid."

"Yeah. It was," Maggie sighed. "And unfortunately, it's a mistake that cost me the love of my life." She walked around the chair, stood directly before Colleen, and raised the gun. "And now it's going to cost you yours."

Maggie squeezed the trigger before Colleen could respond. The silencer attached to the gun allowed the bullet to whistle through the air as Colleen's body slumped against the chair. Blood began to ooze above Colleen's right eye, coating her cheek and soaking into her sweater. "Sorry, I meant to chat longer, but I can't stand talking about that cunt anymore." Maggie put the chair back, pulled a pair of gloves from one of the bags and a damp towel, and wiped down the chair. She grabbed the paper bags and turned to look at Colleen before opening the door. "Don't worry; I'll make sure your daughter knows what your last words were." She smiled and listened into the hallway before stepping out. As she neared the front door, she saw the pieces of trash still holding the door open, but the woman who had placed it there earlier was no longer there. "Could this have been any easier?"

She got into the old truck and tossed the bags in the passenger seat. Killing Sam's mother was a bonus. She had been so busy with the grand plan but then just happened to stumble upon this treasure. Maggie cackled behind the wheel at the whole situation. Sam was killing everyone in her life and she didn't even know it.

Chapter 48

Sam's internal alarm woke her up at the usual time Friday morning. The sky was still dark, with just a hint of purple haze hovering on the horizon. She started to roll out of bed to start her workout but felt a strong arm wrap around her with a grumbled moan and pulled her back in. She attemped to roll out once again, but he flexed once more, pulling her back to him. She chortled at the absurdity of this tug-of-war. She was about to attempt once more, but he snuggled up behind her, molding into her body. Giving in, she let her body melt into him.

"You can skip a morning workout, you know," Casey muffled into her hair.

"What if the world ends?" she asked.

"It will not."

"It could."

"It won't. You've had a couple crazy, intense weeks, Sam. You're allowed to skip a workout."

Sam spun around and faced Casey, nose to nose. She wasn't about to admit to him that she already had skipped one. Instead, she squeezed her hand between them and placed her palm on his chest. The hair on his chest was as dark as it was so soft, and she loved letting her fingers trace against it. She looked up and saw his eyes were closed as he was trying hard to continue to sleep. She moved her hand further up and ran her fingers through his scruffy beard. She traced his chin line until her fingertips found his lips, and she traced them, watching the corner of his lips perk to one side. She wanted to kiss that smirk off his lips, but she whispered to him, "Not all of the intensity these past couple of weeks has been bad."

Casey replied by kissing her fingers. He opened his eyes and found hers. "Good or bad, it's still been a lot."

"What day is it even?" Sam asked.

Casey looked at his watch to confirm. "It's Friday." Casey rolled over on his back and stretched his arms over his head. "Which means," he yawned, "I have to get my ass to work early with our tournament tomorrow. So, I'm going to beat you to the bathroom to get ready if that's okay?"

"Sure." She smiled at his thoughtfulness, then added, "As long as the world continues to spin, I'll allow it."

Casey rolled back over to Sam and kissed her with a quick peck. "It will."

He stood, stretched, and Sam admired his bare bottom. She couldn't believe that ass was real, and she got to touch it. Casey cocked his head around and caught Sam.

"Are you ogling my ass right now, Ms. Reeves?"

"Yes, I am, Mr. Parks."

He turned around with a grin, and Sam's eyes drifted immediately down to his hard cock.

"Morning wood?" she chirped.

Casey placed his hand around his cock and teased himself a few times. Sam wasn't able to stop the moan that escaped her mouth as she watched him.

He walked slowly around the bed keeping his eyes locked on hers as he kept his hand on himself. Sam's body followed his movement like a cat watching a mouse cross the floor. He stood just in front of her and growled her name, "Sam."

She licked her lips, wanting her own hands to be on him. "Yeah?" she responded.

He bent forward, hovered above the edge and whispered back, "I hope you have enough visuals." He laughed, spun on his heels, and went into the bathroom. He turned on the light, stood in the door, and threw up his middle finger as he closed the door shut on her.

"You asshole!" she shouted as she tossed the pillow at the closing door.

She heard him laughing through the door as the shower turned on.

She sat up on the edge of the bed and grabbed the workout clothes she always kept bedside. She slipped on her shorts and bra. "Like I would skip a workout twice in a week."

Sam looked up from her sit-up position to see Casey towering by her toes with a smirk. His dark navy polo did nothing to hide his bulging biceps as he crossed his arms across his chest. "I should have known better."

"Yup." She fell back and pulled herself back up. "What did you expect, getting a girl all hot and bothered and leaving her to her own devices?"

Casey cocked his head to the side as he considered this. "Most women would have found a release," he said with air quotation marks, "in other ways."

"Who says I didn't?" she teased with a wink before falling back and crunching back up.

Casey shook his head as he watched her continue to knock out full crunches.

"What other things are you going to do today that you shouldn't?" he asked, as he still hovered.

"Dig further into my past. Find more unprocessed trauma. Probably have another mental breakdown." Sam rolled over and popped up to stand toe-to-toe with Casey. "But maybe find a murderer. Or at least a motive."

"How do you not know the motive already?" Casey offered

"What?" Sam plopped back down and put her hands on her hips. "What the hell do you mean by that?" she retorted.

"Jealousy," he said casually. "It's always jealousy." He

pointed in the air. "Or revenge. I've seen enough movies to know that." Casey toiled with his trimmed beard as he thought. "I'd go with revenge *and* jealousy." He smiled like he had solved the whole case.

Sam stared wide-eyed at Casey. "It's not always revenge or jealousy."

"Someone left a picture at a crime scene and literally pointed a big arrow at you and said, murderer." He grabbed her shoulders. "It's fucking revenge, Sam."

Sam walked over to the dresser, grabbed the military police patch, and held it in her hands so Casey could see what it was.

"After talking to Chief Crane and my mother yesterday, I know." She ran her hand over the patch lightly as she spoke. "I know someone wants me dead for the deaths I caused in Afghanistan, but why now? Why nearly ten years later? Revenge is obvious. The question is, why now? Any family member or angry wife or girlfriend would have already acted on it. I think if I focus on the why, maybe I'll find the motive which will lead to the killer."

Sam could feel Casey's eyes on her as she studied the police patch that meant so much yet provided no answers. She carefully put the badge back on her dresser and was quiet for a moment before she said, "Someone wants revenge. Bad."

Casey put a hand on her shoulder but said nothing.

Sam spun and looked at Casey. "I'm overlooking someone or something. Something has to have happened recently to bring this all up after so many years." Sam nodded, mostly affirming for herself. "I need to research my team and their families again."

Casey nodded in agreement. "I'll get the coffee going for you." He grabbed her and kissed her softly, then pulled away. "Go brush your teeth, nasty." She laughed as he stuck his tongue out in disgust. "Yuck. Then go get your research on." Sam shoved Casey as she walked past. She felt a lightness flood her as she grabbed her toothbrush, and Casey headed down the stairs.

Chapter 49

The light tendrilled between the shades as Maggie awoke from a deep sleep. A deep sleep she hadn't experienced in so long. As she lay there, the memories of the dingy apartment, the pretend grocery bags, and Colleen's perplexed face crept into her mind. At this point, she wasn't even sure if she killed Colleen to fuck with Sam or for herself to finally be able to sleep. Sure, she intended to get more information out of Colleen that she could use to inflict more suffering on Sam, but the greed to feel the sense of killing again took over. And with her body fully relaxed, she wasn't even mad it went so quickly. "It won't be like that with her, though," she said to herself with a satiated smile beaming across her face.

She was so close now to ruining Reeves's life that nothing else mattered.

Maggie sighed as she sat up and slipped her feet into the fluffy slippers. She grabbed the silk robe that matched her pale pink slip as she made her way to the bathroom. She had created a new life of luxury and filled it with caviar and comforts. Unfortunately, none of it helped her recover from the loss she felt in Afghanistan. For many years, she was just numb. Then, seeing Reeves opened up something inside her. Whatever it was, it steeled the darkness to her core. It spread like a shadow until she knew nothing would comfort her until Reeves was dead.

"But having control of Sam's life." Maggie's smile remained

as she made her way to the bathroom. "That feels delightful."

It was like killing a part of Sam. She was taking little bits of her life from her, and the more she took away, the fuller Maggie felt. She was almost complete.

But then what? she thought as she brushed her teeth. *Then what?* Her kids were a byproduct of a fake life. Her in-laws were already raising them; why not let them continue? Maggie rinsed her mouth, and a fresh idea popped into her head. "A new identity." Start a new life out on the East Coast. No kids, no connections to the Midwest. She could move back to New York. She knew some of Jeffrey's acquaintances would be more than happy to comfort a lonely widow. Maggie touched her face. "A facelift with some eye enhancements." She fingered her mostly-natural fiery red hair. "My hair..." Maggie loved her hair more than most things. She didn't change it when she became Maggie and hesitated at even thinking about it. "Maybe I'll just add some dark tones to it."

Maggie resolved to her new plan as she smiled at her reflection. Just a few more things to prep for today. "By the end of tomorrow, Sam will be dead, and I'll be somebody new."

Chapter 50

Sam sat in front of her computer and searched the archived newspapers for events and stories related to her service time in Afghanistan. Her hand ached at how long she had been scrolling and scanning documents.

The first article she came across that morning was a headline article about the attack and the men who died. Their DA photos were front and center on the front page. Their life filled eyes seared into hers. She stood from her chair, wanting to escape their stare. But as she stepped back, she paused. Those pictures weren't going to hurt her.

She inched back toward her desk and looked the photos straight on. She was never scared of these men when they were alive. Why should they scare her now?

She sat down and realized tears had started rolling down her cheeks as she remembered their laughs. She grabbed a tissue from the box on the desk. "I can do this."

By the time she opened the last file she had archived to review, she was spent. Her nose was raw from all the tissues. She'd cried more this morning than she had in the past ten years. "This whole feeling feelings is quite annoying," she said as she blew her nose and tossed the tissue in the trash.

The last article she had to review was a cover story about

the non-profit foundation created in memory of Brian Lewis. It provided support and resources to families who had lost a loved one who served overseas. Sam reached for a tissue on her desk to find the box empty, and she saw that her trash can was full of crumbled tissues. She sniffled as she stood. "I think that's enough memory lane for today."

She went to the hallway cabinet where she stored the extra tissues and saw one last box tucked back at the top. "Alexa, add tissues to the shopping list," Alexa confirmed the shopping list as she stretched up to pull the tissue box down. Out of the corner of her eye, she saw the edge of a dark blue box tucked in the back corner of the shelf behind some extra linens. She couldn't remember what was in the box. Curiosity got the best of her as she scooted the box off the shelf and brought it down. Sam set the box on the kitchen island before restocking the desk with the fresh box of tissues. She grabbed the small trash can by her desk and emptied it into the bigger one at the kitchen island. After returning the empty bin to her office, Sam returned to the dark blue box. She slid it closer as she popped off the cardboard lid. Inside, she saw two thin four-by-six photo albums, loose photos, folded newspaper clippings, and old army coins and ribbons.

She felt her breath catch in the back of her throat at the same time as her heart dropped into the pit of her stomach. "It's Afghanistan." Sam slammed the lid back on with both hands grasping the edges. She took a few deep breaths to regain control. *No. I can do this*, she reminded herself. *I got this.*

She lifted one corner ever so slightly and peeked inside— *But not today*—and closed the lid. "Memory lane is closed," she said and slid the box across to the other side of the island.

She looked at her watch and saw it was lunchtime. She needed to get out of the house. She wanted to solve a murder today, but it seemed the only thing on the docket was experiencing a mental breakdown. And she was tired of those.

Casey answered on the second ring, "Hi, Sam."

"I need a break from today. Want to grab lunch?"

"Hey, you remembered to eat." Casey praised.

"I'm just as surprised as you are." Sam grinned into the phone.

"Well, I would love to grab lunch with you, but I'm having lunch with my sister in a bit. She called this morning and doesn't believe I still exist. So, I said I prove to her I'm here."

"Oh."

Sam tried to hide her disappointment in her voice, but she couldn't muster what else to say.

Before Sam could think of what to say, Casey chimed in, "Why don't you join us?"

"Oh, I don't want to ruin your time with your sister. It's fine."

"Don't be ridiculous. You can't ruin anything," Casey said.

"Are you sure that's a good idea? I don't want to put your sister in danger. There is a killer after me."

"Yeah, she knows that, and now that I think about it. It's probably best that you tell the story instead of me. She'll likely listen to you more than me."

Sam sighed into the phone, unsure of what she wanted to actually do. She really wanted to get out of the house, and she felt she had been stuck in it for too long. She wasn't sure meeting Casey's sister was the best option.

Casey interrupted her thoughts. "You're coming," he said in a matter-of-fact tone. He waited a beat before adding, "That's what she said." Sam could hear the smile through the phone.

She laughed. "Technically, it would be that's what *he* said joke."

"Oh, you know it's going to be both of us coming tonight," Casey smirked. "But for now, lunch."

She rolled her eyes at Casey's words but knew he meant it, causing her cheeks to flush. "You're ridiculous," she said through her smile. Casey gave Sam the location and time before they hung up.

She wasn't solving any murder today, but maybe the bright side was she was processing some emotional trauma as she dug through her past.

Now, she seemed forced to process some emotional hurdles by meeting Casey's sister. *How is this my life right now?*

Sam began to pace back and forth from her kitchen to the back of the sofa. *My life was so easy and predictable.* She continued pacing. *But that was before this case. Before Jeffrey Lindahl.* Sam's pacing now added arm flailing. *No drama.* She spun on her heel. *No unpredictability.* She was living in her comfort zone of repetition and consistency. Her life had been nothing but chaos and mystery since this case started.

Yet. Sam slowed her pace. Somehow, Casey was there. *How does he make me feel calm and cared for in the middle of all this hell?* Sam ran her hands down her face. *Emotions are a pain in the ass. Argh!* She dropped her arms on the kitchen island, and her head rested against her folded forearms.

After gathering her thoughts, she pushed away from the kitchen counter and made her way upstairs. Meeting Casey's sister meant she needed to put a little effort into her appearance before leaving the house. Sam changed her shirt into a button-down denim shirt and freshened her face with mascara and bronzer. She inspected the tiredness in her eyes as she dabbed a bit of concealer on the fading scar on her cheek. She thought of how Casey was there in the hospital with her. How, after just a single meeting at a golf course, did he fully infiltrate her life? Her fingers traced her damaged cheek. It dawned on her just then that she was reflecting on something positive and not the trauma of the explosion that almost killed her.

"Holy hell!" Sam brought both hands to her cheeks, looking like Kevin in *Home Alone*. "What is happening to me?"

Since Casey, she was reminded that there was so much more in the world of emotional experiences than being numb to it all. Casey Parks made her feel everything but numb.

Chapter 51

Sam walked into the sunny restaurant with black wooden chairs and oak-topped tables. It was warm enough that the wall of clear garage doors was open, letting the warm breeze blend with the smoky smell of the wood fire grill. She greeted the host with a nod and quick greeting before she made her way to the black-painted wooden booths toward the back per the instructions from Casey's text. Sam spotted Casey's smiling face, and she couldn't help but smile back. It was unsettling how he could disarm her with just a look. Casey slid out of the booth as Sam walked up.

He engulfed her in a bear hug. "Hi," he said into her hair. Slightly embarrassed by his public display of affection, Sam pulled back with a quick hello in return, wanting to acknowledge his sister. "Hi Nikki, I'm Sam. Thanks for letting me barge in on your lunch with your brother."

Nikki smiled with a dismissal wave as Casey and Sam slid into the booth. "No worries. He gets kind of boring anyway."

Sam smiled at the sisterly jab at Casey and settled into the booth. She took in the woman sitting across from her. Nikki's dark navy scrubs did nothing to distort the woman's beauty. She had the same intense green eyes as Casey, but hers were softer and more feminine. A few wisps of hair had escaped her bun and framed the dark tones of her face with the grace of a portrait painting. Her plush lips were dark-stained in a natural way that Sam was immediately jealous of. Nikki

Parks, Sam thought, might be the most beautiful woman she had ever met. She looked at Casey and realized then, that she was, in fact, dating the most beautiful man she had ever met.

Nikki clasped her hands in front of her as she leaned forward on the table. "And I hear your life is anything but boring," she said with her eyes on Sam.

"Nikki," Casey warned.

"What?! I mean, besides the almost-dying part, I'm sure it's a great story. I need some excitement and distraction right now anyway."

"It's okay," Sam said with a laugh as she rested her hand on Casey's arm.

Sam caught the subtle way Nikki said she wanted some distraction. PI Sam filed that away for later, but right now, she needed to be in friend mode, not in private investigator mode.

A chipper server in a branded t-shirt and jeans approached and took their drink and food order. After the server left with the menus, Sam updated what she could with Nikki while being careful not to overshare and get another person involved and potentially hurt. Their food came, and the conversation changed over to Sam asking questions about Nikki's work at the hospital and how school was going as they ate. Although Nikki was genuine, Sam thought something else was on Nikki's mind. The slight darkness around her eyes told Sam that Nikki hadn't been sleeping.

Sam took a long sip of her water as she glanced at Casey. Casey looked at her and then back at her sister. "Oh, do I finally get to talk now?" he said, teasing.

"Again," Nikki said. "Sam here is a lot more entertaining than you."

"Sorry, Casey," Sam said as she waved her arm out in front of her. "You may have the floor." She bowed her head toward him.

Nikki laughed and pointed her finger toward Sam as she looked at Casey. "I like her."

"Me too," he said.

Sam's face beamed at the pure kindness directed at her. She tossed another yuca fry into her mouth to try to hide the flush on her face.

Casey updated Nikki on the golf tournament happening tomorrow.

She wondered if he could see all the signs on Nikki that she did. Casey could read her like a book, but from what she could tell, she didn't think Casey could do the same with his sister. After a few more minutes of watching the siblings converse, she knew her answer. "He doesn't," she said to herself as she brought the glass up and caught her straw in her mouth.

"He doesn't what?" Casey asked. Sam put her glass down and saw Casey carefully eyeing her and Nikki looking curiously at her.

So, my inside thought was an outside thought, Sam realized. *Shit.*

"What doesn't Will do," Casey asked, emphasizing Will, knowing that Sam had never met Will before.

"Oh, Will!" Sam feigned. "I thought you meant someone else." Sam shrugged as she felt her face heat once again. "Carry on." She waved her hands as she smiled. "Just ignore me."

Casey kept his eye on Sam for a few more moments before turning back to his sister. "Anyway, speaking of Will, you two have been spitting fire at each other lately. What's up with that?"

Sam saw a fraction of a flinch from Nikki as Casey brought up Will.

Her eyes darkened as her brows narrowed. Sam smiled. She was pretty sure she knew what was up then.

"He's a dick."

"Christ, Nikki..." Casey shook his head and threw his hands up in surrender. "You know what, never mind. I'm not getting between you two." Casey stood. "If you'll excuse me, I'm going to use the restroom before we leave." He took a step before turning back, "If the check comes, feel free to pick up the tab, sis."

"Ha, ha." Nikki's head shook like a toddler as she gnarled her lips into a fake smile.

Sam waited for Casey to be out of earshot before blurting out, "So, what did Will do to break your heart?"

Nikki whipped her head up and stared wide-eyed at Sam.

"Come on. I won't tell your brother," Sam coaxed with a Cheshire cat grin.

"You really are a private investigator then, huh?" Nikki asked with an arched brow.

Sam sat with her unwavering grin and shrugged. "I notice things."

Nikki looked back toward the restrooms and then at Sam before taking a deep breath. "He didn't break my heart, just pissed me off. He showed up at my house with a date waiting in the car." Nikki shrugged. "He was looking for Casey. It wasn't like he brought her on purpose, but it still sucked." Another deep breath. "We argued and blew up at each other as usual."

"I'm sorry, Nikki."

"It's fine. It's been like this for years now. He broke my heart once, and I'm never giving him the opportunity to do it again." Nikki sighed and played with the straw in a water glass." It's just that..."

"He's coming back." Sam said to cut her off.

"I'll fill you in with the whole story next time," Nikki whispered with a wink.

"You know," Nikki said as she looked at Casey as he sat down before turning to Sam. "I always wanted a sister instead of a brother." Nikki smiled. "So, thank you."

Sam felt her face flush for the third time during this lunch. An overwhelming sense of joy flooded through her at being called a sister.

Chapter 52

The day was done. Sam sat at one end of the sofa with her legs stretched out, her laptop in her lap, and her feet resting over Casey's lap. After their lunch, Sam spent the rest of the day running errands, researching, and avoiding the Afghanistan box, waiting for Casey to finish up work. She moved the box back into the closet. It was a future Sam problem now. Her day was already a spectrum of emotions. Avoiding the box was best.

She watched Casey as he read a book and absentmindedly rubbed Sam's feet. His thumb ran circles at the base of her toes, which sent relaxing waves of calmness all over, like he was massaging every inch of her body. She studied the sharp line of his jaw that managed to cut through his beard. I bet he's stunning with or without the beard, she mused. His long, dark lashes were of the kind that women would pay for. Lucky for his sister, Nikki, who was blessed with the same lashes. She smiled and stared fondly, thinking she would never tire of looking at him.

"I thought private investigators would be a bit more subtle at observation than you are," he said without peeling his eyes away from his book.

Sam snapped her laptop shut. "I'm not trying to be inconspicuous."

Casey smirked but kept his eyes on his book.

"How many times have you had to reread that sentence you're on?"

"Seven." Casey tilted his head nonchalantly. "Maybe more."

"You haven't turned a page in a *really* long time," Sam needled.

Casey kept his head in the book. "Well, my mind is betraying me. Instead of comprehending the words on the page, I just keep thinking of all the other parts of your body that I would rather be touching." Casey moved his hand from her foot and trailed it up her leg and back down with fingers gracing the outside of her black leggings.

"Mmm... I think," she said as she put her laptop on the coffee table, "you should give up reading then."

In a split second, Casey threw the book like a flying disc across the coffee table, sending it across and right off the edge on the other side. It was such a quick and sharp movement that Sam jumped, squealed, and laughed all at once. "Oh!"

Casey was on top of her, with his knee on the outside of Sam's hip, between the sofa back, and the other leg braced on the floor. He hovered just above her face, his white teeth gleaming wide with mischievous eyes. His eyes drifted down to her flushed lips. Casey brought his hand up to her face.

"I was thinking," he said, his voice husky and low, "of my hands touching your lips... like this." He slowly traced her bottom lip and watched the wetness from her breath color her lips a glossy red.

Sam could feel her chest expand as Casey moved his hand down from her lips along her neck. "I was thinking of my hands touching that sensitive spot behind your ears that makes you respond to my touch." Casey trailed his fingertips down her jaw to the sensitive nape of her neck, just under her ear. His head followed his hand, trailing his breath along the path after his touch. He felt her body quiver, and her breath increased with each touch. "Hmmm... Good girl," he whispered on her skin. "I love how your body needs me."

Casey's hand found the hem of her black t-shirt, and he pushed the shirt up; it bunched below her chin. Her black satin bra was now exposed for his hands to explore.

She gasped as the rush of air cooled her sensitive skin.

"I was thinking of my hands..." He followed her décolletage down and traced the outside bra line, his fingertips just caressing the uncovered skin "...on one of my favorite parts." He cupped her breast over her bra and squeezed his thick palm over it. He felt her breath catch sharply as she arched into his touch. He looked up and saw her head was back with her eyes closed. "Look at me, Sam." Sam opened her eyes, meeting his hungry emerald stare. "Watch me touch you," he growled.

He cupped her breast again. Sam did what she was told and watched. It was incredibly sexy how his hands roamed over her and demanded her attention. She had no choice but to pay attention to every sensation that rocked her with his every touch. An uncontrollable moan escaped her mouth as her hands went into his hair and relished in the thickness of it.

"Mmm. That's my girl." Casey's voice was deep and feral, like Sam had not heard before.

Casey's hand slid under Sam's bra and found her nipple taut and hard. He squeezed it playfully, again making Sam's breath catch and body arch. Casey's mouth continued over her skin. He slid the strap of her bra off her shoulder and pulled down the cup, exposing her breast fully, his mouth hovering just over her. He looked up to make sure Sam was still watching. His gaze locked on Sam's gaze, and he exhaled a long, drawn-out breath over her. His lips barely caressed the edge of her nipple. "You're perfect."

Before Sam could respond, Casey sat up, brought Sam up just enough to reach behind, unclasped her bra, and removed her shirt. As she collapsed back down, she watched Casey's eyes widen and focus on her breasts. His hands were on them at once, and his mouth quickly followed after. It was like he couldn't get enough of her as he devoured her entirely. Sam's chest lifted as she arched instinctively, giving Casey full access to explore her. Casey moaned as Sam's hands found his hair again, and she gripped it tight as she tried to gain control of her body. Casey's lips slid down Sam's body, and his hands trailed over her black leggings. His strong fingers ran up and down her inner thighs with enough force to create heated friction that spread throughout her body. Again, she arched at his touch. Casey's hands slowed as he circled back around her innermost thigh, and he let his thumbs tease the outer edge of her center. Casey watched Sam as she responded to each roll of this thumb over her.

"Casey. Please." Sam whimpered.

"Not yet." Casey swapped his circling thumbs with his full palm over her center and massaged her deeply through her leggings.

"Casey," Sam cried as her head rolled back. She began to move in rhythm with his hand.

"Yes. Fuck yes," he groaned as he increased the speed of his hand.

"Oh, my God!" Sam screamed as her legs quivered and squeezed against Casey. In a flash, Casey had her leggings down, and his mouth found her swollen center, wet and ready. He replaced the quick motion of his hand now with rapid movements of his tongue. The rapid change of sensations sent Sam over the edge.

She cried out his name as the blazing heat spread across her body in waves of explosions and colors. She had never known such a level of ecstasy. Just as her body started to arch down, she realized Casey's mouth was still on her, and he wasn't done. He began again, and her body hummed for a moment more before another wave vibrated through her.

"Casey!" She screamed.

Sam finally collapsed and tried to catch her breath. Stars? Did she really see stars during sex? She'd never experienced anything like that. She decided that not only would she not tire of looking at him, but she didn't think she could ever tire of orgasms like that.

After catching her breath, she opened her eyes and looked down and saw the mischievous grin on Casey as he hovered between her legs. "I could watch you come all day," he rumbled.

Sam laughed. "I don't think I could handle coming all day." Sam sat up, pulled Casey toward her, and kissed him. Her sex, mixed with the taste of his mouth, ignited her insides. She wasn't even sure how that was possible since she just came twice. She looked at Casey, and she should have said, "I should go to bed now." But instead, what came out was, "I could handle another one or two right now."

"What my lady wants, my lady shall receive."

"I don't want," Sam said. "I need," she whispered alongside his ear. "Inside me." She bit his earlobe. "Now."

"Fuck me," he groaned as Sam's hands dropped to Casey's belt, and she worked at getting the clasp undone. His hands met hers there, and within moments, the belt was undone. Sam's fingers unbuttoned the strained jeans. Casey stood off the sofa as Sam sat up, swinging her legs over the side of the couch and placing her legs between Casey's as he stood facing her. His hands found her hair as Sam's hand rubbed against his jeans as she followed the length of his steel-hard erection. Casey rolled his head back as Sam teased him. She leaned forward and gently bit the bulge over his jeans. She heard Casey's hiss as he cursed something inaudible. She smiled against his jeans before she stood. She wrapped her arms around Casey's ass and pulled down jeans and underwear in one swoop. She playfully pressed her palms into his ass and squeezed as his clothes fell to the floor in a heap between them. Casey's arms wrapped around Sam's slim waist as he stood and brought her up to stand with him. His mouth found hers and devoured hers on contact. Sam could feel Casey's now free erection pressed hard against her lower stomach. She moved her hand from his chest and grabbed his cock, causing another hiss to escape from the back of Casey's throat. She positioned him directly between her legs. Sam gently moved back and forth, letting her wetness coat and tease his cock over her clit and center. "Hmmm..." Casey moaned. "How does it feel this good every time?"

"And we haven't even gotten to the best part yet," Sam smirked between her gasps for air.

With that, Casey's hands tightened around her waist as he spun Sam around and sat on the sofa, pulling Sam on top of him. Sam straddled him, hovering above his lap. Casey grabbed a handful of her hair and pulled her head back. She arched forward as Casey's mouth burrowed into her breasts. "Yes, please," Sam cried as he bit into the soft fullness of her breast. He moved his hand from her hair and used both hands to pull her face down to his as they kissed with unsatiated need.

Every nerve ending on Sam's body was engulfed in flames. Everywhere he touched would surely have burn marks tomorrow. She ached for every inch of him to be closer. So fucking close. "Casey, please," she begged.

Casey's hands traced down her sides and stopped at her hips. He looked up at Sam. "Put me in," he growled.

Sam's hand wrapped around his cock, and she centered him on her. And as soon as she moved her hand, Casey thrust up as he pulled her down, causing them both to cry out in pure pleasure. He stilled momentarily, waiting for Sam to focus back on him. When she finally did, he asked, "You good?"

"Yes. Fuck, yes."

"Good." He grinned as he spanked her ass and thrust in again. And again. Their rhythm was entirely in sync. Sam felt the sweat bead down her back as she rode against him. Everything and anything she ever thought she had control over was gone. She wanted nothing but sensations rocking through her body. She felt Casey's hands holding her hips as he helped lift her at a pace that seemed torturous. She needed more. Without thought, she used her hands to explore her breasts, and then she slid one hand down her front as she teased her clit as Casey thrust into her. Sam cried out at the overload of sensations.

"Yes, Sam. Keep touching yourself," Casey panted out. She screamed his name at his command. "Ah, fucking hell, Sam," Casey growled. Sam felt every inch of him shudder into her as his orgasm climaxed just as hers overtook her once again before they both collapsed on each other.

They both sat satiated until their panting turned into even breathing. Sam rested her forehead on Casey's shoulder, still together, with his hands wrapped around her back in a soft bear hug.

How can this be real? Sam thought. There was no way sex was this good. Without warning, Sam sat up, flung her hair back over her shoulders, and pinched Casey's chest.

"Ow!" he screeched as his hand flew up and rubbed the spot where she pinched. He stared dumbfounded at Sam. "What the hell was that about?!"

Sam then pinched her forearm. "Ow!" she cursed under her breath.

Her eyes widened as she looked at Casey. "It's real." Her shoulders slumped. "This is all real, isn't it? You, me, the murders. My life."

Casey cupped his palms on Sam's cheeks and waited for her mind to settle and focus on him. "Sam," he said softly, "it's all real. And I am real. And what we have is real."

Sam shook her head. "I'm so mentally fucked up; it's not even funny." She looked at Casey again. "Why are you here for this..." Sam gestured to herself from head to toe with her hand. "This... this emotionally unstable shit show called Sam?"

Casey looked at her and realized why. He saw her as a whole, not just parts.

Casey took Sam's hand. "You've been through a lot. You are going through a lot."

Casey sqeezed her hand, "I don't know if I fully understand why I'm here now. I just know there is no other place or person I want to be with." He grinned and lifted her chin to force her to look at him.

"I would actually be concerned if you weren't a shitshow right now. It's okay to be a hot mess. Emphasis on the hot part," he added with a wink. "I can only speak for myself, but I have had some of the most amazing sex of my life these past couple of weeks and specifically like 2 minutes ago." He put his hands to his lips. "Chef's kiss."

Sam coughed a laugh. "Murder, Bombs, and Sex: The True-Life Tragic Story of Samantha Reeves."

"I'd read it."

"It's not a picture book," Sam clarified.

Casey eyed Sam up and down as she sat straddling him still. "I already have plenty of visuals to help me."

Chapter 53

Chief Crane awoke to his phone buzzing early Saturday morning. He let it buzz and rolled over, and threw his arm over his wife instead. The phone stopped the insistent buzzing. But only briefly before it started again. His wife whimpered a sound that he construed as an annoyance. She looked over her shoulder. "Just answer the damn thing."

He groaned as he rolled away from the warmth of his wife. He picked up his phone and saw it was the station. Retirement couldn't come soon enough.

"Hello," he grumbled as he threw his legs over the side of his bed.

"Chief, sorry to bother you. We just got a call for a health and welfare check that I think you should know about."

He dragged his hand over his face and through his thinning hair. "Now, why in the world would I ever need to know about a health and welfare check?"

"Ah," the officer stumbled. "Hmm…"

Crane usually had all the patience in the world, especially for his younger officers, but his was worn thin. It was his first day off in about two weeks, and he was upset their Lindahl murder case wasn't getting anywhere.

"Get on with it, son," he said.

"Sir, we got a call a couple of minutes ago for a check on Mrs. Colleen Reeves."

"Son of a…" He dropped his head into his hands, and he

rested his elbow on his knee. "This case just keeps getting worse."

"Should I send the officers over now, sir?"

"No. Tell them to send the SWAT team first. It could be nothing, but we don't need another Lakeside Motel situation. Get a hold of the apartment manager, evacuate the building and secure the area. I'm on my way."

He hung up the phone and turned to find his wife watching him. "You need to retire after this one, you know," she said flatly.

"I know."

His wife rolled out of bed and straightened the bed covers. "I'll get your coffee ready."

The chief nodded at her in appreciation as he headed to the bathroom to get ready. It was just a welfare check right now, but he knew better. He knew she was either dead or about to be dead. Not that Sam ever had a close relationship with her mother, but still. His heart hurt for her. Ever since she was a little girl and he was called on that first case, he knew Sam was something special, and her mother was anything but. He assumed Colleen knew that Sam was smarter than other kids, and that's why she did everything to keep her down. You can't control someone who can outsmart you.

He made his way to the kitchen just as his wife filled up the oversized travel mug with the coffee and handed it to him. "Tahiti soon?" she asked dryly.

"Tahiti soon," he said as he kissed her goodbye and headed out. He planned to call Sam once he knew what was going on. He didn't want to sound any alarms if he didn't have to. But first, he needed to know where Colleen Reeves was and if she was alive.

Chapter 54

Maggie watched as the dwellers of the apartments scurried about half asleep, wearing stained and torn shirts with cartoon character pajama bottoms. Everyone either looked pissed or confused. Maggie laughed at all of them from the safety of her dependable beater truck. She put the call in about twenty minutes ago to the tip line. She couldn't risk her not being found this morning.

"Colleen was a sad fucking waste of space." She took a sip from her Stanley before propping it up along the back of the bench seat.

"No wonder her only kid was also a waste of space." If she could go back in time, she'd put that bullet in Colleen's head when she was pregnant with Sam. "The world would be right, and I would be with Justin."

Tap. Tap. Maggie jumped as she turned and saw a police officer knocking on her passenger window. Panicked filled her, but she gave away nothing. She rolled down the window with the crank handle just enough to talk through.

"Ma'am, I need you to move out of this area. It's closed until further notice."

"Oh yes, thank you. I'll move." Maggie nodded and got the truck started. All for the best anyway, she thought. She wanted to stick around and see the whole show, but with everything in motion and the police tape going up, she knew her plan was taking shape. Maggie checked her watch. She only had a small window to make the next step work. She wasn't too worried though, she knew the dumb bitch would come running.

Chapter 55

"Sam, slow down now," Chief Crane said after he told her about the health and welfare call this morning. "There's nothing down here for you to do but get in the way. Teams already cleared the area of any potential explosives, and from where I'm sitting, they are about done."

"I can't just stay here, Chief. I can't sit here and do nothing."

"I'm not asking you. I'm telling you to stay away."

"Fine. Just, um... Just call me as soon as you hear anything." She was about to hang up when she heard Chief Crane's police radio mutter something. "What they'd find?" she asked after the squawking subsided.

Chief Crane took a long, deep pause. "I'm sorry, Sam."

"She's dead, isn't she?" Sam asked.

"I'm sorry," was all he said.

"Oh, God. Shit." Sam stood at her front door. Ready to leave but froze in place. "I just saw her yesterday."

"I'm sorry, Sam. This must be difficult on many levels. I know you didn't have the best relationship with her."

"Any!" Sam interrupted. "I didn't have any relationship with her, Chief. You know that. And you suggested I should investigate my past, so I did. I talked to her because I thought maybe she knew something or had something from my past that could connect me to the case, and now she's dead..." Sam trailed off.

"Fuck me!" Sam yelled as she smashed her palm to her

forehead. "They followed me," she whispered as the realization hit her that her mother was dead because of Sam.

Sam slid down the closed front door and tucked her head into her knees. Tears fell, but she wasn't crying. She couldn't cry over her mother. She knew that was what daughters were supposed to do when their mothers died. But nothing came.

The tears that spilled out of Sam's eyes were from being overwhelmed with emotions. They were not because her mother was gone. Her mother made her who she was, and not because Colleen empowered her daughter. No, Sam thought. *I am who I am today because I learned to survive my mother.* How do survivors process the death of their abuser? Sam reminded herself to Google that one later. Much later, when she was ready. Right now was not the time to mourn the loss of someone that she never had a loving relationship with.

"Sam," Chief Crane said. "Colleen's dead because somebody killed her. Not because you visited her."

"But what am I supposed to do?"

"There is nothing wrong with doing nothing."

"When I did nothing in Afghanistan, people died. When I do something here, people die. I can't win."

"You win when we find out who is doing this. We'll find them, Sam." Chief Crane's radio cracked again. "I have to go. Is Casey with you?"

"No. He's at work for a tournament today."

"Give him a call or go talk to him. He seems to be good for you."

Sam exhaled, resting her head against her knees and then against the back of the door. "He is. Thanks, Chief."

She wiped the tears off her cheeks and ended the call. "And that terrifies me just as much as this killer."

Chapter 56

The chief had told her not to come down to her mom's place in Hastings. She tried to settle herself down, waiting for him to call her from the station. It took every ounce of her patience not to jump in her stupid rental and drive down there, but she decided to pace around her house instead.

Her mom was dead.

She tried watching TV. She tried scrolling social media and even attempted to read, but nothing moved time faster.

She lost count of how many times she picked up her phone to call or text Casey but put it down instead. He had already sacrificed so much of his time for her. He already knew she was a shitshow. Adding a dead mom to it wasn't something she was looking forward to doing. He would say the right things, no doubt. But dammit, she thought, she was fine handling things on her own. She could still do it.

You didn't handle shit. You were numb, she heard a disgruntled inner voice tell her.

"Shut up," she told that inner voice.

She shook her fist in the air. "Damn, everything." She poured herself a glass of water, huffed down on the sofa, and stared at nothing.

By about ten, she hadn't heard from the chief, and she knew Casey would be expecting her soon. She had no choice but to text him.

> Sam: Hey, I'm on my way to the course for now, but something came up this morning, and I can't promise to stay. I'll explain everything when I get there.

He responded before she even got to her rental. Sam read it as she crawled into her rented tin can.

> Casey: Are you okay? Do I need to worry?

Sam typed the automatic reply of "I'm fine" but paused. Even through text messages, she felt Casey would see through her. She deleted the text and started again.

> Sam: Well, no, but don't worry. I know you are busy, so we'll talk when I get there. See you soon.

Sam knew this was a big day for Casey. It was a big tournament with a significant impact on veterans. She knew it meant a lot to him, and being a veteran herself, she knew how important events like this were for people.

All she had done since meeting Casey was drop these huge life-changing bombs on him. First Jeffrey. Then Juan. Now, her mom. "Fuck." She punched the steering wheel in frustration as she drove out of her neighborhood.

I'm going to have to start therapy again, she thought as she rolled her eyes.

It was just a flash of movement out of her left peripheral. She turned fully to the flash of bright headlights on a dark-colored truck, but it was too late. She felt gravity lift before it smashed her back into her seat, and the seat belt tightened against her chest. Her head smashed against the door window as the airbags deployed. Then everything went black.

She was awoken by what she thought was shouting, and her body ached as she felt quick pulses against her shoulder. It sounded like a woman, she thought. A woman was talking to her. Was she lying down? No. She wasn't lying down; she was sitting in her car. She could feel shards of glass around her and a sharp pain in her left arm.

Her eyes fluttered open as she felt hands on her face. "Good. You're alive," she heard, but there was no softness to it. Sam moaned in agony as she felt her body being pulled from her car. "Can you walk?"

All Sam could do was nod as she climbed out and stood outside of her smashed-in driver's door.

"Then move. We don't have all day."

Nothing felt right. Sam's body was tingling with warning and danger signs, but the pain in her head and left arm made it impossible to register anything.

"Ow!" Sam shrieked as this stranger pushed her into what Sam presumed was another car.

"Oh, shut up. You'll be fine." The thundering bang of the car door felt like it slammed on her head. She moved her arms up to grab her head, but her left arm didn't move. She looked down, and the swelling of her arm confirmed that it was indeed broken.

Sam heard some rustling to her left and saw a woman get into the driver's seat of a car. Her mind was still foggy as she took in her surroundings, trying to clear her mind and notice things. She shuffled her feet, felt paper, and heard grinding like sand and dirt underneath her shoes. She was in a car: no, she thought, a late-model truck. Finally, the images cleared a bit, and she got a clear image of the driver. "Maggie?" Sam said, groggy.

"Oh dear, yes." Maggie reached for a small black bag on the dashboard. "Well, not really." Maggie withdrew her hand from the little bag and swiftly stuck the needle into Sam's neck. "You may remember me as Lane."

Chapter 57

"That's it. I can't handle it anymore," Will declared as the master of ceremonies of the Tee It Up For The Troops Tournament closed the opening ceremony. Casey looked over his shoulder as Will stomped away from him.

"What are you talking about?" Casey asked as he pulled his shoulder back to stop him from walking away.

"You," Will said. "You can't stop fucking moving or checking your phone." Will shivered. "It's making my skin crawl."

"Sorry. It's just that Sam said she was on her way almost an hour ago, and she isn't here yet," Casey said as he pulled out his phone and checked it again.

"Maybe she is with Nikki." Will shrugged. "I haven't seen her either."

"Nikki is already here, dumbass." Casey nodded his head up to the big windows on the second floor. The same spot where he saw Sam for the first time. "She's just avoiding you, would be my best assumption."

Will followed Casey's gaze and looked up to see Nikki looking down at them with her arms crossed in front of her chest. She smiled a tight-lipped grin when she met Will's eyes. Nikki extended the middle finger nonchalantly on her outside crossed hand but never moved her arms from in front of her. Will threw his arms out to the side in a WTF motion. Nikki narrowed her brows before she spun around and walked away.

"Fuck me," Will said as he turned back to Casey. "What

the hell did I do wrong this time?"

Casey shrugged, took his phone out, and hit the call button before saying, "Knowing Nikki, everything."

The line went right to voicemail. "Something isn't right." Casey looked around. "All the golfers are headed out." He turned to Will with a pained look. "I have to go find her."

"Ah… fuck me again." Will threw his hands up in surrender. "First, your sister's throwing her fucking attitude at me for no apparent reason, and now you're leaving me to go find your girl all because she is probably ignoring your dumbass." He started walking away from Casey. He turned his head back around. "A fine fucking family you both are," Will emphasized his point as he spun back ahead and threw up his middle finger salute over his shoulder back toward Casey.

"Will, I'm sorry," Casey pleaded as he chased up after him. "I have to know…"

"Go, dipshit," Will interrupted and stopped walking. "Go find your girl before she gets into more shit and takes you with her. I don't want to ever have to tell Nikki her brother is dead, and I don't want her to ever have to tell me the same."

Casey grinned, and he jogged away. "I love you, man, you know that?" he hollered over his shoulder.

"You're a fucking lucky bastard that I put up with your shit." Will shouted back before muttering under his breath, "Be safe, dipshit."

Chapter 58

Thinking she might still be at her house, Casey drove north to White Bear Lake to Sam's townhome. He called her number a few more times but yielded the same result.

He drove faster than he should along Highway 61. He seemed to get stuck behind every Buick sedan and hit every red light.

After what seemed like hours, he finally turned east off the highway and made his way to the left turn off the main road toward her place.

As he turned the corner, his heart dropped to his stomach. He took in the sight of multiple police cars with lights flashing, an ambulance with open doors, and a fire truck blocking the intersection. He pulled up as close as he could.

Deep in his core, he knew whatever happened, it involved Sam. He instantly regretted never telling her he loved her.

He knew it was stupid; he'd only known her for two weeks, but he knew. He loved her beauty, raw honesty, and vulnerability when she didn't want to be.

"Fuck me," he said as he realized he was in love.

A thousand curse words came to mind as a million stakes drove through his heart when he saw the small gray car smashed in on the driver's side door. It was upright but slammed against some bushes, and a white fence snaked around the front end. "Sam!" he shouted as he jumped out of his car. "SAM!" he screamed more frantically.

Heads whipped in his direction as two police officers started toward him.

His eyes darted around to try and find her. "Sam!" he shouted again.

"Sir," one of the officers said. Casey met the officer's eyes, and he jogged over to meet her halfway. "Where is she? Where did you take Sam?"

"Sir, there was nobody here to take anywhere." The police officer introduced herself and her partner. Casey gave her his name, but confusion still filled him. "Mr. Parks," Officer King said as she wrote down his name in her notebook. "Looks like we have a hit-and-run situation, but we can't find either party."

"What do you mean you can't find either party? Where is Sam?"

"Who is Sam? Was she driving this car?" she pointed to the crushed Prius. "What is Sam's full name?"

Casey nodded his head. "Yes, Samantha Reeves. That's her rental car. She lives in the townhomes just a couple blocks up this road." Casey pulled out his phone. "I've been trying to call her, but her phone goes right to voicemail." He could hear the panic in his voice, but he didn't care. He had to find her. She had to be okay.

Officer King took down the address and sent an officer to the address. Within a few minutes, they called back and said the house was clear. Nobody was there.

"What about the other vehicle?" Casey asked.

"A witness said it was an old black truck when she looked out her window, but by the time she got to the scene, the truck was gone."

"Does Chief Crane know about this?"

"Who?"

"Right." Casey scrolled his phone. He realized this wasn't a movie where they all knew each other. He put his phone to his ear just as the chief answered.

"There's been an accident, Chief, and Sam is missing. I don't know what to do. I'm at the scene right now, talking to the police here, and they don't know you, and they don't know where Sam is," Casey said in one breath.

"Oh. This isn't..." the chief mumbled. Casey could hear him mutter something but realized he wasn't talking to Casey but more to himself. "Give your phone to the officer, please, Casey." Casey nodded without a word and held his phone out to Officer King. "It's for you."

She took the phone and turned her back as she talked to Chief Crane.

Casey paced and was lost in his thoughts for long enough that he didn't realize his name was being shouted. "Mr. Parks," Officer King sternly said as she held out the phone.

"Hello?"

"Casey, when was the last time you heard from Sam?" Chief asked.

"She texted me about ten this morning and said she was on her way. But she said she wasn't okay and that she would explain what was going on when she got there. That was it." He hung his head. "She didn't explain any further."

"Interesting," Chief said. "Casey, why don't you meet me at the station? I'll get more details about the crash and fill you in on what's happening when you get here." Before Chief Crane hung up, he added, "Let me know right away if you hear from Sam."

Casey nodded at the officers and took off.

Casey was back in his car, heading south now on Highway 61. No Buicks slowing him down this time. Or maybe he didn't notice. All he could think, see, and feel was terror for Sam.

Chapter 59

The first thing Sam noticed was the cold metal against her arm. The air smelled like old, gritty fryer grease. She moaned and tried to move but found her hands and legs were restrained. And her body hurt. Everything hurt. Her eyes finally obeyed, and she fought against the harsh fluorescent light to open them. She was faced with a dusty steel cabinet in front of her. Her head moved to the side and found more dusty and filmy steel. She saw a few metal pot hooks mounted on the wall and a small TV in the upper corner of what seemed to be a long, narrow room. She looked up and noticed a square plastic hatch in the roof.

Reality dawned on her.

She was in a food truck.

She followed the length of her arms to see they were tied around the thick handle of a small oven that her back rested against. Her feet and legs were laid out and were bound in front of her. *What the hell was happening?* She wanted to say it out loud but couldn't because of the duct tape across her mouth.

She remembered the flash of headlights and then airbags blasting in front of her. A car accident. She had gotten into a car accident. Then how did she end up in the back of an old food truck?

The needle.

Maggie.

No. The name. Lane.

Lane. She didn't know any Lanes. Nothing came to mind Sam's fuzzy mind. Maybe a former case she worked on. No. She thought it would have to be connected with Jeffrey Lindahl. It all started with him.

A deep fog started blurring her vision. She couldn't stop it. Afghanistan. Yes. It started with Afghanistan.

Justin sat across from Sam with such concentration she couldn't help but laugh. "It's Rummy. Whatever you discard isn't going to set off a UXO (unexploded ordinance)."

"You always beat me. Every card I throw, you pick up and use it against me."

"Hate the game... not the player," Sam taunted. Justin finally threw down a ten of hearts and cringed as Sam laughed, picked it up, added it to the two tens from her hand, and threw them down on the piece of scrap plywood that rested on stacked milk crates that made their table. Justin tossed his cards at Sam, and she laughed even louder.

"You're the worst," Justin proclaimed. "I'm never playing cards with you again." He crossed his arms over his tan shirt making his dog tags clank with the motion. "Besides, I have a new friend I can play cards with." Justin dipped his head and relaxed his arms. "Actually, Sam..." He looked at her more seriously. "I can play a lot more than just cards with her."

"Oh?" Sam said with raised eyebrows. She admitted she liked Justin, but it was brotherly and not lustful. She suspected he wanted more initially, but she was an NCO in charge of her squad. She didn't want to cross any boundaries. And she knew he didn't either. So, they settled with family love instead. She smiled once she realized he was waiting for her approval. "That's awesome. Tell me more."

"I met her a couple of weeks ago during an EOD unit mission. They were tagging along on a convoy, and she was part of the team. I mean, those EOD guys are nuts. And I couldn't quite wrap my head around why

a female was with them. So, we started talking, which turned to flirting, which turned to, holy fuck, this girl can kiss."

Sam laughed. "We're in the middle of a war in Afghanistan. I bet you'd love the way a dog kissed right now."

"I actually would. I miss my dog's slobbery kisses." He pointed at Sam. "But that's not the point." He tucked his hand under his chin. "She is a little odd, says weird shit about blowing things up, but it's EOD stereotype, I guess. And she is a little obsessed with me. It's too early to tell in a good way, obsessed or bad way, but we have a few more months here to figure it out." Justin shrugged. "At least it's fun for now."

"Good for you, Justin," Sam said, and she meant it as she shuffled the deck. "I hope she is at least super hot, too."

Justin laughed. "Oh, she is. She has this fiery red hair like I've never seen before."

"You mean like Maggie Lindahl's hair?" Sam asked. Justin looked at her, confused. "Who's Maggie, Sam?"

"Maggie Lindahl. You know the case I'm working on. Maggie has fiery red hair," Sam explained.

"I don't know a Maggie," Justin said. "My girl's name is Lane."

Sam's eyes flew open. "Lane," she said, but her mouth was taped shut. Lane was Justin's girlfriend from the other unit. Sam's mind cleared as this revelation took hold—Jeffrey's death. Maggie, well, Lane hired her. It was a setup. The motel. All of it. It was because Justin died, and she blamed Sam.

Chapter 60

"I see someone finally decided to wake up."

Sam's eyes settled on the fiery red hair that moved from the shadows and was now hovering over her. She thought about kicking her bound legs but wasn't sure she could count on her strength or what would happen next. The stove handle held her captive. She'd likely lose that fight, especially if Lane had a gun.

"I can see from your eyes that you've finally pieced together who I am." Lane clasped her hands, and Sam noted the pistol she held between them. "Congratulations, you dumb cunt." She dropped the feigned smile and kicked Sam. Sam cried out in pain, muffled by the tape over her mouth.

"Took you fucking long enough." Lane spun, and Sam watched her shoulders roll back as if Lane was trying to gain control over an edge she was losing. Lane turned to face Sam. "I don't have all day, you know." The maniacal smile returned. "I have places to go. People to blow up." Sam saw it in her eyes. There wasn't much control left in Lane. Terror ran through Sam for the first time. She had to figure a way out.

Sam noted the truck wasn't moving, but she also didn't hear any noises from outside the truck. She had no idea if they were still in the cities or in a secluded area. Whatever Lane had drugged with could have put her out for ten minutes or ten hours.

"Confusion seems to be still lingering in your tiny little

brain." Lane stepped back, taking a few small steps to the back of the truck before turning back at Sam. "Let me clarify what's happening right now."

"Justin loved me. I loved Justin. I forgot about you. You ceased to exist. I wasn't whole after you killed Justin, but I created a life of comfort. Lane died when Justin died. Those army doctors said I wasn't fit enough to serve anymore. But they were wrong! Tried to send me away, but I wouldn't allow it."

Lane shook her head from side to side. "Why should I be locked up for something you did? You. Killed. Justin." Lane pointed the gun at Sam's head.

Sam shook her head.

"Yes, you did, you fucking bitch!" Lane rushed forward and pressed the gun against Sam's head. Through gritted teeth, Lane growled, "He'd be alive if you would have done your job." She paused and took a deep breath before she stepped back and pulled the pistol back into a shrug.

"And you know what? I was fine. But then you showed up in my life again. And once again, you didn't do your job, did you?" She pointed the pistol back slowly at Sam. "You ruined my life." Lane pressed the tip of the barrel into Sam's forehead.

Sam clenched her eyes shut.

"Relax, dear," Lane said, dropping the gun from Sam's head. "As much as I want to shoot you right now. I can't. That's too simple."

Lane turned and fiddled with the TV in the corner for a moment. The little monitor flashed and blinked before it focused on what looked like a lobby or a storefront. Sam's eyes widened with realization. She was looking inside the Lakeside Motel's lobby.

"You need to understand what it's like to hurt like I did. You didn't know Jeffrey, so that didn't hurt you. That was mostly for me, anyway." Lane laughed at her little joke. "That was just a fun little way to bring you closer to me and take care of that asshole." Lane chuckled. "Two birds with one stone, am I right?

"And Juan, remember sweet Juan?" Lane asked as she tapped on the screen. "He used to sit right here and help people keep their dirty little scandals and secrets, didn't he? I wanted him to share my secret with you. Send you that little gift. Did you like that gift, Sam?"

Sam didn't move. Lane kicked her ribs with the bottom of her black boots. "Answer me, bitch. Did you like your gift?"

Sam nodded.

"Good," Lane smirked with zero glee in her eyes. "And I wanted to be sure you got the message, so I threw in a little explosion for fun. Relive my EOD days, you know."

Lane paused, and her smile faded into a thin, pressed line. "What I didn't know was that fucking minivan would ruin it all."

Lane continued pacing the tiny space.

Sam fidgeted with the zip tie restraints as they held her hands around the handle. She knew breaking the restraints like she was trained was out of the question with her broken arm, but perhaps it was possible to wiggle out her intact right arm.

Lane gestured toward Sam. "You were supposed to die in that explosion, you know. If you had just been blown into tiny bits of nothing like I'd planned, think of how many people would still be alive. Juan. Your mother. Sorry about your mother." Sam locked eyes with Lane even as she discretely tried to loosen her right wrist.

"That was just for funzies. I hadn't even realized your mother was still around until you showed up at her place. What a piece of white trash she was. She was just as much of a waste of space as you are."

Sam watched as Lane's frenzied eyes flicked up at Sam's wrist. Sam froze, but it was too late. Sam saw the flash of anger cross Lane's eyes just before her heavy boot rose and came crashing down on Sam's broken arm. Sam screamed, but the tape muffled it. She squeezed her eyes as tight as possible, hoping to stop the tears that the searing pain produced.

Lane leaned down into Sam's agonized face. Sam could smell her high-end perfume mixed with the lingering odor of dried sweat. Lane, as petite as she was, had carried the dead weight of Sam from the accident. And unless she had someone to help her, she carried Sam's dead weight into the truck where she currently was. It was safe to assume this woman was not above carrying Sam's dead weight again.

"Do you know what the last thing your mother said was?" Lane leaned in further. "She said you were the biggest mistake she made."

Lane shoved off and laughed. "Isn't that hilarious? A mother is about to die, and she confesses she hates her only child. I almost felt bad putting a bullet in her head. She would have always been a solid source of pain and suffering for you." Lane snapped her fingers. "But then I remembered. You wouldn't live long enough to suffer properly."

Sam didn't know whether that was true or not or if Lane was trying to get in her head, but she wasn't going to allow it. She shoved aside the notion and refused to be distracted from finding any potential options she had to escape this truck. She had compartmentalized pain before, and she could do it again.

"But enough of the chit-chat. The sooner you're dead, the better." Lane checked her watch. "Now, where would Casey Parks be right now?" Lane tapped her lips while she pretended to ponder.

Sam froze and her eyes widened at the sound of his name.

"Oh, I know, dear," Lane said, feigning sympathy. "I know the pain of losing a loved one, remember?" Lane reached behind her back and pulled out Sam's phone. "Shall we give our lover boy a ring?"

Chapter 61

The city seemed to pass in a snippet of colors as Casey sped along the interstate and rushed to meet Chief Crane at the police station. He couldn't shake the nervous energy that consumed him until he knew Sam was okay. He wished the chief would have told him more over the phone, but he'd be there soon enough. The silence of the car ride was interrupted by an incoming call. He looked at the display on his dashboard and saw Sam's name in bold white letters.

A wave of relief quickly washed over him. She was calling him back. "Finally," he said as he accepted the call. A prickle at the back of his neck reminded him that he still didn't know what was going on.

"Sam," he answered but didn't wait for a response before the wave of relief turned into a stream of worried questions. "Are you okay? Where have you been? I've been trying to call you..."

"Calm down, Romeo."

Every nerve in Casey's body flared with warning. That wasn't Sam. He wasn't prepared for that. His worry morphed into complete terror. He braced himself before he asked, "Who is this?"

He heard a soft chuckle. "It's not about who, dear. It's about where."

I know that voice, Casey thought. The way she said "dear" and how it was enunciated with an eye-roll.

Be careful with that golf bag, dear. It's expensive.

He sat stunned, his knuckles turning white as he gripped the wheel, trying to understand how Maggie Lindahl was on the other end of the phone.

He cleared his throat. "Okay. I'll bite. Where is Sam?"

"Where is..." Casey heard a loud thump followed by a muffled moan. He flinched. "This bitch," she continued, "was supposed to die." Maggie paused. "Well, close enough." She chuckled before her voice turned cold again. "Come alone. Call no one, especially that fat fuck guard dog of Sam's. If you do, a lot more people will die than just your precious Juliet."

The line went dead, and the silence returned to the car.

Casey tried to control the panic that threatened to spill out of him as he changed the destination on the navigation map from the police precinct to the Lakeside Motel.

Chapter 62

His white Audi seemed out of place in the empty parking lot of the Lakeside Motel. Ripped police tape scattered around the burnt edges of where room 7B once was. The room he had watched Sam walk into after that first night he dropped her off.

He couldn't lose her. He loved her.

"I love her," he said out loud. His hands twisted around the steering wheel as he processed this. How long had he really known her? Had it only been two weeks? How had Sam permeated his life so much that he loved her? Could you love someone in such a short amount of time? Images of Sam laughing with him filled his vision. Then, she was crying and vulnerable in front of him. Then he flashed to her teasing, sexy smile he craved constantly. He loved every part of her. He wanted to share more and more with her. He fell in love with her in two weeks, and right now, he planned to love her a lot longer.

Casey's eyes traced around the motel parking lot and saw the lobby across the way. He saw the curtains in the window to the lobby were open enough to see no lights were on inside, but he had a feeling Sam was in there. He tried to control his shaky hand as he grabbed his phone and tapped on Sam's name.

"I'm here," he said after he heard it connect after the first ring.

"Excellent," Maggie answered. Casey heard some shuffling.

"Why don't you make your way into the lobby? It's open. Oh, and dear, hands up where I can see them."

"Is Sam in there?" Casey asked. "Is she safe?"

He heard Maggie laugh into the phone.

"Are you being serious right now?" she chided. "Of course, she's not safe."

Maggie laughed a bit more, but nothing was funny for Casey.

His blood boiled as it raced through his core. What the fuck was he going to do?

The pulsing blood in his ears quieted enough for him to notice she was no longer laughing.

He heard an annoyed-sounding grunt seep through the phone. "Ugh. She's alive for now if that's what you're asking," Maggie said. "I'm running out of patience with you, however. Move."

The phone went silent as she ended the call.

Sweat beaded down his spine. He looked down at the phone in his hands, wanting to call Chief Crane, but knew it was too late, and he was running out of time. Maggie had said that Sam wasn't safe. He had to figure out something quickly. He slid his phone into his pocket. He went to open his driver's door, but an idea dawned on him that made him pause.

He thought about the classic movie troupe of people secretly recording the bad guy's confession in these types of situations. He pulled his phone back out and hit record before shoving it back into his pocket. He closed his eyes and took a few deep breaths to calm his breathing and his pulsing heart before he climbed out of his car. He eyed the lobby door as if it was his mortal enemy. He squinted, trying to see if he could see any movement through the lobby window, but the bright, cloudless sky's reflection made it impossible to see inside.

He took a few steps before it dawned on him that bad guys usually confess right before they shoot the good guy. He stuttered his step before he stopped. "Shit." He wasn't sure what to do about that part. He had no weapon. Nothing in his car to help him out. Maybe a golf club, but she'd said hands up; he couldn't hide that.

He took a step.

And then what? he thought. She probably had a gun, and he'd have a nine iron.

Another step.

I'm not an action hero in a fucking movie, he thought.

Step.

This isn't a movie.

Step.

He put his hands up and out to his sides with his palms out.

Step.

I'm just a guy that works at a golf course.

Step.

He felt his heart begin to race faster than it was already. The mid-day sun reflected off the cracked and broken asphalt of the parking lot as sweat beaded across his forehead and poured down his back.

Step.

He swiped his hand across his forehead, taking a deep breath as the lobby door loomed ahead. It sat partially ajar, but not enough to see anything on the other side.

Step.

He had no clue what he was doing, but he knew he loved Sam. He knew he needed to do something to try and save her.

"Here's hoping this movie ends with the good guy winning," he whispered to himself before he took the final step and pushed the door open.

Chapter 63

When Sam heard her phone ring and Casey's voice on the other end, she knew he was there. Her heart leaped with relief at first but then filled with terror as Lane opened the back of the truck and stepped out. Sam caught a glimpse of the backside of a white-bricked wall with a service entry door before the door slammed shut. Her food truck prison had to have been parked behind the motel office lobby.

Sam was left alone with just the monitor focused on the inside of the Lakeside Motel's lobby.

With Lane gone, Sam leaned her face close to her hands and peeled the tape off her mouth. She inhaled sharply, letting a full expansion of her lungs give her new energy. She spun her legs under her so she could sit up better and look around. Her arm protested by sending sharp stabbing pain with every moment, but she had no choice but to push through it.

She couldn't let Casey die. Lane wanted vengeance, and Sam knew Casey was walking into Lane's plan to make Sam pay. Eye for an eye, Sam thought.

Justin died, so Casey had to die.

"No!" she cried out.

She kicked at the closest cabinet door and cried out as pain sliced through her. The door flung open, but it was empty. Nothing was in there that could cut the zip ties holding her hostage. She opened the oven she was strapped to. Nothing. After a few more attempts to kick open another cabinet just to find it also barren, she took a second to look around.

She caught movement on the monitor and saw Casey in the motel lobby. She didn't see Lane on the screen, but seeing the frozen features on Casey's face, she knew she was there and had her gun pointed in Casey's direction.

"Casey!" she cried out.

Casey was right there. He was in the lobby. He was so close to her, and yet she couldn't free herself to help him. She failed another person she loved.

Loved.

Tears stung her eyes as she realized she loved him but had never told him. She couldn't admit it to herself until now, and it was too late to tell him.

Love wasn't for her. Nobody loved her. She never let herself love fully. The likelihood of loss and pain and hurt was too great to risk for love. It had been a decade, but she hadn't recovered from her grief. It was an everyday battle.

But in the past few weeks, Sam realized, her battles felt less intense.

Sam stared at the blurry image of Casey on the screen. Maybe it felt less intense because she felt love. Her battle against love and relationships was to recover from her grief maybe wasn't the right answer. The answer was to allow herself to love again. The answer was Casey. She loved Casey.

She focused on Casey again and could see his mouth moving, but there was no sound.

"No," she said out loud as tears rolled down her cheeks. "I'm not giving up on him or myself." She pulled her eyes away from the TV screen. She had to find something here.

Casey's eyes took a second to adjust from the sunny sky outside to the dark, unlit room of the motel lobby. A beam of light from the open curtain lit up the corner edge of a faded chair and wooden coffee table. As soon as his eyes adjusted, he searched the room to find Sam, but he couldn't see her, and he didn't feel the familiar energy of her when they were in a room together. The only thing out of the ordinary he saw was the shadowed figure toward the back of the lobby. It didn't take long to figure out he was at the firing end of a gun. Behind the gun was a silhouetted woman with fierce red hair. "Maggie," he whispered.

She took a step forward, out of the shadows and into the light.

"It's Lane, actually," Lane corrected with a coldness that froze the sweat on his back.

"Lane?" he repeated, trying to make sense of it. He didn't know anyone named Lane, and this was Maggie. He was sure of it. Could it have been a twin, he thought?

"Yes, Lane, you imbecile," Lane huffed, annoyed. Casey shook his head, trying to understand. "Good God, dear, you're not getting this, and I don't have time for it."

"Who are you?" Casey asked hoping he sounded more confident than he felt. "Where is Sam?"

"So many questions, Casey." Lane rolled her eyes. "Let me see, the short version is," Lane sighed, "I'm Lane. I was told to join the army or go to jail. I went army because at least then I was allowed to play with explosives and guns." Lane lowered her tone in a mocking voice, "They'll teach her how to use them responsibly and not blow up our house." Lane laughed, "Can you believe how stupid my parents were? They thought it was an accident that I set their house on fire?" She chuckled some more. "They thought we just had bad luck with pets running away or mysteriously dying." Lane shook her head. "Fucking idiots. So anyway, I joined the army, learned to blow things up, shoot things—oh, and found the love of my life."

Casey watched as Lane's face shifted from a false bravado of cheery to darkened notes of evil.

"She ruined it, though," Lane hissed. "Justin and I had just started to get to know each other. It was just a few weeks, but I knew he'd love me eventually as much as I loved him." Lane seemed to fade into her thoughts of the past.

Casey looked around the room to see if there was anything he could use to throw or distract her without getting shot first.

"Justin loved listening to me explain how we used explosives in my unit. He had passion like me. He appreciated my love of watching things being destroyed. He loved to watch things die, too. He didn't say that, but I know he was a military police officer because of that."

A shadow swept around Lane's face, and it seemed to snap her out of her past. Her eyes focused back on Casey, and her knuckles tightened once again around the handle of the gun.

Casey froze, knowing his chance to make a move was gone. He'd have to figure something else out.

"Where is Sam?" he asked again.

"Oh, she is right here," Lane nodded over her shoulder.

Casey followed her nod to the camera set on a tripod next to her.

She is, Casey repeated in his head. *Lane said she is, so Sam is alive.*

"But I don't know why you are so concerned about Sam," Lane smirked. "If I were you, I'd be worried about all those veterans at your golf course today."

Casey felt the bile rise in his throat as his lungs constricted. Terror coursed through his veins as Lane's smile widened with malice.

"How is your little charity event going?" Lane looked at her watch. "Geez, in just a few hours, everyone will be sitting around enjoying a nice dinner, and then…" Lane let her hand go up and explode open in front of her. "Poof."

Casey couldn't move. Couldn't breathe.

Lane took another step toward Casey, her face now clearly visible in the light from the lobby window. Her eyes still held the darkened shadows, though. Casey saw her lips pressed in a thin line. "More veterans dead because of Sam," she snarled. "You'll be dead. Then Sam will dead. Then I'll be gone."

Lane took another step closer to Casey. "After Sam watches this bullet plaster your brains on the wall, I'll make sure your event ends with a bang," Lane emphasized the word bang with a slow, drawn, deep tone.

"How could you?!" Casey whispered.

"Easy," Lane said straight-faced. "I mean, I've been out of practice, so I had to do a bit of testing and fine-tuning. I wasn't used to rigging cars, but the second time, I think I got it right, I mean..." Lane tilted her head toward the window. "That worked out better than I anticipated. It stayed so isolated, and the blast radius was almost perfect, and someone actually died." Lane smiled. "I knew I was ready for a bigger bang after that."

She was just a few feet from Casey now.

"So, let's see." Lane tapped her finger on her chin. "Jeffrey," Lane took her free hand, formed a finger gun, and dropped her thumb to her palm as she said, "Bang."

She fisted her hand and said, "Then there was a bomb." She exploded her hand. "Then another bang." She pulled the imaginary trigger again.

"There was supposed to be another bomb before the bang, but I had to change my plans a bit, but there will still be the bomb," she said with her hand exploding.

"And so, you know what that makes you, Romeo?"

"No," Casey pleaded.

"Yes, you're the bang," she said as she centered the gun on Casey. "Her mother had an opportunity to say final words, so being a generous person, I'll give you a chance as well."

"Sam," was all Casey got out before a startling crack ripped through the air. Casey dropped to the ground as glass shattered around him. He heard a loud crash from behind him and felt the floor vibrate as footsteps surrounded him. He popped his head up as the gun that once was pointed at him lay limp in Lane's hand before it fell to the ground. She looked down at her chest as the blood began to flow and stain the front of her black shirt. She stood, eyes wide for a moment, before she collapsed forward. Shadows and figures surrounded him and Lane in the motel's lobby.

Casey was pulled to his feet and dragged backward out of the motel. The heat of the sun momentarily blinded him as he lay on the heated asphalt. Two figures hovered above him.

His eyes adjusted to the light, and he saw bold white lettering on black uniforms—SWAT. "Sam's alive!" he shouted to the uniformed officer at his side. "Find her."

"We already did," a familiar, calm, even-toned voice echoed behind him. He watched as Chief Crane came to his side. He stood as relief flooded him, and tears welled at the sight of the chief and his calm demeanor. Without a thought, Casey pulled the chief into a hug. "I'm so glad to see you," Casey said.

The chief cleared his throat as he stepped back. He smiled at Casey. "Come on."

Chief led Casey through the lobby and out the back door, careful to keep clear of the lifeless body of Lane as a few SWAT officers flanked it. Casey couldn't see the body, and he was grateful for that.

Out the back door, Casey watched as two officers lifted a distraught yet beautiful Samantha Reeves out of the back of the old, nondescript food truck. She held her arm close as tears streaked her face. "Sam," Casey called out.

She looked up and met Casey's gaze. He watched relief wash over her as she cried out. He was certain if the officer hadn't been holding her, she would have collapsed. He ran to her, and, careful of the arm she held, he wrapped his arms around her and cried with his face buried into her hair.

"I love you," Casey said. "I love you so much."

Sam laughed through her tears.

"What's wrong with you?" Sam asked, laughing.

Casey pulled back and looked at her through his teary eyes, his eyes brow arched in surprise.

"First, you ask me out while I lay in a hospital bed. And now you tell me you love me when I get pulled out of a food truck prison with a broken arm?"

Casey laughed. "I just always say the right things at the right time."

Sam shook her head. "I love you, too."

Chapter 64

One Month Later

"I still can't believe he found us," Casey said as they passed the sixth or so sign telling drivers along the interstate that Jesus Saves. "I thought the phone tracking trick was just in television shows."

"Well, you didn't show up at the station; he knew something was up." Sam laughed. "Chief Crane may be old school, but he isn't that old."

She turned her body as much as her seat allowed, reached across, and put her right hand on Casey's thigh. "And I know you are tired of me saying this, but I am truly sorry about everything—Lane, me, the tournament being shut down—everything."

"Nobody else got hurt, Sam." Casey put his hand on top of Sam's. "And besides, Will said it was almost funny watching all the veterans not even flinch when the bomb squad showed up. He never saw so many people want to hang around to see if there was a bomb or not."

"That sounds about right." She smiled.

"Now, will you stop apologizing for it? It's been over a month now. It's okay to let it all go," he said as he squeezed her hand.

"After today, I am letting it all go. And starting therapy again."

She smiled as she moved her hand back to the bundled package she held in her lap. With everything finally settled and the case closed, she had one more final thing to do before moving on.

An hour later, Casey slowed at the rusted milk tin mailbox with a wooden sign etched with the name "Sommers" in aged letters. He turned onto the gravel road that led up to an old farmhouse with a small dairy barn behind it. A few milk tins lined the front porch, and fall-colored mums held onto the fading colors of the season.

Casey stopped, and the dust around the car settled as the front door opened. An older woman stepped out with a towel over her shoulder. She pressed her hand over her brows to shield against the sun.

"That's Patty."

"Do you want me to come with you?" Casey asked.

Sam shook her head. "No. I'll be okay. I should have come out here a long time ago." Sam stepped out. "Just wait here."

Casey watched her walk up to the porch, her arm in a sling. He saw Sam introduce herself as she held onto the little package in her hand, wrapped in tissue paper. The older woman's eyes widened with acknowledgment. She unwrapped the tissue, and Casey watched as her hands shook. She held Justin's military police patch in her hands. Tears streamed down woman's blushed cheeks as she began to weep. Justin's mother threw her arms around Sam. Casey watched as Sam leaned into the embrace without hesitation.

Epilogue

One Year Later

Sam stood next to her kitchen island as she wrapped the packing paper around the lone framed photo from her desk. Nearly everything else in her house had been packed, but this photo she purposely left for last. It had taken her a few months after the Lindahl case closed to settle down and weekly therapy appointments to get herself to unpack the blue box with all of her Afghanistan memories, but she finally did. "It just felt silly to pack it up so quickly after it took so long to pull it out," she had told Casey when he asked why that was the only thing still unpacked.

And as if she summoned him by thinking about him, she heard Casey's familiar gait stroll down the stairs.

She set the frame in the open box on the island and threw the lid on. She turned in time to meet Casey as he approached her. Sam took him in with an appreciative look. He truly was embarrassingly handsome in his crisp white button-down shirt untucked, paired with dark blue shorts with tiny little golf clubs on them. From afar, they looked like just a little embroidered cross design, but Sam knew better.

"You ready?" he asked as he pulled her into a hug.

"For the move or for the party?"

Casey cocked his head to the side as if he were thinking deeply about her question. "Both?"

"Yes, and yes." Casey kissed her forehead and said, "Let's go then."

They pulled up to Chief Crane's house a short time later. Cars lined both sides of the street, and a huge banner with balloons ensured that everyone knew which house hosted the retirement party. They walked into the big backyard and found it jam-packed with friends and family and familiar faces.

Chief Crane had a beer in his hand that matched perfectly with his creamy white Hawaiian-style shirt full of palm trees and beaches. He must have seen them come in because he excused himself from his conversation and came over and wrapped them both in a big hug.

"It's good to see you both." He pulled back. "Here, let me get you folks a beer." He leaned over and grabbed two beers out of the cooler that sat in the shaded areas of the newly remodeled patio. "It's beautiful back here, Chief," Sam said as she grabbed the bottle and took it all in.

"It's just Mark now."

"Sure, Chief," Sam said with a wink.

"Hey, dipshit," Will's voice called over from the door behind them. He bounced his shoulder off Casey's as he joined them.

Sam rolled her eyes but smiled at Will. She loved Will and knew that despite his brooding bravado, he was a gentle and kind soul.

"Good to see you, son," Chief said as he handed Will a beer. He accepted the beer and pulled Chief into a hug. "Ah, congratulations, Mark. You'll have all the time in the world now to put those golf lessons to work at the club."

"I nearly got a hole-in-one on seventeen last week," Chief told the group with a beaming smile.

"It's true," Will said. "I witnessed it myself."

Another group of well-wishers stepped into the backyard, and the chief excused himself to greet them.

"How is everything going?" Casey asked Will after taking a sip of beer.

Will shook his head. "No amount of Blue Label will ever make up for this bullshit," Will said dryly.

"Dude, your house is massive. You probably won't ever see my sister."

"I feel terrible," Sam added, putting her hand over her chest.

"Fuck that," Casey said as he smacked Sam's down. "Don't feel bad."

"You should feel bad, Sam." Will pointed the beer bottle at Sam. "Your happy-ass romance is the reason Nikki is being kicked out of her home with apparently nowhere else to go."

Sam laughed. "I feel bad that Nikki has to deal with your bullshit," she said. "But I don't feel bad for moving in with Casey." She smirked at Will before turning to Casey. "I like our happy-ass romance."

Casey grinned. "Me too." He turned back to Will. "And dude, we offered for her to stay until she found a more permanent solution, but she refused."

He continued, "You've had your mom's house now for almost a year, dude, and it's just been you in there, and you aren't getting any closer to selling it or fixing it or claiming it as your own. You have a big house with lots of room. And Nikki needs a place until she finishes med school and gets her residency."

Will scuffed at his buddy's lecture even though he'd heard it several times over the last two months after Casey and Sam announced they were moving in together.

"This isn't going to end well," Will said before he tipped his bottle back. He smacked his lips after he drained it. "I give her two weeks before she moves out."

Sam looked at Casey and grinned. "I give it two weeks before something happens."

Will glared, Casey laughed, and Sam raised her bottle and toasted the two men.

Acknowledgements

To the reader who took the time to read my book, I'm eternally grateful.

To the kid in my writer's group who asked after I read my first chapter, "Why is she (Sam) so paranoid?" I'm also eternally grateful. That question opened a whole new perspective for me that helped me recognize my own PTSD & my own healing journey.

To the Tee It Up For The Troops nonprofit organization, especially Rick Dale, Jodi Baer, and every golfer I've had the honor to team up with. Your support of me and thousands of veterans brings me to tears more than I will ever admit.

To Atmosphere Press and the entire team, thank you for making this manuscript into a beautiful and profound novel that I can't believe I wrote.

To my test readers, Maddie Rudawski and Melissa Liebold, and my ShitShow writing group. And to the many, many friends who believed in me and helped me through all the mental breakdowns while writing this book. It would have never come to fruition without your love, encouragement, and advice.

To my two favorite people in the entire world, my kiddos. Victor and Lily. You have been nothing but supportive and my cheerleaders throughout this whole process. I love you both more than words can express.

Resources

The hardest step is the first one. Please reach out to any of these resources for any concerns you may have with your PTSD or a loved one's.

- **988:** Call or text 988 to speak with a trained crisis counselor about mental health-related distress. Veterans can call 988 and press 1 to speak with a responder who can support them.

- **Veterans Crisis Line:** Call 1-800-273-8255 (press 1) for 24/7 confidential crisis support for veterans and their loved ones. Veterans can also chat online with the Veterans Crisis Line.

- **Veteran Center Call Center hotline**: Call 1-877-927-8387 to speak with another combat veteran.

For more information about **Tee It Up For The Troops:** https://teeitupforthetroops.org

About Atmosphere Press

Founded in 2015, Atmosphere Press was built on the principles of Honesty, Transparency, Professionalism, Kindness, and Making Your Book Awesome. As an ethical and author-friendly hybrid press, we stay true to that founding mission today.

If you're a reader, enter our giveaway for a free book here:

SCAN TO ENTER
BOOK GIVEAWAY

If you're a writer, submit your manuscript for consideration here:

SCAN TO SUBMIT
MANUSCRIPT

And always feel free to visit Atmosphere Press and our authors online at atmospherepress.com. See you there soon!

About the Author

REBECKA LASSEN debuted with a nonfiction semi autobiographical in 2019 before she found her storytelling passion with fiction and humor. An army veteran, Rebecka draws from her own experiences to create lighthearted stories that bring a touch of brightness to even the darkest of worlds.

She lives in St Louis Park, Minnesota, where she can be found procrastinating writing, dishes, going for a run, or putting actual pants on.

CONNECT ONLINE: